Safe Harbour in Sandy Bay

BOOK 3 IN THE SANDY BAY SERIES

EMILY HUSSEY

WINSOME BOOKS

Note that Australian English is used for this book, as it is set in that country. Spellings will be different to standard spellings used in the United States.

Copyright © 2025 Emily Hussey
ISBN 978-0-6482972-8-4
Cover Design: Winsome Books
Image: Depositphotos

Published by Winsome Books 2025

Adelaide, South Australia

Contents

Also by Emily Hussey

The Red Centre Series
Journey to the Heart
The Red Heart
Trust Your Heart
Follow Your Heart

Harrow Series
Wild Spirit
Wild Destiny
Wild Tempest
Wild Fire

Sandy Bay Series
Secrets in Sandy Bay
Escape to Sandy Bay
Return to Sandy Bay
Safe Harbour in Sandy Bay

1- Arrival

HE HAD RUN OUT of choices. Adelaide was so near, but so unreachable. Anchoring at Sandy Bay was the best option. Harley consulted his charts, grateful he still had the paper variety, even if they were ancient and creased from multiple folds. By his estimation, he would tie up around mid-afternoon.

He peered at the coastline, and then back at his chart, aligning what he could see with the two-dimensional version before him. Leaving the safety of the chart table, he stepped onto the deck and scanned the horizon, watching for marker buoys and other boats in the area. After everything else that had happened, the last thing he needed was a collision with another vessel or with submerged reefs. Sailing without the security of the radar and depth sounder left him feeling incredibly vulnerable.

It shouldn't do that. He'd sailed often enough, reliant mostly on wind and sail, and without sophisticated electronics, but that had been close to home in familiar waters. Now, he was feeling his way, and reliant on skills he'd almost forgotten. He cast an anxious eye at the sky and the looming clouds. The sooner he docked, the better. The forecast was not in his favour.

The sea rolled with restless energy, its once calm and serene expanse now transformed. Muted colours reflected the sombre hues of the sky. A heavy mass of clouds stretched towards the coast and beyond, bringing to the watcher the threat of rain. The slap of the waves against the hull gave further indication of the churning he could expect if he didn't head for the protection and shelter of the Bay.

His wasn't the only boat heading towards the marina. A fishing trawler followed him in, motoring with the assurance of a skipper on his home turf. Harley nudged Ocean Dream closer to the dock. He'd been unable to radio ahead, but with mobile coverage, could call Dennis, the marina manager, requesting a berth and a helping hand on arrival.

Dennis stood at the allotted berth, hands on hips as he waited for the yacht to approach. He wore white trousers topped with a navy blazer and a captain's peaked hat. Harley took that detail in with a sideways glance as he spun the wheel, and judged his speed and the current, waiting for the bump against the timber supports. He cut the motor and flung the stern mooring rope towards the other man, who caught it and wound it around the cleat on the pontoon. Harley hurried to the bow and flung the next line with a practiced aim. Dennis hauled on it, dragging the bow in before securing the rope around the next cleat.

"Thanks for that," Harley sprang from the deck onto the weathered pontoon. "Much easier than doing it myself."

The boat gently rocked in response to the wash from the vessel chugging past. Dennis gave a small nod of acknowledgement as he cast an eye over Ocean Dream. "Nice looking vessel. I gather you've had a spot of bother."

Harley noticed the manager's hat was a well-worn relic from decades prior. "You could say that. The electronic system crashed earlier today. I hoped to be in Adelaide tonight, but I'm reluctant to keep going without functioning equipment. I have no communications… nothing! Do you have a marine technician in town?"

"We do. Roger Marriot of Sandy Bay Electronics. He covers a range of equipment, so he's quite busy."

The pontoon heaved gently beneath Harley's feet as he adapted to terra firma again. He took stock of his surroundings. The heavy clouds overhead cast a dim grey light over the scene, lending an air of sombreness to the setting. The tang of salt hung heavily, mingling with a faint odour of fish and the inevitable diesel fuel. It appeared to be a busy marine facility, given the number of boats moored at the three pontoons jutting out into the bay. A sign on the low-set building read Sandy Bay Marina and gave the phone number of the manager if the office was unattended. A cluster of seagulls hovered hopefully close to the fish café trading on the other side of the carpark behind the office. Much like any marina anywhere else.

Harley directed his attention back to Dennis. "Do you have a mobile number for this guy, or is he in walking distance? The sooner I get him to check out this problem, the better."

"I've got his number, but you won't find him today. He went to the city early this morning for a family funeral. I doubt he'll be back before tomorrow, if not the day after. Stan might know."

The fishing trawler he'd seen earlier had now docked as well, and the skipper and a deckhand made their way towards them, pushing a trolley laden with plastic tubs. The squeaking wheels announced their approach.

"How's your day been?" Dennis called out as they drew closer. "Tubs full, I see."

The skipper grunted. "Not too bad. Typical for this time of year."

Dennis rolled his eyes. "Harley here is looking for Roger Marriot. He's got some trouble with his electronics. Do you know when Roger's due back from the city?"

Stan's glance slid over Ocean Dream and Harley before returned to Dennis. Harley felt himself to be dismissed, probably for being an outsider. He stepped forward and held out his hand. "I'm Harley Mendelson. I lost the electronics a while back and put into Sandy Bay rather than continue to Adelaide. If this Roger Marriot is away, is there anyone else who can look it over for me?"

"Nope." Stan didn't acknowledge the outstretched hand, and Harley dropped it again. He pushed his sunglasses on top of his head, enabling him to see the trio in front of him with greater clarity. If they could see his eyes, they might be more friendly. *What is it with small-town people?*

"Flash boat. Pity it doesn't work. Perhaps you shouldn't stray too far from familiar waters, not unless you've got reliable equipment. Are you sure you turned everything on?"

Harley turned to the deckhand in annoyance, surprised to see it was a woman. He hadn't noticed that initially, as her hair was tucked under the cap pulled low on her head. She pursed her lips as she gave the boat an appraising look. Harley shifted uncomfortably under her scrutiny, feeling a combination of self-conscious and annoyed. Was she jealous perhaps? The boat she'd disembarked from looked weathered and battered by comparison. He noted the name of the boat with bemusement: Sea Witch. He snorted inwardly at the appropriateness of the name.

She crossed her arms over her chest. "Must have set you back a bit. Shame when you have to fall back on old sailing skills. I assume you can at least read a compass and follow a chart."

"Some other time, I can give you a tour and show you my charts, but first, I need to address this problem. Is there anybody else local, or do I need to bring an electrician down from the city?" His voice betrayed his irritation.

Unexpectedly, Stan grinned. "By the time you did that, Roger would be back, so you might as well wait. Hope you don't have to be anywhere in a hurry."

Harley didn't. Not really. His time was his own. He'd expected to be dining at the South Australian Yacht Club that evening, but it could wait. He just had to adjust his mental plans. He took a breath and exhaled slowly. "It looks like I'll be here for at least a couple of days, then. I assume there are no problems with me living here on the boat for the duration?"

"I'll give you the key to the gate. Come up to the office, and we'll sort out the details. I'll give you Roger's number as well. Bathroom and laundry facilities are in the main building. Don't use the head while you're moored here."

Harley nodded. "Okay. I'll see you there shortly." He needed his wallet and the ID details he knew Dennis would ask for. Like it or not, he would be in Sandy Bay for a couple of days. He sprang back onto the deck of Ocean Dream, noticing as he did the sardonic expression worn by the woman. She didn't comment, but seizing the handle of the trolley, began pushing it towards the gate at the entrance of the marina, and presumably the carpark beyond. Unusual occupation for a woman.

After grabbing what he needed and securing the door to the cabin, he headed towards the office building. Despite the overcast weather, reasonable activity was taking place in the marina and beyond. Seagulls free-wheeled in the air above, monitoring the action below, and calling to each other in high-pitched squeals.

He noticed a boat ramp, where two men were engaged in the business of securing their launch onto a trailer. Others, perhaps tourists, meandered along the water's edge. He hadn't intended making the stop in Sandy Bay, but spontaneity was what this trip was all about. He would keep telling himself that while still maintaining the quiet solitude he craved.

∾

Lily observed the newcomer with a critical eye. He sauntered up the pontoon towards the office, looking polished and neatly pressed even though spending time at sea, and on a not-so-pleasant day at that. His wrap-around sunglasses made him appear secretive. He looked out of place among the fishing trawlers and the usual charter boats that regularly docked at the marina. It would kill her to admit it, but she was curious about where he'd come from and why he was travelling alone. The boat looked to be reasonably new, so it would have cost a few pennies. There was still a glossy finish to the hull, and everything on the deck had looked to be pristine. Nice if you could afford it.

"Are you going to daydream all day?"

"What? Sorry, dad. I was just wondering why a bloke like that sailing on his own."

"Presumably he has nothing better to do, but we have. The co-op will be closed if we don't get this load there in a hurry. Get your skates on."

Father and daughter worked in practiced harmony loading the tubs into the back of the van before Lily pushed the trolley back to where it lived overnight in a fenced enclosure. They had to lock it away, or the local lads might take it for a ride in the middle of the night, or push it into the water. It had happened before. She jumped into the passenger seat beside her father, and they drove the short distance to the co-op. Here, catches were unloaded and weighed, and gossip exchanged with others who relied on the sea. Lily was a rarity on the boats. Women worked on the receiving and sorting side, but not at sea. Except for her.

"G'day darlin'. Did you bring me back a nice cray? You and I could have a cosy dinner for two."

"In your dreams, Evan. You'll have to catch your own cray." She bit back the response she really wanted to make. Evan Peters bordered on being a pest, but never got the message. She did, in fact, still have a cray in the van, but it would make a meal for her parents. Under their contract with the co-op, they were supposed to hand over all their catch, but sometimes something ended up on their dinner plate.

"Leave the girl alone, Evan. She's told you before, she's not interested."

Thank you, Mavis. Lily flicked the older woman an appreciative wink, without drawing attention to the gesture. Standing in her gumboots, with hands on hips, her hair tucked under a plastic cap and wearing a white plastic coat that stretched around her ample middle, Mavis looked capable of gutting the man as easily as she gutted and filleted the fish.

"I was only asking." Evan sounded surly at the reprimand, but Lily knew he would soon recover. The conversation would probably be repeated tomorrow.

Mavis turned back to Lily and Stan. "You two were late back today. You wouldn't want to have left it much later. Looks like we're headed for a bit of a squall."

"Bit of a squall wouldn't worry us much," Stan said, blowing his nose on an enormous cotton handkerchief. "Might have worried the bloke who limped in behind us though."

"Oh? Who was that?"

"Harley someone. I didn't pay much attention. He's moored down at berth sixteen. Lost his electronics. That's the trouble when you have a boat as flash as his; there's too much can go wrong."

Mavis moved to the open door, and shielding her eyes against the late afternoon glare, peered towards the boats moored in the marina. "Hmm. He didn't pay for that filleting fish, that's for sure. Where's he from?"

"No idea. I didn't give him the third degree. Dennis will probably know. The bloke will have to stay a couple of days at

8

least to get it fixed. Roger Marriot is in the city on family business."

"Yeah, I heard about that."

Lily knew there was not much that Mavis didn't hear about, and it would not be long before she knew everything possible about the skipper of Ocean Dream; where he was from, where he was going, and where he derived his money and much more besides. She made her way to the office to sign the paperwork for the day, leaving Mavis and her father to continue their conversation. A hot shower called her, and the sooner she arrived home the better.

She paused beside the van before getting back in, looking out over the harbour. She knew every nuance of the waters around the bay, but it could be treacherous for someone without local knowledge. It would be a pity if a nice boat like that had run aground on the reef. With no working radio and no sonar, finding him would not be so easy at night. The man was a fool for travelling on his own. He must be running from something—a wife, gambling debts, or perhaps the mafia. Maybe he was drug running. That would be one way of affording a boat like that.

She knew she was being judgmental, but this Harley didn't look like a real sailor. Boat too new, outfit too pristine… didn't have the sun-weathered look that most of the sailors around the Bay sported. The sea was an unforgiving mistress, and could easily destroy man and boat alike if he didn't know what he was doing. He would have been better off staying in his local pond.

"I thought you said you wanted to get home."

Her father sat in the driver's seat, peering out to where she stood. She turned her back on the sea and slid into the passenger seat, still buckling the belt as her father began driving out of the carpark. Whoever he was, it was no concern of hers.

2 – Marina Operations

THE SHOUTS AWOKE him, underpinned by the noise of the trolleys bumping over the wooden planks on the pontoon. Harley kicked off the covering blanket as he sat up in his berth and pushed open the hatch in the ceiling above him. The cool night air rushed in, an antidote to the stuffiness of his cabin. Still dark. Not even a glimmer of light. The odd star was visible. What time was it, for fuck's sake?

As he peered at his watch, he heard the first of the trawlers rumble into life. Diesel fumes floated through the hatch, and reaching up, he slammed it shut. He didn't need to lie in that stink. Realistically, there would be no more sleep. More trawlers would follow, as would daylight, and then the marina would be a hive of activity.

Giving in to the inevitable, he eased himself out of his berth and padded into the galley, with the boat gently rocking from a combination of tidal activity and the wash from the motoring vessels. He yawned, scratching his belly as he took stock of the scene on the wharf. Floodlights illuminated the marina, allowing him to observe the activity as fishing crew readied their vessels for departure. Might as well brew a coffee.

Harley was glad he wouldn't be staying long. He'd never get a good night's sleep if he was. Carloads of youths had congregated in the carpark late the previous evening, and after they'd driven the inevitable donuts with showers of gravel and exhaust fumes, he'd had a hard time getting back to sleep. After breakfast, he would look for the technician.

He took his coffee up on deck to drink, checking out the surrounding activity. Sea Witch was still tied up at a berth. Perhaps they weren't fishing today. As he watched, four men climbed into a launch, loading eskies and fishing gear into the boat. He could hear the chiacking between them, no doubt hopeful of a successful day's catch. They cast off and chugged past him, with the skipper raising a hand in acknowledgment.

Daylight cracked to the east, with a faint glow toward the hills that bordered the coast. The top of the range was outlined in a muted pink, heralding the change that was about to come. It was too early for breakfast. Harley dragged on a pair of tracksuit pants and a windcheater and stepped off the boat onto the wharf. He'd gone to the nearest pub for a counter meal the night before, but hadn't seen much of the town. He would leave checking out the main street until after opening time, but for now he could stroll along the beach. It would soon be light enough to see where he was going.

He pulled a beanie from a pocket and jammed it on his head, tugging it over his ears. The morning breeze kept him walking briskly and his breath came with small puffs of vapour. A few people already fished on the jetty under the lights, no doubt hoping for an early morning catch of squid or perhaps crabs. A woman walked a dog along the sand, and an exercise group ran through their paces on the grassed area by the Esplanade. That was keen! It still wasn't properly light. Security lights showed their sweaty bodies and the pain of effort on their faces while the trainer bellowed instructions. He had left behind that world of self-punishment with no regrets.

By the time he wandered back to Ocean Dream, his stomach insisted it was time for breakfast. Sea Witch no longer sat at her mooring. He made a second cup of coffee and devoured fried eggs and grilled tomatoes with a slice of toast. After he washed his dishes and tidied the cabin, the marina was in full swing. He wandered up to the office, where Dennis sat at a desk covered in a mess of papers.

"G'day, Mate. Sleep well?"

"Aside from the antics of the local lads, and then the pre-dawn departures that threatened to throw me from my berth, slept like a baby. Can I get the contact details for that electronics bloke?"

Dennis frowned and pursed his lips as he looked at the chaos on his desk. "I should have a spare business card here. I doubt he'll be back yet, but if you call him, he can tell you himself."

He thumbed through a pile of cards on his desk and, with a grin of satisfaction, extracted one, passing it over. Harley glanced at it. Roger Marriott. Sandy Bay Marine Electronics. "Thanks. I'll call him shortly. Aside from that, what are the highlights of Sandy Bay? What brings people here from the city?"

"It's a quiet town, and we like it that way. Swells a bit on weekends and in the holiday season. Some people come because it's quiet, and they want a break from the hustle and bustle. Others like the fishing or the surfing, or perhaps to tour the local wineries and gourmet establishments. If you're looking for the Gold Coast Mark Two, you've come to the wrong place."

Harley raised his hands as though rejecting the suggestion. "That's the last thing I need. Quiet will do me just fine. I'll catch you later."

He shut the door of the office carefully so that it didn't bang behind him and made his way back to Ocean Dream. The calls he wanted to make were best done in comfort and while sitting down. A couple of people passed him on their way back to the carpark, pulling small trolleys loaded with their fishing gear. He peered into their buckets as they passed. Both seemed to have done well for themselves. They had their catch for the day and were heading home.

His call to the technician was answered quickly. "Marriott Electronics." The voice was abrupt.

Harley explained his problem. He heard a weird noise, as though the man at the other end of the call was sucking his teeth. "Should be back tonight. Contact me in the morning." The call was disconnected, leaving Harley staring at the mobile in surprise. Not a loquacious chap then. That meant another night sleeping in the marina.

Next call was to Bryan in Adelaide. He and Meredith had expected him to stay with them for a few days.

"Hey, Bryan… there's a slight disruption to plans. I'm going to be held up in Sandy Bay for a couple of days."

"Meredith will be sorry to hear that. I think she was planning a dinner party in your honour. What's the problem?"

"It's going to take longer than I thought to get the electronics on the boat sorted. I can't speak to the technician until tomorrow. God knows how long it will take to get fixed. He wasn't very communicative."

"There are worse places to be stuck, but I hope you don't die of boredom."

"Not me. I'll find a quiet spot and get out the paints. Give my regards to Meredith and apologise for me. We'll do that dinner some time, but I'm not expecting her to pull out all stops for me."

"You know what women are like. Once they've got an idea in their head, there's no stopping them. I think she has a friend she wants you to meet."

"Bryan, don't let her get any ideas. This is a solo trip, and that's how it's going to stay."

"This woman has a gallery, so Meredith thought you would have something in common."

"Once maybe, but not anymore. I'll call you again when I know what's going on. Enjoy your day."

Harley disconnected the call. He was fond of Meredith, but sometimes she became carried away with her great ideas. Fortunately, they didn't last long when her attention was taken by something or someone else. It looked like the day was his. Not having transport, he couldn't explore any of those wineries or venues far from the coast. That left a day of sketching. He grabbed a sketchbook and his case of pastels and clambered off the boat. He cast around him looking for subject matter and inspiration. Terraced lawns behind the marina looked out over the bay and the associated activity. There was no point in wandering too far. That would detract from the time available for sketching, and he wouldn't be in Sandy Bay for long.

Having made that decision, he found a shaded patch of grass, and even a picnic bench. He cleared off the remnants of a fish and chip meal that someone had left behind, and after sitting down, opened his pad. He sat for a while, absorbing the scene before him, noting the movement and colours before he picked up a pencil and began outlining the parameters of what he could see.

Early start and early finish. That suited Lily, as she had errands to run that afternoon. After an early lunch, she would drive down to Port Reilly where she had an appointment with a masseur. Working on the boat could be hard on the back and shoulders, and her muscles let her know about that. The therapist would get stuck into the knots, bringing her some relief. She rotated her shoulders, squeezing her shoulder blades together to ease the tension.

Her father cut the engine as she stood, poised on the deck and with the line coiled in one hand. She eyed the closing gap between the boat and the dock. As he edged against the bollards, she sprang ashore and quickly wound the line around the cleat. When she ran down to the next cleat lined up with the stern, Davey, their other deckhand, threw the next line to her. While her father busied himself on the boat, Lily walked up to the wire-mesh fenced enclosure to grab the first of the trolleys.

A couple of people sang out a greeting as she passed. She knew most of the locals who frequented the marina. The people who were strangers were probably tourists. Victor, the Fisheries Inspector, passed her on his way to chat with her father. The underlying purpose would be to check the catch and ensure that the fish was appropriately stored for transport to the fish co-op. He could also ask to check which species of fish were in the tubs or the size of any crays, but he rarely did that. Victor and her father had a working relationship spanning a couple of decades.

Her eye was caught by a figure on the lawned area beyond the carpark. It was the yachtsman who had come in the day before with Ocean Dream. She'd forgotten his name, though not him. He was good looking in a metro sort of way, if you liked that sort of thing. Different to the honest and open features of the men she usually associated with. He carried an air or assurance that came with affluence and expectations that everything around him would go according to plan… his plan. Bad luck about that.

Now and then he looked up, peering at the scene below, and then looked down again at whatever he was doing. Even from this distance, she could see that he appeared to be frowning in concentration. She didn't have time to ponder the issue. Lily unlocked the gate and grabbed the trolley.

By the time she got back to the boat, Davey and her father had the plastic tubs lined up on the wharf. Her father and Victor were still engaged in discussion, mainly about the season and recent changes to the fishing regulations that affected marine fisheries.

"Looks like you're busy. I'll get out of your way," Victor said as Lily and Davey began loading a trolley. "See you next time." He wandered down towards the next trawler that had docked behind them. Lily knew that although the conversations he had with the crew were general in nature, Victor didn't miss much. He did his job without being obvious, unless circumstances required it.

Dennis wandered over as they loaded the van. "Productive day?"

"Can't complain." This was Stan's usual response. He nodded his head toward the figure seated at the bench on the on the lawns. "What news of that fella? Did he get hold of Roger Marriott?"

"I passed on the number, but I'm not sure what happened. He's up there sketching the harbour. He's quite good. I just had a look."

Stan's eyebrows shot skywards, surprised at this information. "When we're finished here, we can take a gander."

"Dad, we can't just stare over his shoulder. That's intrusive."

"If he didn't want people looking at his work, he wouldn't be sitting up there in a public park. Pass me the next tub."

Her father's pragmatic approach to life could be exasperating. Lily helped Davey to finish loading the van and then took the trolley back to the compound. When her father took off up the slope towards the figure at work, she hurried after him. The only way to control his intrusive behaviour was to stick close.

"Dad, wait. You need to get to the co-op. Don't forget, I'm not coming with you today. I've got my car here. Davey's already left."

Her father waved in acknowledgement without looking around. When she caught up with him, he stood behind Harley, looking at the drawing unfolding on the paper and then squinting at the scene below. She wanted to look as well, though she drew back, reluctant to appear a sticky beak. Her father turned to her.

"Came and have a look, Lil. He's even sketched an outline of Sea Witch. It's not very big. You'd hardly know it was our boat."

Lily drew closer, unable to contain her curiousity. Her father was right. Sea Witch was identifiably there on the paper. Harley worked quickly, and the scene developed depth and definition as he outlined and shaded the work in front of him. He glanced at them with a brief nod of acknowledgement, but focussed on his work. It impressed her that he didn't appear to be put off by spectators.

"Is this a hobby, or are you a proper artist?" Stan asked.

Lily felt a rush of embarrassment. Honestly, her father had no tact. "Dad, that's not an appropriate question. Leave the man alone. You need to get the catch to the co-op."

"You're right," he said, not in the least phased by being chastised. "I just thought we could get a painting of the boat."

"But you've got hundreds of photos."

"Yes, but it's not the same, is it? I'll be off then. Perhaps you can ask the questions."

He strode back down the slope towards the van, leaving Lily and an uncomfortable silence behind him. Harley paused, watching as Stan climbed into the driver's seat and drove out of the carpark.

"Sorry, dad's sensitivity meter is non-existent. We don't need a painting of the boat." She squinted at the drawing in front of Harley. "Looks like you work in charcoal and crayons, not paint. I'll tell Dad that, and then he'll drop the subject."

Harley tilted his head as he turned to look at her. "Actually, I do… paint, that is. I often sketch a scene first and then paint the same subject later in water colours. I use oils or acrylics as well, but not on this trip. Just the water colours. I doubt I'll be here long enough to take on any commissions."

"Commissions?" Her tone rose, reflecting her surprise. "So, you are a *proper artist* then."

"I'm probably not the right person to comment on that. It's a pastime that I've had more time to explore recently. I doubt I'll ever win any awards, but I do exhibit and sell work occasionally."

"Your electronic problem is under control, then?"

"Not yet, but the technician should be back in town tomorrow. Hopefully, he'll find the cause quickly and then I'll be on my way. The marina isn't the best place in which to get a peaceful night's sleep."

"I'll have to take your word for that. I've never slept down here. Roger Marriott knows his stuff, so he should diagnose your problem once he looks at the boat. You could always stay a night in the local pub if you want something quieter. The Regal Hotel has accommodation." She glanced at her watch. "I need to get moving. I have an appointment in Pt Reilly."

As she climbed into her car, she could have sworn she felt his gaze raking her body, just as she had seen him watching her father. She drew a quick breath accompanied by a surge of adrenaline, but resisted the urge to look around to check if he was really looking, or if it was just her imagination. As she turned the ignition key and eased the car onto the access road, she risked a glance in his direction. He was absorbed in his work. He wasn't paying her any attention, and probably never had.

Lily chided herself for being silly. Why should an affluent stranger, who, judging by appearances and the money his boat represented, pay any attention to a deckhand? No reason at all. Strangers came and went in Sandy Bay and never stayed long. They came for the change in pace, but after a while, became bored and hurried back to the lights and action. She'd learned that the hard way, and wouldn't be taken for a ride like that again. Once bitten, twice shy.

3 – Exploring the Town

THE THOUGHT OF a night in a local hotel was tempting, but Harley told himself that this night would probably be quiet. Besides, the boat would be more secure if he slept on it. He had a hot shower in the bathroom attached to the administration block and treated himself to a nip of whiskey before retiring. Both, he reasoned, should facilitate a good night's sleep.

Thankfully, the local lads didn't return, but the anticipation kept him awake longer than he would have liked. At twelve thirty, he climbed out of bed and sat and read for a while, before conceding that the lines on the page were blurring, and he was now tired enough to retire again.

It seemed he had only just done that when the first of the early morning activity woke him. In reality, he had probably been asleep for a few hours. He stretched out his legs, seeking a new position of comfort, all the while keeping his eyes closed. He had a childlike thought that if he kept them closed, he could convince himself that it wasn't time to wake yet, and he could drift back to sleep. The rumble of a diesel engine put paid to that.

Voices carry so clearly at night. Nobody kept their voices down. Why should they? They were starting work for the day. The voices were the same as the day before, and so was the banter. He thought he could hear Stan, but couldn't be sure. If his taciturn daughter was with him, she was being quiet.

Harley lay for a while longer, thinking about the day ahead. As soon as reasonable, he would call Roger Marriott, but until then, he could go for a walk again. If the problem with the electronics couldn't be fixed before mid-afternoon, he would check into the local hotel. He preferred leaving the last leg of the trip into Adelaide for daylight hours. If the town was big enough to have a car hire facility, he would explore the region. Might as well now he was here. Only after talking to Marriott, of course.

With those decisions made, he eased himself out of bed, grabbed a towel, and ambled up to the bathroom to freshen up. A couple of blokes messing around on their boats recognised him from the day before and called out greetings as he passed. He couldn't fault the friendliness of the town, just the noise level. He raised his hand in acknowledgement, noticing as he did that Stan's daughter—*What was her name?*—trundled towards him, pulling the trolley loaded with empty tubs behind her. Her long hair was braided into a single plait, and a thick beanie that could have been knitted by someone's grandma covered the top of her head. Her jeans were tucked into a pair of rubber boots, and she wore a weatherproof vest over her sweater. She looked ready for her day on the boat.

He stepped to the side, giving her clear passage. "Morning."

Her eyes flicked sideways before returning to straight ahead. "Morning," she replied, without looking at him.

Not as friendly as the blokes then.

"Bit of an early start, isn't it?"

"Looks that way."

"I s'pose the first boat out there gets all the fish, or something like that. Sort of like an early bird gets the worm."

She gave him a look that made him feel a total idiot. "The sooner we leave, the sooner we get back."

"Makes sense. Have a good day," he called to her back. There was no reply, but he hadn't expected one. He glanced at his watch. Five-thirty. There was a twenty-four-hour service station a short walk away. He knew they served coffee, as well as basic take-away food. The coffee that someone else made always tasted better than what his did. He could fill in some time by walking up there and buying one of theirs.

By the time he'd finished his ablutions, pulled on warmer clothing and grabbed his phone and wallet, the time was closer to six. As he walked up the main street towards the servo, the door opened at Maisie's Café and a staff member started dragging out tables and chairs for the diners who preferred eating outside. Maybe he could get a coffee here instead. He hadn't expected to find a café open this early.

"Need any help?"

He held the door open while the young man shuffled out, clutching a tower of four chairs, which he distributed around one table.

"We're not officially open yet, but if you could hold that door for a moment, that would be helpful."

Harley reached up and secured the door in the open position, and then grabbed another pile of chairs. He had nothing better to do at this hour of the day. In a couple of minutes, they had four tables set up on the footpath, chairs arranged around them, and market umbrellas sprouting from the middle.

Harley dusted imaginary dirt from his hands. "When are you officially open?"

The young man consulted his watch. "I reckon in about one minute."

"Is it okay if I come inside and wait for one minute?"

The kid grinned. "I reckon you've earned it. Take a seat."

Harley took a seat inside the cafe and picked up the menu. Now that he was in the cafe, the thought of a full breakfast appealed. The menu offered an extensive breakfast selection, but the choice was easy.

"When the kitchen's open, I'll have the big breakfast and a mug of flat white."

"You must be hungry. Coming up." The kid scribbled the order on his pad before commenting, "I haven't seen you here before. Are you staying in a holiday rental?"

"No, my boat is moored in the marina. I need some repairs so I'm waiting for Roger Marriott to look it over. I suppose you know him?"

"Sure do, not that he's in here much. He's not very sociable. Good at his job, though."

"I'm pleased to hear it. I'm Harley, by the way."

"Jordan. Welcome to the Bay." He hurried back to the kitchen to file the breakfast order and then fired up the coffee machine. Already, a couple of other people had come through the door. The day began early in these parts.

Harley scrolled through his phone while he waited, checking on the news of the day and his emails. Tolhurst Gallery in Sydney advised him that one of his pictures had sold. Funds would be transferred to his account at the end of the month. That was a win.

Another email was from his broker, with recommendations for changes in his portfolio. He would think about that before responding. He wasn't risk averse, but considered the placement of his financial assets carefully. The last email was from Ralph, the CEO of his tech company. Until recently, that role had been his. Now he had taken a back step to silent partner and minor shareholder. Ralph was doing an excellent job, according to the latest financial statements. Harley scanned the attached report and turned his attention to the daily news instead.

When Jordan delivered the mug of coffee to his table, it occurred to Harley that if anyone knew what was available in town, it would be him.

"Is there a car hire company in Sandy Bay?

Jordan laughed. "Not here. We're not big enough for that. There is one in Port Reilly, but you need a car to get there."

"What about bicycle hire, then?"

"Nope, not one of those either. How long did you need a car for and where did you want to go?"

"Only a day. As soon as the boat is fixed, I'll be off again. I'll find out later today when that is likely to be. In the meantime, I thought I would follow the local gourmet trail. I saw some posters about it in the town's information centre."

"Hmm… leave it with me. I might have a suggestion." Jordan hurried back to his station behind the counter to deal with other early morning customers. The kitchen hand delivered his breakfast, and Harley turned his attention to the meal. According to the menu, the eggs, sausages, bacon, and mushrooms were all locally grown produce. If he ate like this for too many days, the boat would sink under the weight.

When Jordan returned to clear away his plate, he placed a piece of paper on the table. "This is my dad's address. He has an ankle injury and is stuck at home. Driving is not allowed. If you feel like some company, you can drive his car and take him with you. He's been going stir-crazy. I've called him, and he's expecting you."

"Wow, that's going above and beyond. Thank you so much… I'll go there now, if it's not too early. I should let your boss know what an asset you are to the business."

"Yeah, do that. She needs to be reminded occasionally. Maisie's my mum."

Harley snorted. "In that case, she probably already knows. Not much gets past mothers."

He left a sizeable tip on the table. The address Jordan gave him was within walking distance, so he went straight there. It was still too early to call Roger Marriott. Adam, for that was the name of Jordan's father, met Harley at the front door with his foot in a moon boot. He sported the same grin as his son, confirming the paternal relationship.

"Jordy told me the sad story about your boat. He said you need a set of wheels for the day. I'm not allowed to drive, as you can see."

"Well, if you'd like a chauffeur and to get out of the house, I'm your man. I'd love the company of a knowledgeable local."

"You've won me. Fuel tank's full so we can go whenever you'd like. It's a bit early now, so I suggest you come back in about two hours."

Harley was astonished at the friendliness of both father and son. You wouldn't find such trust in Sydney. He decided to give Adam the painting of the harbour before he left the town. That was the least he could do. It needed some work, but he could manage that. He finalised arrangements with Adam before walking back to the marina. The phone call was next on the agenda. Seven thirty… the man should be up and available by now.

❧

Roger Marriot was no more communicative in person than he was on the phone. "Yeah, you've got a bit of a problem there."

"How long to fix it?"

Roger sucked his teeth in what Harley was to learn was a frequent habit. "Depends. Needs a replacement part. I haven't got one. I'll have to get one in."

"From Adelaide? If it needs to be couriered down today, I can pay for that."

"Depends. They might not have it in stock. If not, it will have to come from interstate or overseas."

"Can you find out? I wasn't planning on holing up in Sandy Bay."

The other man turned an enigmatic look on him. "Life's what happens in spite of our plans. I'll get back to you. I've got your number." With that, he jumped off the boat and ambled off without any words of farewell.

Talk about a contrast. The impression he'd gained of the town earlier that day was tarnished by that one taciturn interaction. Once Marriott had left, Harley sat down and worked on the watercolour version of the scene he'd sketched the day before. He'd done some work on it the previous evening, but it wasn't finished. He had some time before walking back to pick up Adam. He sat down and reached for his brush.

Lily noticed that Ocean Dream still sat at its mooring in the marina. It was there when Sea Witch docked mid-afternoon and was there still when she returned to the marina an hour later to pick up a jacket she'd left on the boat. As she walked along the boardwalk past the yacht, Harley startled her by popping up on deck from the cabin below. He gave her a nod.

"Hello again. Finished for the day?"

"Yes… a couple of hours ago. I just came back to fetch something from the boat." She felt gauche around this man. She hadn't just looked at his sketch the day before; she'd taken the opportunity while standing behind his shoulder to study him. He was handsome in a rugged sort of way, though not magazine perfect. A bump in his nose prevented that. His hair curling over his collar might need a haircut, but it wasn't just his physical appearance that took her attention. It was his eyes. The deep brown pools looked right at you, through you even.

Expressive eyes that showed what he was thinking. When he looked at her, her legs went to jelly, and she feared he could see right through her. There would never be secrets from a man like that.

Lucky she didn't have any secrets, not from him or anyone else. Hers was a simple life. She was a deckhand on a fishing trawler and he was an affluent sailor with a self-assured aura. Here he was, seemingly with no obligations, sailing where the whim took him, and she was sailing to wherever the fish were and back again. She had no intention of getting closer to someone like him.

She squared her shoulders and looked at him directly. "I thought you might be gone by now."

He gave an ironic laugh. "So did I. At least I hoped that would be the case. It seems fixing this electronic problem won't be so simple. The replacement part I need isn't readily available, and has to come from interstate, or possibly from the manufacturer in Europe."

"That's bad luck." It sounded like a lame response, but what else was there to say?

"I was about to have a gin and tonic. It's that time of day. Would you care to join me?"

Lily looked at him in surprise. Was there a motive? Come and look at my etchings, perhaps? He answered her unspoken question. "I don't like to drink alone. I've toured some of the local wineries today, and picked up a bottle of boutique gin, flavoured with local native plants. It seems a shame not to share."

She surprised herself. "I could be persuaded. I've always wanted to try it, but that gin doesn't come cheap. Just one drink, though."

She made the leap onto the deck of Ocean Dream, ignoring the hand he held out to her. He must have anticipated company, or else he regularly treated himself. When she entered the cabin below the deck, she saw he had laid out a platter with a couple of fresh cheeses, some olives, and dried tomatoes and dried apricots. Slices of lemon sat on a chopping board, and he had opened a bottle of elderflower tonic. This was not a man who did things by halves.

He noticed her looking at the platter. "I didn't just purchase gin today. I have a couple of bottles of merlot put away, and I found a variety of tasty treats. I was just debating whether I wander up town for another pub meal this evening, or stay here and graze of the spoils of my trip. I have food in the fridge of course, so I can easily cook. I was feeling lazy, as well as disgruntled."

He fetched a couple of glasses from a cupboard and poured a generous slug of gin into each. He dropped in a slice of lemon, then topped the glass with the tonic. He passed her drink over. "Cheers" They clinked glasses. "Did you want to see over the boat?"

He must have seen the apprehension that caused her to hesitate. He held up a hand as though to ward off her thoughts. "I thought you'd be interested, that's all. This boat's my pride and joy. I'm always happy to show her off."

Lily flushed. Of course, he would want to show off his boat. She wanted to see the chart table and the navigation equipment. It wasn't often she could look over something as modern as this. It was top of the range for its size. Pity about the electronics. He talked her through the various features of the boat, and then showed her both cabins, fore and aft, and the bathroom. The galley was well equipped with both a fridge and a freezer.

"I was given the option of an ensuite bathroom when I commissioned the boat, but I thought that was a waste of space on a boat this size. Better to have more storage."

Lily noted the well-made bed in the cabin he obviously occupied and observed how well appointed the boat was. It had been designed with maximum storage and comfort for someone living on it for an extended period.

Her attention was taken by the painting sitting on the far end of the bench that ran along the wall opposite to the galley. "Hey, that's the scene you were sketching yesterday. You've coloured it in."

"Not quite. That's a watercolour, and it's an additional work. See?" He showed her the sketch for comparison.

"So, what are you—a sailor? An artist? Some sort of tycoon?"

He gave a bemused smile. "A bit of everything. Painting is my guilty pleasure."

"Why guilty?"

"I had ideas of going to art school when I was younger, but my parents wouldn't hear of it. They wanted me to pursue study in an area that was more practical and financially rewarding. Now, I can please myself with what I do, but there's still that feeling that I might be wasting my time."

"Doesn't look to me like you're wasting your time, but I'm not a knowledgeable critic. If you enjoy it, why not? Do you still do what your mother says?"

He laughed. "Sometimes, but not in matters relating to my future and what I do with my life."

"You're obviously a sailor, so that question's answered. You do well to sail a boat of this size by yourself."

"Sometimes a friend joins me for part of the trip. He can't stay all the time, and I don't want him to stay either. While he's here, it's good, and when he's gone, it's better. I don't mind my company. If the weather's bad, I find a safe mooring and wait it out. I'm not stupid."

Lily gestured as she looked around. "You have well-appointed living quarters. Wherever you drop anchor, at least you're going to be self-contained and living with reasonable comfort."

Harley screwed up his face slightly at that comment. "Yes, but it can be noisy here. It's not like dropping anchor at a deserted beach. Late night cavorting in the carpark, and then the early departures mean that sleep gets disrupted. I had thought about booking a room in the hotel as you suggested before, but left it a bit late. It's booked out tonight."

Lily tilted her head to one side, considering what he had just said. "What about a holiday cottage? It's off season now, so a few will be vacant."

"I didn't think of that. I'll do an internet search to see if I can find one."

"I can do better than that. My friend runs Professional Coastal Rentals. I'll call her."

The call was connected after a couple of rings. Maddie sounded breathless. "Lily! You just caught me. I'm locking up for the day."

"Don't go just yet. I have someone looking for a bed for a couple of days." She outlined Harley's situation, and why he was needed alternative accommodation. "You have? ... I'll let him know. If you can wait a few minutes, he'll pick up the key."

She disconnected the call and turned back to Harley. "Seaspray Cottage is available. While I grab my jacket from Sea Witch, put together whatever you need for tonight. I'll take you to get the key and to sign Maddie's paperwork, and then I'll drive you to Seaspray. You should have a better night's sleep tonight." She glanced at the platter on the table. "Take that as well. It would be a shame to leave it behind."

She noticed that the first thing he did was gather up his painting gear and the watercolour he'd been working on. It only occurred to her later that he hadn't told her what sort of tycoon he was. Perhaps he had won the lottery or inherited his money. Half his luck. That sort of good fortune was the stuff of dreams.

4 – Seaspray Cottage

MADDIE MASTERS LOOKED up with a smile when Lily and Harley pushed open her office door.

"Hey, Lily… lucky you rang when you did. It's been so quiet; I was going to close early."

Harley extended his hand. "I'm grateful you stayed. I wasn't looking forward to another night sleeping in the marina. Lily tells me you have a holiday cottage that I could use for the time I'm here."

She grasped his hand with a warm smile and a warm palm. "Do you know how long you'll be staying? It's off season, which is why it's available, but it's a popular property. It's right on the seafront and doesn't have close neighbours."

"I hope not more than a couple of days—I think Lily explained about my unscheduled visit to Sandy Bay. I'm waiting for parts to fix my boat. Let me know if you get other requests for it. I can move back to the boat if I have to."

"That won't be a problem. I've prepared the paperwork. If you like to sign here," she pointed to a place on the form with the pen she was holding, "and I'll get the key. If you have your credit card handy, I'll take a deposit and we'll finalise the account when you check out."

While Maddie processed his credit card, the two women chatted. They looked to be of a similar age, so it wasn't surprising they were on friendly terms.

"How's Alex?" he heard Lily asked.

"He's away at the moment. His job takes him all over, but he gets back to the Bay whenever he can. Actually, he stayed in Seaspray Cottage when he first arrived in town. That's how we met. I have fond memories of that place."

"So that's where you and he…"

Both women broke off and looked in his direction, Lily with a grin and a sparkle in her eye. By this stage, Harley had wandered over to the display of real estate photos on the wall, and pretended to be absorbed in all the property descriptions. Whatever they were talking about, he didn't need to know, but it was obvious there was some history associated with this rental.

"That deposit's gone through now."

He looked around to see Maddie holding out his credit card.

"Let me know if there are any problems with the cottage. There is a list of instructions inside—where to find everything you need, and how to lock up, etc."

Harley took one of her business cards from the stand on the counter. "I'll be fine. Thank you once again. I'll let you know my movements as soon as I know them." He looked at Lily and she took the hint, moving back towards the door.

"I'll drive Harley out there. We must catch up for a coffee sometime."

The two women paused at the door to kiss each other on the cheek, with more murmurings of future plans. Harley heard the office door being locked behind them. Maddie's immediate plans appeared to be going home.

The cottage was further from the town than he had expected, but Maddie was right. It was on the seafront. Lily drove into the parking space, which was at the rear of the building. The front faced the ocean, with only the dunes separating the porch from the water. Without noticeable distractions, he could work on his painting.

While Lily unlocked the back door, protected by a covered veranda, he grabbed his packed bag from the rear of her car. He dumped that just inside before going back for his painting gear and the platter he'd brought at Lily's suggestion. He'd also filled a shopping bag with food from the boat and some contents from his fridge. In the meantime, Lily had walked through to the front door and thrown it open, allowing the late afternoon breeze to carry in the briny tang of the sea.

Harley joined her on the front porch. The breeze ruffled her hair about her face, as she stood, one hand grasping the veranda post and the other hand jammed in a back pocket. It bemused Harley that even though she worked on the sea, given the opportunity, she still stared at it. Not for the first time, he thought about the tenacious hold the oceans had on those who were caught within its grasp.

A couple of flower pots containing succulents sat under a window, and beyond them was a wooden table and four chairs. The furniture looked weathered, and not in any danger of being stolen, despite being readily accessible to anyone who wandered along the foreshore. Although it was late afternoon, the day still held some warmth. It was a good place for a sundowner.

"I could bring that platter out here. I grabbed the bottle of gin as well, so I can refresh your G and T. That's the least I can do after you organizing this option for me."

Lily looked away from her reverie and turned to face him. "It was no trouble. I should leave you to get settled in."

"There's not much settling in, as you call it. I'll throw my bag in one bedroom and put the perishables in the fridge, and that's it."

"I thought you wanted to work on your painting."

"I do, and I will, but I put out too much food on the platter. You'll have to help me eat it."

"For a little while then. I'll feel guilty if I've been a distraction."

"Sit down, and I'll be right back."

He left her on the porch and made his way back to the kitchen. It was stylish in a rustic sort of way, with framed posters on the walls featuring inspirational quotes, and the colour scheme in shades of blue, white, and yellow. Typical beachside décor. He rummaged in the cupboards and found a couple of side plates and some serving cutlery. He also found tumblers for their gin. A tray was propped on its side at the back of the bench, so he loaded everything onto that and carried it out to the porch, kicking the screen door open and then backing through the opening.

"Wow… this is service! I didn't expect you to go to any trouble." Lily straightened up from where she had been leaning against the post and followed him to the table. She plonked herself down on a chair, moving it so she still faced the ocean. She looked at the platter, eyebrows rising in appreciation. "Everything is so nicely arranged. Did you work in hospitality or something like that?"

Harley laughed at the suggestion. "I try not to be obsessive, but I like food to be visually attractive, not just a jumbled mess. The appearance is half the appeal of a meal, though it still has to taste good."

"Perhaps you should go on MasterChef. The contestants get points for how they present the food."

He handed her a plate, suggested she should help herself. "My cooking is not up to that standard. If I want that level of presentation in a meal, I'll order in from a gourmet chef."

Her eyebrows rose at that comment, but she merely said, "Well, I hoped you're accomplished at cooking fish. Fishing is a major industry around here. You can always go to the pub in town for a meal, but it's a fair walk, there and back."

"I've already thought about that. There's a bus that runs to Port Reilly on its way to other towns further south. I'll walk into town tomorrow in time to catch it. I'll hire a car in Port Reilly. That will give me transport."

"I love these olives." Lily cut off a chunk of brie and carefully balanced it on a rice cracker. "You're all sorted then. You can—"

Harley's phone ringing interrupted the conversation. He dug it out of a pocket and glanced at the screen. Meredith.

He debated a second about ignoring her, but knew she would keep on calling and he didn't want to turn the phone off in case Roger Marriott called.

"Sorry, do you mind if I quickly take this?" He didn't wait for Lily's reply but stood up and walked a few steps away on the porch and answers the call. "Hi Meredith. If you're calling to ask, yes, I'm still in Sandy Bay and I'm not sure when the part will arrive for the boat. Can I call you back later? I'm with a friend at the moment."

"Friend? Who do you know in Sandy Bay?"

"I've met a few people since I've been here. It's a friendly town. I'll call you, okay?"

"Darling, don't go. We're talking about driving down on the weekend. I need to let Bryan know it's okay with you."

"What? Probably. We'll talk about it later. Bye."

Meredith was never one to take no for an answer. He disconnected the call and threw his phone on the table.

Lily pushed her chair back. "You've obviously got things to do this evening. I won't hold you up. Thank you for the drink. No doubt I'll see you at the marina."

The easy camaraderie that had been developing between them was gone. She stood stiffly, and shunted her chair noisily back under the table. Harley followed her through the house to the door leading out to the carpark, with the uncomfortable feeling that somehow, he'd messed up. Did she always bolt like this? He wanted to say, *don't go yet,* but also didn't want to sound needy and therefore pathetic. He put on a courteous smile.

"Thanks again for organizing the cottage. I really appreciate it."

She gave him a brief nod and climbed into her Hyundai. She reversed out of the carpark and drove off without looking back.

❧

The fading evening light crept around her. Birds rose into the air as she passed the trees in which they sat, screeching their evening chorus. She could hear them, even with the windows up. Lily turned on the headlights and gripped the steering wheel tightly as she replayed their conversation. *Did you work in hospitality?* What a stupid question. Someone who dressed as Harley did, wore designer sunglasses, and sailed a yacht worth north of four hundred grand would not have earned that sort of money working in hospitality. Perhaps he came from a wealthy family. He must have laughed to himself at her naivety.

Then there was the phone call. From a woman. Meredith, she heard him say. Although he had moved away from the table, she could still hear the other half of the conversation. Whoever the caller was, she sounded upset that he was stuck in Sandy Bay. Just as she began to relax in Harley's company, she received a potent reminder that he was only visiting. Best not to get involved, particularly when there was another woman on the scene.

She had helped him out, and that was a friendly thing to do. That was what he'd said on the phone; it's a friendly town. He was right about that. The town looked after its own, and extended a hand to visitors in need as well. He had somewhere quiet to sleep. Tomorrow he would have a car, and in the next day or so, Roger Marriott would fix the boat. Then he would leave.

The part that had surprised her was his artwork. He didn't look like an artist, whatever that was supposed to look like, but to her uneducated eye, he appeared to have talent. She would like to see the painting when he finished it, but that was unlikely.

She slowed down as she reached a T-junction and made the turn onto the main road leading into town. A small sigh escaped, a huff of envy and regret. Imagine having the freedom to sail where you wanted and to paint as well. Choices. Some people had choices and the means to achieve them. She sometimes wondered if she'd made a conscious decision to remain in Sandy Bay, working with her father, or if that decision had been made for her through indecisiveness. It was too late to do anything different now. Her father depended on her, a substitute for the son he never had.

When Sea Witch docked the following afternoon, Lily found Harley busy working on the deck of Ocean Dream. His usual pristine outfit had been swapped for baggy shorts and a t-shirt that had seen better days as he applied a coat of wax to the deck, rubbing vigorously to distribute the paste.

"He looked up with a grin. "I always know when you're coming. Those squeaky wheels broadcast your arrival. I've got some oil here. Do you want to de-squeak your trolley?"

Her first reaction was to feel embarrassed. She'd meant to do something about those wheels for ages, but bringing the can of oil with her continually slipped her mind. In time, she had become used to that irritating squeal. Not as bad as fingernails on a chalkboard, but perhaps Harley thought so.

He held out an oil can. "I've been fixing a few persistent squeaks myself. I might as well put my time to good use while I'm here. There is a myriad of minor jobs on the boat that have had my name on them for far too long."

"You're right. I should have done this ages ago. I was always going to do it the next day, but that day never came."

Harley stood up from his crouched position on the deck and extended an arm towards her, holding the can. She had to adjust her balance first before reaching out and taking it from him. As she did, their hands brushed against each other. His felt warm from the work he had been doing in the sun. Hers were wet, cold, and probably smelled of fish. She glanced at him to gauge his reaction, half expecting him to wrinkle his nose, or at least wipe his hand on the back of his shorts. The deep brown eyes that met hers looked amused, as though able to read her thoughts.

Lily looked away and applied herself to the task, generously dispensing blobs of oil at each of the wheel joints, and then jerking the trolley backwards and forwards to distribute the oil around the axle shaft. The squeals subsided, and the trolley moved more smoothly as well. She should have done this before, instead of waiting for a someone else to point it out to her, especially when that someone was a suave-looking stranger like Harley.

"Well… isn't it amazing what a little oil can do?" Stan had approached while she tested the trolley. "Makes a world of difference. You could have done that ages ago."

"Yeah, right Dad. So could you."

Stan grinned, not appearing in the least perturbed. Lily handed the can back to Harley, who had been watching her work on the trolley. He placed it on the deck before wiping his hands with a rag. He then massaged the small of his back, leaning over backwards as he did. A small frown crossed his face.

"I've been bending over too long. My back is letting me know about that."

Stan snorted. "That's what you get for owning a boat. There's always something to do. You could always pay someone else to do it," he suggested.

"I could, but my boat, my responsibility. I'm not throwing money away on something I can easily do myself. Unless it involves electronics. That's where I defer to the experts."

"What's the story with Roger, then? Has he provided an estimate of how long before you'll be on your way?"

"Sadly, no. He didn't get back to me today. Communication doesn't seem to be his strong point. I think I'll be here for a while yet."

"It's not all bad news then. Gives you time to get to know the town."

Harley gave Stan a wry look. "I think I've seen most of what there is to see. I've walked up and down the main street, and tried out a local café and a local hotel for a meal. I've even driven around the gourmet food trail."

"Hmph."

When her father gave one of those grunts, Lily knew it was time to move her father on. He was known for blunt talk, and you never knew what he was going to come out with next.

"C'mon, Dad. Look at the time. We need to get the van loaded."

Stan held up a hand as though warding her off. "That's all land-based. That's only half the story. Come out with us for a day. Then you'll learn what fishing's all about."

Lily couldn't believe what she had just heard. Her father never took other people on the boat, let alone strangers. He said they got in the way and were a liability. Most likely they would get seasick and moan until they were on shore again.

"Are you sure?" Harley looked as though he was taking the idea seriously. He clambered off Ocean Dream and stood facing her father with his hands on his hips. "I'd appreciate that. Tomorrow?"

"If you like. Be here in time for cast off. Dress warmly. Bring whatever you need."

"Just my camera and my life-jacket."

"Fine. We'll see you tomorrow."

Lily waited until they were out of Harley's earshot. "What did you do that for? You never take people out with us."

"He's a sailor, Lily. He's won't become seasick. He could make himself useful and might even learn something."

"Sailing a luxury yacht is vastly different to hauling up nets in the middle of a swell with a freezing breeze that's swept up from the South Pole. He might be in for a shock."

"He might be. Nothing much we can do about that."

Secretly, Lily didn't mind. Previous interactions had been on Harley's turf. Tomorrow would be on hers. Then she would see what sort of man he was.

5 – A Day's Fishing

HARLEY SAT BACK on his heels, thinking about the day. He'd been busy, but in a good way. He spent another fifteen minutes on his task before packing up. There would be a few more days in which he could catch up with the maintenance. Next job would be to chisel off any barnacles that had attached themselves to the hull. He never enjoyed that one, but it had to be done.

He had picked up a vehicle. The car rental firm in Port Reilly only had a ute available. He didn't need anything more salubrious. After he drove back to Seaspray Cottage, he had picked up the finished water colour and delivered it to Adam. The other man had been surprised, but thrilled, or so he had said. Privately, Harley thought it was one of his better works.

"Mate, you didn't have to do this." Adam had led the way, stomping into the dining room where he could lay the picture down on the table and examine the detail.

"I didn't have to, but I wanted to thank you for your generosity. Sorry it's not framed, but you might not want to hang it anywhere. I enjoyed our outing the other day, and this is my way of saying thanks."

"Not half as much as I did. This bloody foot has really cramped my style."

"I've got wheels now, so I can always pick you up. Not sure how long I'll be here, but I can take you to have a look over the boat if you're interested."

"I'd like that. I've got a physio appointment today, but perhaps in the next day or so?"

"Sure. I'll call you and we can take it from there."

After he left Adam, he had dropped in at Maisie's Café for a late-morning coffee. It was while he was sitting there with his mug of coffee and a cinnamon scroll that Roger Marriott had called him, giving him the news.

"This mob in Sydney are very particular. They reckon you shouldn't have had this trouble, and as I said to them, no argument with that. They want it sent back to them for their technicians to investigate. Can't do it today. I've got other jobs on, now. I'll be there in the morning."

"How long's all this going to take?"

"No idea. We can send it by air, but we've no control over how long they take to do their evaluation."

"Damn. Mercury must be in retrograde." He heard a snort at the other end of the call. "I'm staying in a local holiday cottage while this drama is unfolding. I'll leave the key to the boat with Dennis in the marina office. That way, it won't matter if I'm there or not."

"Sounds like a plan. Enjoy your holiday."

Holiday! Harley had to take a deep breath when the call ended and remind himself that this trip was all about de-stressing. His itinerary was flexible. He could take each day as it came. He was still frowning into his coffee when Jordan paused at his table, carefully balancing a pile of dirty plates on one arm.

"You look like the cat just died. No progress with the boat?"

"It seems to be one step forward and two steps back. I'll be here longer than I thought."

"That's good, isn't it? Who wouldn't want a holiday in Sandy Bay?"

Harley had felt the tension dissipate at the young man's cheerful confidence. Jordan was right. He had the opportunity for an unscheduled holiday and should make the most of it. He'd already completed one painting. There was nothing holding him back from working on more.

This invitation to join Stan and his daughter on Sea Witch in the morning had been a surprise. Given the way Lily had looked at her father, he sensed it had been a surprise to her as well. Hopefully not unwelcome. There was something about Lily that intrigued him. She differed from other women of his acquaintance. He looked forward to the day, even though it meant an early start.

A late afternoon breeze whistled around his bare legs. Time to pack it in for the day. He collected a book from the cabin that he had been reading, locked up, and dropped the key off with Dennis on his way back to the ute. He looked forward to a quiet night.

∂

Security lighting illuminated the dock as fishing crew went about their pre-launch business while getting ready for the day. Harley slung a backpack over his shoulder as he made his way to where Sea Witch was moored. Lily and an unknown male were loading the tubs on deck, and he could make out Stan's figure in the wheelhouse.

He hesitated on the dock alongside the boat, not wanting to board until he had specific permission to do so. He didn't want to get in their way. An icy breeze originating from the ocean to the south swept over the dock and wrapped its tentacles around him. He pulled his beanie low over his ears, and cupped his hands over his face, breathing hot air into his palms to stop his nose from snapping off.

"Morning!" Stan now stood on the deck facing in his direction, and waved a greeting. "Welcome aboard."

"Anything I can do to help?"

"Only if Lily says so. She's in charge of loading."

The woman in question gave him a cursory glance before shaking her head. "We've got it under control. We have our system of working together."

Harley took the hint to keep out of the way, and climbed over the side of the boat onto the deck, keeping clear of the work zone. He made his way to the wheelhouse, where Stan obligingly gave him a description of the dedicated electronics, both for navigation and also for fish detection. The console lit up with a variety of lights and screens, all part of the integrated display. Some of it was familiar, but other instruments were dedicated to trawler operations.

"If you're after a coffee, there's a coffee machine down below in the galley. While you're at it, you could bring me one as well. Black with two sugars. Lily will show you over operations in the hold once we're underway."

Harley almost snapped back with *Aye, aye, Cap'n,* but decided against it. Best not to annoy the skipper. He found the galley and also the coffee machine. The facilities were more basic than what he had on Ocean Dream, but were still functional. Bench seats surrounded a rectangular table on three sides. Beyond the galley was the bunk room, with a couple of bunks on either side of a narrow passage.

The engine rumbled into life as he took the mug of coffee upstairs to Stan. He watched as Lily and the other crewman took care of casting off, and after watching to ensure that Sea Witch was tracking safely, headed down to the galley as well. He followed them and was introduced to Davey, the other member of the crew.

"Not too early for you then?" Davey asked as he cradled his warm mug between his hands. "People don't like to come out at this hour when the wind is biting, and the cold is freezing your nuts off."

The man had an insolent grin, as though inferring that Harley might find their working schedule to be challenging. He was a thickset man, with a barrel chest and tattoos covering his forearms. His eyes set in a weathered face gleamed as he sipped his coffee. It wasn't a question that needed answering. Harley believed that the other man was all brawn and bluster.

'It'll warm up soon enough," Lily said. "If you worked harder, Davey, you wouldn't notice the cold."

From that and other exchanges, Harley understood that the pair had an easy and teasing camaraderie. Working at such close quarters and subject to the control of the sea threw people together. Perhaps there was more to the relationship. It was hard to tell.

"It will be a while before we reach the fishing ground. I'll show you over the hold. Bring your coffee with you. It's cold down there."

Davey settled down in the galley to read a magazine from which Harley understood that it would be some time before they reached the fishing site. Lily led the way below deck to where the catch was stored after the nets were hauled in. They were not normally at sea for extended periods, but the catch was kept cool in the chilled plastic tubs. Mostly they caught snapper using mesh nets, which could be hauled in by her and Davey operating the electric winch. Once on board, the fish was transferred via a hatch in the deck to the large tubs in the hold.

Her self-assurance impressed him, particularly when she expertly fielded the few questions he asked. She gave every impression of being competent at her job, and he found that incredibly attractive. He listened carefully to everything she told him, but his attention was drawn back to her, especially when she was looking away from him. Why had a young woman chosen this way of life? Surely, she had other options available?

"That's all I can show you… for now. You might like to help later when we're hauling the nets in. You'll appreciate your next meal of fish and chips all the more when you see the hard work involved in bringing it to shore."

"I do already. I'll go up to see your dad again. He might talk me through how some of the equipment works. At least it does work; not like on that wretched boat of mine.

It surprised her; he genuinely seemed interested. The test would come when the hard work started. Lily joined Davey in the galley while Harley climbed up into the wheelhouse with her father. No doubt, playing with all the electronic toys at her father's disposal was more interesting than processing fish.

Davey looked up from his magazine. "Are we providing real life fishing experiences for rich playboys now? Is this a new business venture?"

Lily rolled her eyes at him as she rinsed out her coffee mug.

"Because if we are, we should probably have monogrammed sweatshirts and a better class of catering. At the very least, we should have chocolate biscuits."

"In your dreams, Davey. Look at the size of your belly. You've already eaten too many chocolate biscuits. Think yourself lucky you get any biscuits at all."

Lily had discussed the charter business with her father as an option in the off-season, but Sea Witch wasn't really furbished for that sort of venture. It would need a different boat and every time they reached that conclusion, the discussion petered out. There was talk of fishing quotas being restricted, and if that happened, their livelihood would be adversely affected. They needed to diversify, but that would cost money.

Her father had suggested on more than once that she should explore other options.

"What about being a teacher? You're bossy enough. Perhaps you could have a little business in town— a cafe or something like that."

"Can you honestly see me stuck in a classroom all day? Teaching people to sail, perhaps. The freedom of the sea has spoiled me for anything else."

"There's that qualification you studied for—perhaps you could get a job in the city. It would be much easier work than this. Your mother has never forgiven me for letting you join me on the boat. She's convinced you'll never settle down with a good bloke, and she'll never get grandchildren."

"There aren't any guarantees of that, no matter what I do with my life."

He had grunted in response. She heard her father throttle back on the engine, and that meant they were nearing the day's fishing ground. It varied from day to day. Davey looked up from his magazine at the same time. They both knew there was work to be done. Harley was still in the wheelhouse, quizzing Stan on procedures and how he was interpreting the sonar readings. Now he climbed down from there and made his way to the bow, peering intently at the sea ahead. If you knew where to look and what to look for, you could see where the shoals of fish were likely to be. That's the way it was done before the advent of modern technology.

The next couple of hours were busy as the nets were cast and then hauled in and emptied. Harley watched initially, but then pulled out a pair of waterproof gloves from his jacket pocket and pitched in to help. He picked up the routine quickly, and to her relief, was more of a help than a hindrance.

The tubs were full, and the weights checked by the time Stan hauled up the anchor and turned the boat around to head for home. Lily sat down to complete her paperwork and fill in the submission data on her iPad. Davey switched on the electric kettle to make hot drinks, and took bundles of sandwiches from the fridge, placing them in the centre of the table.

"Tuck in. It's been a long time since breakfast."

"I should have thought to bring food with me. I don't expect you to feed me," Harley protested.

Lily looked up from her work. "There's plenty. We knew you would be on board today, so brought extra. Mum put in some banana cake as well. You worked also, so you've earned it."

She had seen Harley massaging his fingers. He probably hadn't expected the work to be as tough on the hands as it was. His face was flushed and his eyes were bright from being whipped by the breeze, but he looked happy enough.

Davey picked up the kettle, preparing to pour water into the mugs he had lined up on the counter. At that moment, a rogue wave slapped the side of Sea Witch, tipping the boat sideways with a stomach-churning lurch. Harley gripped the edge of the table for balance as he was thrown forward. He gasped as his knees buckled, and he slumped towards the heaving floor.

"Jeez, mate… I'm sorry."

What the…? Lily stared in alarm as loose items slid around the cabin. All she could do was hang on as the boat pitched perilously in the swell. As the seas settled and Sea Witch righted itself, she realised what had happened. As he was thrown forward, Davey had drenched the back of Harley's legs with the boiling water from the kettle.

He squeezed his eyes tightly shut and appeared to be breathing through the pain. Davey grabbed his arm, trying to drag him into an upright position.

"It just went everywhere. Quick… get your jeans off."

Harley stared blankly.

"Get your pants off, mate. You need to cool down."

Only then did Harley straighten, wincing as he did. Lily galvanised into action, leaping from the bench to grab a first aid kit from a cupboard.

"Quick, Harley… strip off those jeans. Davey, get some cold water." She bent down and unlaced his shoes so that he could step out of them.

With a low breathy moan, he unzipped the fly and began easing his jeans off.

"Let me." Lily grabbed the waist of his jeans and pulled them down. She tried to ignore the fact that she was performing a very intimate task. "Lift your leg."

Harley gripped the table again for balance, facing it as she slid the jeans from first one foot and then the other. She noticed the whiteness of his knuckles.

Davey placed a bucket of cold water and a cloth beside them. "Jeez, mate, that looks sore. I'm sorry, it just went all over you."

Lily seized the cloth and gently dabbed the back of Harley's legs with the cold water. He flinched at the touch. He gripped the edge of the table with white knuckles. Water ran down his legs and dribbled on the floor.

"Towel", Lily barked. Davey disappeared into the aft cabin and came back with a towel. She hoped it was clean. She gently dabbed the back of Harley's legs before rummaging in the first aid kit and locating a tube of cream for treating burns. He gasped involuntarily as she rubbed the ointment onto his inflamed skin.

"Sorry, I'm trying to be gentle. It would have been worse if you weren't wearing trousers."

"That's some consolation, I suppose." The words were delivered through clenched lips.

"You can put these on." Davey held out a pair of trousers, presumably a spare pair of his. "They might be on the big side, but yours are wet. Loose trousers will be better, I reckon."

Lily straightened from her crouched position. "That should do for now, but I'll give you a tube of Aloe Vera to take with you. Put some of that on tonight. It will help with the healing. How does it feel?"

"Better than it first did. The cream and your ministrations will help, I'm sure." He reached for Davey's trousers. "I'll try putting these on."

They appeared to stick to his legs in places, but restored his decency. He gingerly sat down with his bottom perched on the edge of the bench, and his legs extended in front. Lily and Davey watched with concern. He gave a weak smile, which was far from reassuring.

"I'll be fine… really. It was just the initial shock. Cooling the skin with the cold water helped, and I'm sure the cream will work its magic. Thanks for the trousers, Davey."

"That's the least I can do. If it's okay with everyone, I'll try making that coffee again. If you want to stand well clear, I won't be offended."

Harley waved a dismissive hand in Davey's direction. "It was an accident. Go for it."

Of all things to happen… Lily felt as bad as if she'd thrown the water herself. "I'm sorry this was your introduction to our operations." She pushed her paperwork aside. "What did you think of it before Davey scalded you?"

Harley eased his bottom into a more comfortable position. "Interesting. I've developed a new appreciation of the fish that ends up on my plate. I know what an effort is involved in getting it there."

"This is only part of it. After we dock, the catch is delivered to the fish factory, where it's processed, frozen where appropriate, and sent off the various markets around the country."

After cautiously sliding two mugs of coffee onto the table with a nod in their direction, Davey carried a mug of tea and a packet of sandwiches up to Stan in the wheelhouse. Harley slid one of the remaining sandwich packets towards himself and unwrapped it. Judging by the speed at which the first disappeared down his throat, the dousing with boiling hot water hadn't stinted his appetite. He'd started on his second before he drew a breath.

"So, what's a girl like you doing in a place like this?"

Lily gave him the look she reserved for people who annoyed her. "What does it look like to you? I'm working with my dad, and I'm fishing."

He coloured and looked mortified. "Sorry, I wasn't meaning to sound like such an idiot. I'm genuinely curious. What led you to pursue this life?"

"Would you have asked that question if I were a man?"

"Well… maybe. You've made your point. Just because you're a woman, I shouldn't make assumptions about your career choices. I won't ask anymore silly questions."

Damn. Now she felt bad for shaming him. Lily shoved her iPad aside and picked up her own packet of sandwiches. "It wasn't a deliberate choice. I used to work with Dad during school holidays, and then after I left school, I couldn't decide what I wanted to do. I tried retail work, but don't have the temperament for it. I did a bit of work with a landscape gardener, and that wasn't too bad, because at least it was outside and physical. Dad was a deckhand down, so I started helping him out and I never left."

"You didn't think about leaving Sandy Bay?"

"I studied in the city for a couple of years, but it wasn't for me. I was like a fish out of water, and that's not even trying to be funny."

It was time to turn the tables. Lily examined the man sitting opposite. Rugged up as he was in his waterproof jacket and still wearing his beanie, he looked no different to anyone else on the boat, but the Rolex on his arm would not have come cheap. He hadn't volunteered much about himself. Was he running away from something, or running towards something—or someone? Perhaps the woman on the phone the other night.

"What about you? Why are you sailing by yourself around our rocky shores? Don't you have a job to go to?"

He took another bite of his sandwich, and for a while, she thought he wasn't going to answer. "I needed a break, and this seemed to be an ideal way to achieve that. I worked in the tech industry. I was still in my first year of uni when I developed a program to facilitate operations in the logistics industry. It turned into a business and in the end, I dropped out of uni to concentrate on managing sales and expanding the product."

When he looked up, there was a tiredness in his eyes, and possibly not just from his early start. "I worked incredibly long days—never had an off-button. It wasn't a healthy lifestyle. Relationships suffered, and so did my health. I never had time to eat properly, nor to exercise. I began wondering what my purpose in life was. I resigned as CEO and Ralph, my partner, took over. I sold him a fifty-one percent share of the company.

The sum was large enough that I could stop working, though I retain rights over the intellectual property and still derive an income from that. I then had to decide what to do with myself."

"So, you've been confronted with those big questions and choices, too. That doesn't tell me what you're doing here, though."

"I needed a complete break. I knew I couldn't do that living my old life in Sydney. When I was a kid, I used to go sailing with my grandpa. We talked about sailing around Australia… it was his dream, but he died before he could do that. I decided I would do it for him, and here I am. I bought Ocean Dream, did a couple of small trips with her to test myself and get to know her idiosyncrasies, and then set off.

Lily took a moment to digest this. A self-made man… that deserved some respect. More so than if he'd inherited his money. "You were heading for Adelaide on this leg. Did you have a time commitment associated with that?"

"I had promised to drop in on friends for a few days, but it was a flexible arrangement… on my part, anyway."

If asked, Lily couldn't say why she derived satisfaction from that piece of information, except that it meant the woman from the phone call was 'just a friend'. Even she knew the thought was silly. It didn't matter to her who was in his life, even if she did call him *darling*.

6- Visitors

HARLEY HAD HEARD Stan's comment about commissioning a painting of Sea Witch. He hadn't acknowledged the remark, because he'd had no intention of painting a picture of the boat. He wouldn't be in Sandy Bay long enough for that. Except now he was. He didn't want to make any promises, in case plans changed and he left Sandy Bay sooner rather than later, but after berthing, he took photos of the boat from different angles.

"You're not putting us on your socials, are you?" Davey called as he unloaded the deck.

"I'm not in the habit of broadcasting my life to all and sundry, so no… I won't be doing that." Harley opened his eyes wide in mock horror. "Were you hoping I was going to make you Insta-famous? Post videos of a handsome fisherman at work… I can just see you featured there, bare chested, pecs gleaming in the sun, and clutching a fish."

"I'll throw you to the fish if you keep that up,"

Davey didn't look impressed at the ribbing. Harley noticed Lily looking at the deckhand speculatively. Was she imagining him with his bare chest? The two of them had a close working relationship, but perhaps there was more to it. With her reserved demeanour, he could never be sure.

He addressed her now. "I've enjoyed today, even if I'm not publicising it to the world at large. I'd happily return the favour and take you sailing on Ocean Dream, but I guess that would be like a busman's holiday. Besides, she's not going anywhere at the moment. No doubt I'll see you here in the next couple of days."

She nodded at him, but otherwise didn't respond. He checked if Dennis had any messages for him. Roger Marriott had returned the key to Ocean Dream, but otherwise there was nothing to report. Shortly after he arrived back at Seaspray Cottage, his phone rang.

"You still in your little fishing village? Meredith and I are definitely coming down this weekend. Do you have accommodation available in that cottage you've rented? If not, we'll stay in a hotel."

"Bryan… I'm still here and maybe for a few days yet. It's a two-bedroom cottage, so you're welcome to stay with me. It's a short distance out of town, but right on the beach. You'll love it. The break will do you both good."

"Great. We expect a good seafood meal and perhaps some of the local wine. We'll drive down from the city on Friday night. Text me the address."

Harley sent the address and then checked that the bed in the other room was made up. He enjoyed his solitude, but having company for a couple of days would be a change. There was a local farmer's market in town on the Saturday morning, so they could visit that, perhaps have breakfast there and stock up with provisions for the rest of the weekend.

He was about to retire for the night when Lily rang.

"I know it's late, but I wanted to check how you're feeling. How are your legs now?"

Harley slid a hand down the back of his legs, probing the flesh and sliding his fingers over the tender skin. "I'm fine. Your cream worked wonders. The skin still looks red, but no serious damage. Thank you for asking."

He heard the sigh of relief. "I was so worried. You're not just saying that, are you? If you need to see a doctor, I can organise that."

"Lily, I'm fine. The jeans absorbed a lot of the heat. Once I recovered from the shock, the rest was manageable."

After reassuring her still further and thanking Lily and her father for the opportunity to spend the day on the trawler, they disconnected the call. All up, it had been an interesting day.

His visitors brought a burst of noise and disruption to the cottage. Bryan tooted the horn as they drew into the carpark. Harley opened the back door to greet them, and Meredith fell out of the car and into his arms.

"My God, Harley… you've really hidden yourself away. I wondered where we were going when the GPS led us down this dirt road. I don't think Bryan's BMW has ever been off the bitumen. What a quaint cottage. You must enjoy roughing it. You're looking great, by the way."

Harley held the door open as she swept inside. Bryan rolled his eyes as he trailed behind, carrying their bags.

"Good to see you, mate. I'm looking forward to a bit of R&R and a relief to the chatter. You can take over now."

"If you want some down time, you've come to the right place. Dump your bags in the bedroom, and come and sit down. I've got a cheeky red open and airing. I thought you might be in need of some refreshment after the drive."

He had prepared a charcuterie platter, similar to the one he'd prepared a few days before. He still had plenty of ingredients in the fridge from his excursion with Adam.

Meredith laid a proprietary hand on his arm. "We've missed you. What have you been doing while you've been here? You must have been lonely."

Harley handed her a glass of wine and directed her to the veranda, over-looking the sea. Dusk had fallen, but the mild weather made outdoor sitting an option. The tide was coming in and the waves surged over the sand towards them. The outside light sent a soft golden glow over the outdoor setting, while moths and other insects performed suicidal circuits around the globe.

"Take a seat. I'll light a couple of mosquito coils. In answer to your question, I've found plenty to do. I've explored the local region for a start—you can taste some of my purchases—and two days ago, I spent the day on a fishing trawler. That was interesting." He decided not to mention the mishap with boiling water. His jeans had absorbed the worst of it, and the cream Lily had used had soothed his skin.

Bryan looked more interested than Meredith. "You've been making connections, then. Did you bring back any fish?"

"Hopefully, lobster," Meredith said.

"I did actually. I nice big snapper. I thought Meredith could scale and gut it. We could have baked snapper while you're here."

He laughed at the look of horror that crossed the woman's face. "Only teasing. I scaled and filleted it last night. It's ready to go in the oven, but I didn't want to begin cooking before you arrived. It won't take long, but we have plenty to nibble on here first."

"We weren't expecting you to cook for us as well," Bryan protested. "There must be restaurants in town."

"There are, but I thought you might not want to go out again after you finally got here. There's a farmer's market on tomorrow—it's a regular Saturday morning thing—so we could visit that and you can stock up on some local pastries, cheeses, honey, etc. We can have breakfast in town as well."

Meredith held out her glass for a top-up. "That sounds like a great idea to me. We can have a lovely weekend down here, and then you can come back to Adelaide with us. Pick the boat up later when it's fixed."

Harley had no intention of arguing with her, but he wouldn't be leaving Ocean Dream behind. He was fine where he was. He glanced at his watch.

"I'll just turn the oven on. Dinner in half an hour.

They were out the door at seven thirty at Harley's insistence. "I've been warned. The best baked goods go early. We need to hit that stall first, and then can browse the others. I want to get some local olive oil as well, and then there are some gourmet cheeses and other bits and pieces. Maisie's Café is a short walk from the market, and we can have breakfast there. I can vouch for both the food and the service."

Meredith grumbled at the early start, but at the thought of a hearty country breakfast, Bryan had her up and out the door relatively quickly. They browsed the various stalls. Harley bought a loaf of sour dough, the olive oil he wanted, and some almond croissants for later. Meredith found some locally made soaps and natural skin care products, and spent some time at a stall selling handmade jewellery incorporating pearls and delicate shells. Bryan sampled some of the local wines, but agreed to hold off on purchases when Harley said they could tour the regional cellar doors later in the weekend.

A significant number of the townsfolk milled around the stalls. The one person he shouldn't have been surprised to see was Lily. He had to look twice to be sure it really was her. Normally, she wore waterproof clothing and gumboots, and had her hair secured under a beanie. Now, her hair, which was longer than he had realised, was loosely clasped in a barrette. He'd thought it was blonde, but now in the sunlight he noticed it had burnished highlights. She had replaced the gumboots with a pair of sandals, and her snug-fitting faded jeans were topped by a white cotton knitted top, with a gold thread running through it. She didn't look remotely like the deckhand he knew her to be.

"Hi, Lily… I nearly walked past you. At the risk of sounding corny, do you come here often?"

She gestured towards the canvas tote she carried, filled with a range of vegetables, plus one of the sourdough loaves on top. "Not every week, but there were a few things I wanted to get this morning."

Bryan gave Harley a pointed look. He took the hint, although with some suppressed reluctance. "Lily, these are my good friends from Adelaide; Bryan and Meredith. They have driven down for the weekend. Lily's father owns the trawler I went out on yesterday."

"Ah… we heard about that excursion. Seems to have been quite educational, and we dined on one of your fish last night. We're about to have breakfast at Maisie's Café. Why don't you join us?"

Harley stared at Bryan in surprise, but quickly covered his reaction. "Yes, do, Lily… you can advise us on the house specialities."

She looked between them uncertainly. Tellingly, Meredith hadn't said anything beyond a clipped 'hello' at the introduction to the other woman.

"I don't want to intrude on your weekend. You'll want to spend time with your friends."

"No intrusion. After experiencing the offerings at the market, these two are keen to see a bit more of the region. You might have some suggestions on the options. Bryan wants to take home some wines. You've got the local knowledge, so you'd be doing us a favour."

"Okay… I'll take this shopping back to the car and I'll meet you at Maisie's shortly. The café gets busy by mid-morning, so you'll need to hurry if you want to get a table."

She disappeared toward the parking lot, leaving them to head to the café. "What was all that about?" Harley hissed to Bryan. "You'd only just met the woman before you started issuing invitations."

"Only one invitation, and if I didn't, you wouldn't have. I'm looking after your interests."

66

"I can look after my own, thank you very much."

"Bryan," Meredith began, "you don't need to organise Harley's life for him. If he's looking for female company, there are options for him in Adelaide."

"Now who's trying to organise his life?"

"I'm not. I just think I can introduce him to women with whom he will have more in common Louisa, for instance."

Harley saw Bryan rolled his eyes again, possibly for the second or third time that day. He didn't want to engage in the current conversation, particularly when Lily was about to join them.

"C'mon, we need to grab a table."

By the time they had secured a table with Jordan's help and received the menus, Lily wound her way through the crowd. As she sat down, Meredith smiled brightly at nothing in particular. "Well now… isn't this nice?"

Nice? What did the woman mean by that? Lily looked at the immaculately manicured nails and the outfit that was probably purchased in Burnside and knew that she was unlikely to become a friend. Her gut feeling said that a fisherman's daughter would never make the A-List in this woman's eyes. *I'll bet she enjoyed the fish last night, though she probably puts that down to the chef, with no gratitude to the person who caught it.*

Lily gave her a polite smile before turning her attention to Bryan. "Have you been to Sandy Bay before? Perhaps you've heard of some of the local wines. There are several vineyards in the area."

Bryan launched into a spiel about childhood holidays and what he remembered, which seemed to focus on the ice creams he ate, being dumped in the surf, and seeing fairy penguins.

"We've been meaning to come down for ages though, haven't we, Darl?" he appealed to Meredith. "Harley gave us the incentive to get in the car and come."

"I'm good for something then," Harley remarked. "Lily, any particular recommendations on the menu?"

"It's all local produce, so it depends on preference… and the size of your appetite. The big breakfast is enough to feed an entire family."

Jordan took their orders, and Bryan resumed his earlier conversation about Sandy Bay. "Did you grow up here? What made you decide on working on a trawler?"

"Yes, born and bred in Sandy Bay. My father has been a fisherman for decades. Earlier, he focussed on lobster, but the catch is varied now, according to the season. I worked on the boat in my teens during the school holidays and loved the lifestyle. I considered other careers, but always drifted back to the sea."

Meredith looked perplexed. "But didn't you want to leave such a small town and explore the world and opportunities? I don't understand what there is to keep you here."

No, you wouldn't. "I studied computer science in Adelaide. My parents insisted I keep my options open. I got my degree, but couldn't see myself in that sort of job forever. I came back to the bay, worked in a newsagency for a while, and then joined Dad on Sea Witch."

Heartbreak hotel… that's what her apartment had been when she lived in Adelaide, but she was not about to disclose that information. Her explanation was met initially with silence. Harley nodded his head in tacit understanding. "Knowing what you want to do in life is a strength; being able to follow that dream is a privilege. You've done well."

She hadn't expected him to be so understanding. There was probably more to his story than the potted history he'd given her the other evening. She still asked herself whether he was really following a dream, or was he running away from something… himself, perhaps?

"With that background, you and Harley have a bit in common." Bryan beamed as though he had made an astonishing deduction. "Why don't you come with us this afternoon? We've had a discussion since we saw you at the market and thought we'd drive down to Port Reilly. Harley says there is a seafood festival happening in town this weekend. A new art gallery is opening as well, so we can visit that. The town should be buzzing."

"Lily may have other plans for the day," Meredith demurred. "She probably has no interest in art, let along traipsing around with us and the last thing she needs is more seafood. Don't feel you have to be polite," she added in Lily's direction.

She was about to decline, but Meredith's tone was the deciding factor. Why shouldn't she be interested in art? Traipsing around was not so enticing, but the suggestion that Meredith might be put out if she came was enough to swing the balance. "Yes, I'd love to come. I haven't done that for a while. It's about time I re-acquainted myself with a little culture and there are a couple of antique shops you might enjoy."

Their meals arrived, and conversation moved to discussion about the food, and what they might see that afternoon. Bryan insisted they should drive in his car. The ute that Harley had hired was not an option, and Meredith was unlikely to travel in Lily's second-hand Hyundai, that probably smelled of fish. With that arrangement settled, Lily gave them her address and Bryan agreed to pick her up at eleven.

Harley hadn't said a lot during these arrangements, leaving her to wonder if his feelings mirrored Meredith's. He seemed happy enough when she slid into the back seat of Bryan's BMW alongside him. Meredith sat in the front. The leather seats were armchair-soft, and still had a new car smell. Lily relaxed back against the padded headrest as the car glided away from the kerb.

"I hope you don't feel that Bryan railroaded you," Harley said softly, speaking under the music that washed over them from the sound system. "He has a way of assuming that everyone will fall in with his plans."

"I noticed that, but I wouldn't have accepted if it wasn't convenient."

His expression still held some doubt, but he gave her hand a reassuring pat and turned to look out his side window. Lily felt the sensation of his touch on her skin, even after he pulled his hand away. She was conscious of the proximity of their bodies. They had shared space during the day he spent on Sea Witch, but this environment was more intimate. She stole a sideways glance, examining his profile. She already knew that he didn't do physical work, and his hands reflected that. He didn't have the muscular shoulders that Davey sported either. Still, he'd pulled his weight on the boat, and didn't shirk the heavy stuff. He hadn't mentioned the burns to his legs, so she assumed there was no lasting discomfort. His aquiline profile

70

looked strong on a man. Surprisingly, his eyelashes were naturally dark, at a length many women would die for.

Unexpectedly, he glanced her way again and caught her looking at him. She felt a surge of embarrassed heat, and looked away, not before she caught the hint of a smile on his face.

7 – Pt Reilly

"WE'RE IN YOUR hands," Bryan called from the driver's seat. "Tell us to where to park and what we should see first."

"If you become tired of wet, smelly fish, you could always try your hand as a tour guide," Meredith said sweetly. "I know which I would prefer.

That comment didn't deserve an answer. Bumper-to-bumper cars circled the town, looking for parking spaces. Lily directed them to the carpark at the rear of the solicitors her father used, Densley and Associates. She made a quick call to Paul Densley, getting permission for the cheeky move, and promised him a fresh snapper next time she was in town.

"I'll look forward to that. Make sure you don't park anyone else in and don't tell your mates about this option!"

"As if I would. Thanks, Paul. You're a star."

They wandered down the main street of the town. Traffic had been blocked off, turning the street into a mall for the weekend. Cafés and restaurants had established pop-up booths on the footpath in front of their stores, and other businesses or artisans peddled their wares from market gazebos set up in the middle of the road. Progress was slow, in part because Lily kept running into people she knew, and in part because Meredith wanted to browse at every market stall.

The day blessed them with pleasant weather. It put the crowd in a convivial mood, and the food booths did a roaring trade. After Bryan dragged Meredith away from a stall selling more silver and pearl jewellery, he suggested a plan for their remaining time in Port Reilly.

"I'd like to see the gallery next in case they close early. After that, I think I'd like to sit down and rest my feet. Since we're here, we should at least be sampling the local oysters, and a cleansing ale would slide down easily."

Meredith pulled a face. "More food. Didn't you have enough at breakfast?"

"Never! Especially if it means oysters only metres from where they were farmed. You don't get oysters tasting as fresh as this in the city."

Lily had no argument with that. She wholeheartedly agreed, but she was curious about Bryan's interest in the gallery. "Do you paint as well, or are you an art collector?"

"I leave the painting to Harley. I never progressed beyond finger painting at kindergarten. I'm a collector of sorts, but mostly I procure art works on behalf of my clients, be they corporate entities or private individuals. I like to keep an eye on what's available in the market and to monitor any new talent. That's how I met Harley."

She glanced at Harley in surprise, but his attention was taken by Meredith showing him her latest acquisition. "I assumed you must have had business connections, or gone to school with each other, or something like that."

"Yes, it was business, but my line of business, not his. I saw some of his work in Sydney when he first exhibited in a gallery that I monitor. I purchased a couple of paintings and then persuaded him to hold an exhibition in Adelaide. It was a great success. I regard him as my discovery."

Lily filed the information away with other titbits she had learned about Harley. The more she learned, the more she realised that her first impression that he was one of the idle rich with a boat to die for wasn't accurate. The man in question broke away from his discussion with Meredith.

"Are you talking about me? Next thing, Bryan will claim credit for every sale I've made," he chided to Lily

Bryan grinned good-naturedly. "This man does his best work under pressure. That's why he needs me."

"It's a quaint little town, isn't it Bryan?" Meredith remarked after showing Lily her new earrings. "Sort of reminds me of that Greek fishing village on the shores of Syros that we stayed in last year."

Bryan shrugged. "Sort of... this place has an Australian flavour though. Easier and cheaper to get to as well."

Lily knew that the comparison was irrelevant. Meredith had wanted to emphasise that they travelled, and to exotic places at that. The earrings were more impressive, and Meredith hadn't needed to travel overseas for those. The jeweller lived in Port Reilly.

"Any time you want to feel as though you're back in the Mediterranean, you can just come down here for a few days. Much cheaper... closer too."

Harley touched her lightly on the arm. "Why don't you lead the way to this gallery, and then we can check out the competition."

He didn't say, 'Don't stir up trouble', but she knew that's what he meant.

"Sure. This way. We should be just in time for the opening of the exhibition." The gallery was at the end of an arcade and a trickle of people also headed in that direction. They slipped inside the door, picking up a catalogue each, and ducking around a group that stood chatting at the main entrance. A photographer moved through the crowd, taking photos of the patrons and some paintings. Looking around, she realised she knew a few of those taking advantage of the glasses of champagne and the free nibbles. Not only that, she knew the artist as well. He wore a bow tie, and an ear-wide grin. He looked alternately pleased with himself and overwhelmed at the surrounding crowd. When he wasn't being mobbed as he was now, she would have a quick work with him.

Harley stood in front of one painting, examining it intently. She looked at him side-on, absorbing the intensity with which he reviewed the artwork. Bryan and Meredith had helped themselves to a glass of champagne and now stood studying the catalogue, conferring with each other. Lily left them to it and began her own tour of the paintings hanging on the walls. Some were of local scenes that she recognised, but not all. She paused in front of a large painting depicting two children picking up shells on the sand, with the beach scene behind them. It was aptly titled *The Shell Seekers*. It made her think of the book of the same name.

"Lily! Fancy seeing you here."

She knew that voice. She spun around. "Christos! I didn't know you were back in town."

The man grabbed her in a bearhug, rocking gently back and forward. "Filming finished, and I have a break before the next project. I need some down-time, plus I wanted to support Dimitri. This is his first exhibition and I couldn't miss that."

She pushed herself back from his embrace so that she could look up at him. "Of course… I should have expected it. Living in my own little bubble as I do, I hadn't realised that he was exhibiting his work. I'm only here because I've brought some visitors along for the day, and they have a particular interest in art."

She glimpsed Harley politely sliding past, clearly not wanting to intrude. Lily nodded in his direction. "Harley has been moored in the marina for a few days. He also paints."

The two men courteously nodded at each other. At that point, the photographer bustled up. "Christos, can I get a photo - perhaps one with your lady friend, and then one with your brother?"

"I'd rather Dimitri had the limelight all to himself today. By all means, take a photo here." With his arm around Lily, he gestured to Harley to move closer. "You too."

They moved into a huddle and after taking several photos, the photographer noted their names for his records. Not that he needed to ask Christos's name of course. As he checked the spelling of their names, Lily looked up to see Meredith staring at them with mouth agape. She seized the moment to reach up and kiss Christos on the cheek. "We must catch up properly before you leave."

"Sure. I've got your number. I'll call you. Eleni will want to see you as well." The crowd swallowed him. Lily saw

Dimitri grasp his arm, so the photographer got his snap of the brothers together after all.

She turned back to find Meredith at her shoulder. The woman hissed accusingly. "How come you know Christos Antoniou? Why didn't you introduce us?"

"Christos? We grew up together. His dad has a fishing trawler as well. The lead artist today is Dimitri, his younger brother. He just blends into the community when he comes home… doesn't like a fuss. Everyone knows and respects that."

Meredith's eyes followed her quarry hungrily. Lily could sense her brain ticking over, searching for an excuse to push through the crowd and introduce herself. Bryan must have sensed the same for he grasped her arm.

"They'll be starting the speeches soon, and I want to get a good look at everything before that. Some red stickers have appeared already."

He shuffled her sideways. Harley still stood beside her, wearing a bemused expression. "You've gained brownie points because of the exalted company you keep, and lost brownie points because you kept him to yourself. He seems a down-to-earth sort of bloke."

"He is. We spent a lot of time together growing up. His sister was in my class at school. Our families mixed socially as well. It was a great childhood."

"So it seems, and a successful one at that."

❧

Harley chided himself for being surprised at Lily's connections. He had assumed that growing up in Sandy Bay meant growing up in an insular backwater, but that clearly wasn't the case. Christos Antoniou was one of the country's favourite sons, having risen to the peak of fame in the film industry. He was not someone Harley had expected to meet in Lily's company.

He saw Bryan in discussion at the sales desk, so he must have found a painting that took his fancy. Being able to point out that the artist was the brother of a famous film star would probably raise the price in Bryan's future negotiations. Meredith would milk the connection for all it was worth, no doubt dropping that she had been at a gallery opening with the man himself. Whatever. Meredith was a skilled networker, and that was all to Bryan's benefit, and ultimately hers as well.

He and Lily completed their tour of the exhibits together, discussing what they saw.

"I know this scene. It's halfway between Sandy Bay and Port Reilly. I like his use of light. He's captured the essence of late afternoon."

"He has… makes me feel I should put my paints away. When someone else has captured the local scenery as competently as Dimitri, my work feels like a pale imitation."

"Rubbish. From what I've seen of your work, not much of it admittedly, you have your own style that could hang on these walls, yet would be quite different. Anyway, Bryan already told me that you've been exhibiting in Sydney and that you took his interest at that event, so you've obviously been impressing people."

Harley laughs. "And I didn't even have to pay him!"

The opening speeches started, with the gallery owner doing the honours. Harley noticed Christos move to the back of the crowd, where he could still see but where he didn't detract from the attention focussed on his younger brother. Bryan looked pleased with himself, indicating that he had made at least one purchase. Meredith was still casting side-eye glances in Christos's direction, while trying to disguise the fact.

The gallery owner finished up with a comment that Dimitri's paintings were being sought by art dealers in the major cities, but that he wanted to exhibit on his home turf first. Anyone who wanted to hang a genuine Dimitri Antoniou painting on their walls had better act quickly. The number of anxious buyers standing at the sales desk swelled immediately.

His thoughts turned to the suggested oysters and other refreshments. Lily was still by his side, but the other two were chatting to the artist.

"Bryan might want to chat for a while if he is establishing some sort of commercial relationship with Dimitri. Have you seen everything you want to see?"

"I think so."

"I'll let him know we're heading to the catering marquee where we can sit down for a while, and they can follow us when they're done."

He sidled up behind Bryan and tapped him on the arm. "Don't want to interrupt your conversation, but Lily and I will find those oysters you talked about. We'll see you in the catering tent."

Bryan acknowledged him with a quick nod, but Dimitri looked over his shoulder with a look of delight.

"Lily… good to see you." He grasped her by the shoulders and kissed first one cheek and then the other. "Did you bring Bryan to my little exhibition? I should put you on commission."

"Modesty doesn't become you, Dimitri. By the look of all the red stickers, you've done well, and this is just the opening. I've no objections if you want to pay me a commission. I'll see who else I can drag along to see your daubings."

He laughed. "Charming, as always, I see. Did you know Christos is in town? Eleni is home as well. Dad is killing the fatted calf, and Mum is in her element and cooking up a storm."

"I'm sure she is. I noticed Eleni on the other side of the room, but she looked busy. Tell her I'll catch up with her in the next day or so." Her eyes flickered over Bryan, who'd waited politely. "I know you've got things to discuss. We'll leave you to it. Congratulations, by the way."

Harley followed her to the door, where they stepped out into the quiet of the arcade, with the background music in the gallery fading the further away they walked.

"Do you know everyone of influence between Port Reilly and Sandy Bay? First you find us a carpark, then you exchange kisses with a film star and his brother the artist. I'm not forgetting your connection with Maddie, either."

She winked at him. "Need any connections? I'm your woman."

"Thanks. I'll keep that in mind."

They strolled past the market stalls that had kept Meredith enthralled earlier and made their way into the catering marquee. The menu board displayed options such as salt and pepper squid, fresh oysters, and even fish and chips.

"If you want to find us a table, I'll order a mixed platter for four. That should keep everyone happy. Think about what you might like to drink."

Hopefully, her connections ran to securing a table in the crowded venue. He left her searching while he made his way to the counter. By the time he found her again, clutching the number given for his order, she sat at a table with a couple of women.

"This is the man I told you about," she said, nodding in his direction. "Mavis and Stella work at the fish co-op in Sandy Bay. They're happy to share their table with us."

"G'day luv," Mavis said. "I saw that pretty boat of yours in the marina. It's nice that Lily can show you around a bit." Empty plates sat in front of them on the table. Mavis looked as though she enjoyed her food—often.

"I see you've already tried the food here. I assume it's good?"

"Of course. It's all local. I probably handled it myself in the co-op. Anyway, as I was just telling Lily, we've finished here, so you're welcome to our table. C'mon, Stella. We'll leave these young people to it."

They wiped their greasy fingers on the paper serviettes before pushing back their chairs and collecting the cardboard plates from the table. The plates were duly deposited in one of the rubbish bins. Stella was as skinny as Mavis was comfortably plump.

"See ya Monday, luv," Mavis said to Lily. "Nice to meetcha," she added in Harley's direction.

Lily swept some crumbs from the table with her hand. "Sit down before someone else tries to claim the table or steal a couple of the chairs. They are a scarce commodity."

She was right about that. "If you can hold on here a couple more minutes, I'll fetch us a drink. Bryan can sort out their drinks when they arrive." He took her order and pushed his way through the crowd to the bar area. He noticed Jordan with a few mates in the crowd, exchanging passing nods with him. It amused him that now, even he had connections in town.

Lily was leaning back on her chair, chatting to a woman seated at an adjoining table when he returned, carefully balancing their drinks. She glanced around when she heard him place them on the table, before finishing her conversation.

"No promises, but I'll think about it. I'll let you know in a couple of days." She swivelled her chair back to face Harley.

"More friends?" He passed her the schooner of cider she had requested.

"Can't escape them. You must miss yours, sailing on your own as you do."

"Not really. It's not like it once was. With internet technologies, I can keep in touch with most people… those I want to, that is."

"I guess so. There's always something happening here in town. Anh is running a fund-raiser for the neonatal ward at the Pt Reilly hospital. Unless a delivery is really straightforward, women have to travel to Adelaide to give birth, and if we had more humidicribs here, women from Sandy Bay and Pt Reilly could have their babies where they have family and community support. I've been asked to help with the fund-raising effort."

"Sounds like a worthy cause."

"It is. I wanted to think about the time factor before I committed myself."

Sounded sensible. Harley knew Bryan and Meredith wouldn't be far away. He looked in the direction he expected them to come from case they were already close. He leaned across the table towards Lily.

82

"Speaking of friends… I know Meredith can be a bit…"

"…bit of a bitch? Don't worry, the Meredith's of this world don't worry me."

"Once you get to know her, she's really quite sweet. Her insecurities can bring out the worst in her."

"Insecurities? What has she got to be insecure about, particularly around me?"

"For a start, you're a competent and confident woman. You've got a kick-arse attitude and rock your own unique style. That can threaten someone like Meredith."

Her eyes widened. She stared at him, clearly processing what he had said. She sipped her drink before responding. "I don't know whether to laugh or cry at that. You don't have to apologise on her behalf. I hadn't perceived Meredith as being insecure and certainly hadn't thought of myself in the terms you described."

"Is this a private party, or can anyone join in?"

Bryan and Meredith stood by the table. Meredith looked frazzled and dropped into a chair. Harley hoped they hadn't overheard the conversation.

"My feet are killing me. Bryan, be a dear and fetch us both a drink. Something with bubbles."

Bryan obediently disappeared toward the bar. Harley saw Lily looking at Meredith speculatively. No guesses what was running through her mind.

He shifted his position in his chair. The skin on the back of his thighs was still sensitive from the scalding. Thank goodness it wasn't worse. He was doubly relieved that he hadn't worn baggy jocks, or had a hole in the back of them. He flushed involuntarily at the memory of standing in front of Lily in his underpants while she rubbed ointment into the back of his legs. It was not what he had expected when he boarded Sea Witch. He told himself it was no different to wearing his swimmers, and she could have been applying sun cream, but his feeling of exposure remained.

She looked up, and catching his gaze, gave a small smile. Hopefully, she hadn't guessed what he'd been thinking.

8 – Lily Reaches Out

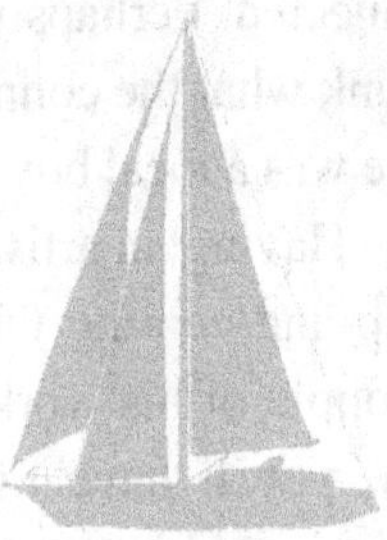

THEY WERE ALL quiet on the drive back to Sandy Bay. Bryan and Meredith discussed dinner options in the front seat, while Lily and Harley observed the passing scenery instead.

"We could get a take-away and bring it back to the cottage," Harley suggested after a while. "What about you, Lily? Would you like to join us?"

I think I've had enough for one day. "That's kind of you to ask, but I'd like to be dropped home. I have a few chores to catch up on."

Meredith was probably pleased. The woman looked over her shoulder at Harley. "Why don't you come back to the city with us tomorrow? There's not a lot you can do here until the boat is fixed. We can bring you back when the work is finished."

He took a moment to answer. "I think some down time in Sandy Bay is what I need for now. I'll spend time with you in Adelaide when the boat is sea-worthy again, I promise."

"At least while you are here, you should get to know Christos Antoniou. Ask Lily to introduce you. I didn't know she was so well connected. Perhaps we'll have to come down here more often. Think what the connection would do for your reputation. I knew he was a local boy made good, but I thought he was from the city. Having an artist brother is a plus."

"Dimitri's an up-and-coming talent," Bryan agreed. I'm sure I can place a couple of his works. If you're staying here for a while, Harley, you'll have time to give the paints a workout. Have you ventured into portraiture? You could do a portrait of Christos Antoniou for the Archibald Prize."

"Whoa… that's getting a bit carried away. I'll leave the portraits to those who specialise in that area."

"How long are you renting the cottage for?"

"It's only short term until the boat is fixed. A matter of days only. I can make enquiries if you think you want to rent it for yourselves."

Lily bit her lip. The way Meredith was talking, you would think she wasn't even in the car. Did that woman only consider others in the light of how useful they might be to her? She kept her gaze fixed on the view outside the window as a strategy to distance herself from the conversation.

Bryan remembered the way to her cottage and pulled up on the verge at the front. "Quaint house. I see you've gone for easy maintenance with the native shrubs."

"Best to use plants that will survive in this area. A new business on the outskirts of town specialises in supplying indigenous plants. I did a complete make-over using their suggestions."

"Makes sense. Thanks for coming with us today. Some local knowledge went a long way. You're always welcome to drop in on us in Adelaide, isn't she Meredith?"

Meredith glanced at her husband before swivelling around from the front seat. "Yes, of course, we'd love to see you. Ring first though, won't you?"

Lily opened the car door, placing a foot on the ground outside the car. Harley reached over to touch her arm. "I'm going to be around for a few days yet. Perhaps we can catch up for a drink or a meal?"

"Perhaps. Enjoy your evening." Lily didn't want to make a commitment for reasons she didn't quite understand. She climbed out and shut the door before standing to one side and watching them drive away. The unexpected day had been interesting, if that was the right term. She had enjoyed spending the day with Harley, but needed time to process what he had said about how others perceived her. It didn't worry her to be thought intimidating, but perhaps that had some influence over the end of her earlier disastrous relationship. The inference then had been that she was cold and distant, and not responsive enough to his charms. He hadn't been as polite as that, but she'd understood what he'd meant. She fled the city with a broken heart and the intention to not let herself be so vulnerable in the future. That applied to Harley and anyone else.

An evening to herself was not to be wasted. Lily ran a deep bath, not worrying for once about wasting water.

She hung a fresh towel on the heated towel rail and placed rose-scented moisturising lotion on the vanity unit as part of her preparations. She chose a playlist on her mobile and brought in the WIFI speaker. While the water ran, filling the room with steam, she cleaned her face and applied a gentle mask to the eye area. The sea air could be harsh on tender skin. She added some rose-scented bath salts, plus a touch of oil that spread in a thin film over the surface. The small room smelt divine. All that was left to do was to secure her hair in a scrunchie on top of her head, shuck off her robe, and step into the water.

Her skin turned a rosy pink in the water, hotter than she had meant to make it, but it felt good. She massaged each shoulder as best she could, noting the tension those muscles carried. The work she did was strenuous, but at least saved her the cost of a gym. Not for the first time, she was grateful that the old-fashioned bath was large enough for her to stretch out.

The water was tepid by the time Lily stepped out and smoothed the moisturiser over her skin, focussing on her arms, legs, and the heels of her feet. She had just slipped on the towelling robe when she heard her phone ringing. For a moment, she was tempted to ignore it, but curiousity got the better of her. Few people had her number. The exuberant voice at the other end could have been heard without the phone connection. The Antoniou family were all rather loud.

"Lily! I saw you across the room today, but when I looked again, you were gone. What did you think of Dimitri's work? Hasn't my little brother come a long way? Do you know, he was approached by some hotshot art dealer from the city?"

"You mean Bryan Wilson? I visited the gallery with him and his partner. I didn't realise that Dimitri was exhibiting until I arrived. Remiss of me, but I haven't been paying enough attention to local news. Lucky that Bryan had heard of the gallery opening from all the way in Adelaide. I loved Dimitri's work. Did he sell much?"

"For an opening day, he had a fantastic result. Lots of red stickers. He's on a high, and Mama and Baba are beside themselves with pride. Thrilled also that we're all home. I've brought Dion down to meet the family as well." Her voice brightened. "Christos isn't here very often. Dimitri gave me your message." Eleni paused long enough to draw a breath. "I've got to return to Adelaide early Monday morning, but the parents are throwing a celebratory barbecue tomorrow evening. Baba's cooking a lamb on a spit. Can you come over? I'd love to catch up and you can meet Dion. Mama will want to see you, of course. She says you are always at sea, and never around."

I'd love to come. What shall I bring?"

"No need to bring anything. Mama will be offended if you do. You'll be insinuating she can't provide enough food."

Lily decided to buy a bunch of flowers on her way. No matter what Eleni said, she knew her mother would appreciate a small gift.

"That wasn't the art dealer I saw standing beside you. Who is he? Is this a new man in your life? Things are looking up. Bring him too."

"He is not a man in my life; he's an acquaintance who is in town for a few days. He's a friend of the art dealer."

"He's a good-looking dude. Up to you. It's about time you got involved. You push men away. You can be so daunting."

"So you can feed him ouzo and retsina and tell him tall tales? I don't think so."

Eleni gave a peal of laughter. "As if I would do such a thing. Anyway, what tall tales are there to tell?"

Lily didn't answer that question, because she couldn't. Her life hadn't been one that featured tall tales, or tales of any dramatic interest. "Can't talk anymore; I've just climbed out of the bath but I look forward to catching up with all the news tomorrow. Give me all the goss then."

She knew Eleni would be full of gossip… who they knew, what they were doing, why and when. As long as the gossip didn't involve her, she listened, deflecting anything she regarded as too personal. The conversation left her with a bit to think about, that and Harley's comments from earlier in the day.

She wasn't reserved with everyone, but took her time getting to know people before letting her guard down. She knew that Mimi, Eleni's mother, would question her about her love life the following evening. Mimi was even more direct than her daughter, expecting that by now, a female of Lily's age should be married with a couple of kids. She had offered to introduce Lily to a good Greek boy on more than one occasion.

Did she really make Meredith feel insecure? It wasn't apparent in her behaviour, but Harley knew the woman better than she did.

&

The thought hung around the next morning, surfacing periodically to niggle at her. She didn't mean to be intimidating, but people like Meredith acted as though she were some lesser species. Wasn't her behaviour reasonable if she stood up for herself, however that came about? It absolutely was, but did everyone else find her intimidating, even people she casually met? Eleni had said that men found her daunting, but that was only because she had never mastered the art of small talk. Why say anything just for the sake of it?

She had boundaries; she knew that. She had allowed Andreas to cross them, but that was when she was young and naive. That lesson had been learned the hard way, and she made sure not to repeat the mistake. No man had come that close since. It made Mimi's interrogations tedious, but she provided automatic responses. She was too busy; she didn't have time; no man liked a woman who smelled of fish. She changed the conversation quickly to asking about one of the Antoniou brood. Mimi loved talking about her kids and was easily diverted in that direction.

Lily couldn't say why the comments rankled now, except that people around her were pairing up, and she was alone. Even Meredith and Bryan looked to be a happy couple. The main street in Pt Reilly yesterday had been full of other couples, all enjoying a day out in each other's company.

Her thoughts turned to Harley. She didn't know him well, but he hadn't pushed the boundaries. Inviting him to the Antoniou dinner would keep Mimi happy. Bryan and Meredith were driving back to the city after lunch, so if she rang him mid-afternoon, he would be free to talk. With that decision made, she put her ruminations aside in favour of a cup of coffee. That, and those domestic chores that had a habit of reappearing each weekend.

Harley sounded surprised when he answered her call, though not unreasonably so. "I hope spending the day with us wasn't too much of an imposition?"

"Not at all. I might not have seen Dimitri's exhibition if I hadn't joined you. I hadn't known he was being featured in the gallery. His mother would never have forgiven me if I hadn't seen it."

"From what I saw of the brothers, they are a supportive family."

"Yes, and that is what I am calling about, sort of."

"Oh?"

"I've known the family since forever—being fishing families, we all grew up together. Mimi and Nico are holding a celebratory barbecue tonight, because their offspring are all home. Would you like to come with me?"

There was a moment's silence as Harley processed the invitation. "I know Meredith was blathering on yesterday about making connections with Christos Antoniou, but don't feel you have to listen to her. Won't they think it strange if you turn up to their family gathering with a stranger in tow?"

"In part they'll be delighted, particularly Mimi, the matriarch of the family. You'd be doing me a favour. It will get her off my back. It will be a very casual affair, and as far as the family are concerned, the more the merrier." She shook her head. That wasn't what she had meant to say. "I'm sorry, that came out wrong. I just thought that while you're stuck in town, you might like to meet a few more people, and you and Dimitri will have a bit in common. He might want to know more about Bryan. I'd hate him to be taken advantage of by someone more experienced in the art world than he is."

"I don't think that Bryan would—"

"Probably not… he seems a nice bloke, but I'm sure Dimitri will have some questions."

If she let Harley think Dimitri was her primary concern, he might feel more comfortable about coming. It would make her feel more comfortable too.

"Okay, that would be… nice. What time and where?"

"Do you remember the way to my cottage? If you can be here by six, we can go together."

"Sounds like a plan. I'll see you then."

After they disconnected the call, Lily realised it was the first time she had ever invited a man anywhere. It was a sobering thought.

෧

The blast of music hit them as soon as they turned in at the front gate. The lights that could be seen at the end of the driveway flagged that the party was in full swing under the back veranda. Voices carried on the night air, and as per usual, mostly at full volume. The smell of barbecued lamb greeted them, and probably had carnivores salivating for blocks around.

"Lily! Welcome! Give me a hug!"

Eleni bustled up, drink in one hand and gave her a one-arm hug. "I haven't seen you for ages. You really should come up to the city sometimes." She released Lily and looked over her shoulder in open surprise. "You brought him! You had better introduce me."

Lily flushed inwardly. Eleni's comment made it obvious that they had been discussing Harley. She hoped he had missed the inference. "Eleni, this is Harley. He's stuck in Sandy Bay while his boat is being repaired. He came out on Sea Witch the other day to learn about trawler operations."

"Stan took you out? You must have got on his right side. Welcome. Any friend of Lily's is a friend of ours." She turned to call out to a man standing in a group. "Dion, come and meet Lily and Harley. Lily and I grew up together."

Lily could see as the man broke away from the Antoniou brothers and ambled over, that Lily had chosen a man with Greek heritage. Her parents would be happy. He approached with an easy smile, his dark, deep-set eyes sparkling with friendliness. He slung one arm about Eleni's shoulders and extended the other to Harley, and nodded to Lily.

"Pleased to meet you. I have enjoyed meeting Lily's friends this weekend. Can I fetch you both a drink?"

"We'll say hello to Mimi and Nico first," Lily said, "and join you for a drink after that."

"Sure. I'll be by the fire."

Lily regarded the cluster of men around the barbecue. *These men may be Greek, but they've still picked up Australian habits*. Mimi embraced her in an enormous hug, kissing one cheek and then the other before burying her nose in the bunch of flowers that Lily gave her. She then turned to give Harley an appraising look.

"Lily… it has been too long. You should come to visit more often. Who is this young man? This is your boyfriend? It is about time."

"No… not a boyfriend, I mean… we're friends. Harley is a sailor. He's only here for a few days."

Lily didn't look at Harley but could feel her ears going red.

"A sailor… well, that's a start. Your dad needs someone to help with the fish."

"He's got all the help he needs. Harley's not in town to fish. Anyway, I help with the fish."

"Ach!" Mimi waved a hand dismissively. "This you cannot do when you have a family."

"Mama, don't give Lily a hard time. Come on, we'll get the drink that Dion promised." Eleni looked as though about to break into giggles. "You should have seen your face. Sorry, Harley… my mother is likely to give you a grilling at some point this evening. She will want to know that your intentions towards Lily are honourable."

"Tell her Harley doesn't have any intentions towards me, honourable or otherwise."

"Whatever you say."

Lily resisted the urge to thump her, only with supreme effort. Too late, she remembered Eleni's propensity for teasing. Harley looked bemused, but refrained from commenting beyond shaking his head slightly, as though trying to digest the nuances of the conversations. She should have warned him of the reception he was likely to receive from Mimi.

They joined the group of family and friends milling outside, and Eleni effected the introductions, while Dion kept his promise of fetching them each a drink. Feeling a sense of duty, given Meredith's comments the day before, she also introduced Harley to both Christos and Dimitri. The latter was very interested to learn that not only was Harley also an artist, but that he was friends with Bryan. The two men sidestepped into their own huddle as they discussed the intricacies of the art world.

Lily left them to it, and instead caught up with some of the cousins. Although most of her cohort had grown up in either Sandy Bay or Pt Reilly, some had moved elsewhere. They rarely saw each other, but it might as well have been yesterday when they last connected. The same jokes and memories surfaced, as did the gossip about people they knew. Lily listened mostly, not being inclined to share much beyond superficial detail about her life.

She was about to check if Harley needed rescuing, when someone tapped her on the shoulder.

"Have you had time to think? I could really use some creative input on the fundraiser."

Lily turned to find Anh standing beside her.

"Maybe you could donate a fish, or something. We could auction it if you catch a really big fish."

"Anh... I didn't know you were coming this evening. I assume that is not a serious suggestion, but the answer is no. A fish auction won't earn you much. What ideas have you come up with so far?"

"We're thinking of a fund-raising dinner, perhaps held on the autumn equinox. On a more serious note, perhaps you could donate the fish as one of the menu options."

"Where would you hold this dinner?"

"The local technical college has a restaurant where the hospitality students can put their learning into practice., whether working in the kitchen or serving tables. It's not as expensive as a conventional restaurant. If your family could supply the fish, that would cut costs even further."

"I'd have to ask my father about that, and we'd also have to clear it with the fish co-op. Under our contract, the catch goes to them for processing. I might be able to pull some strings in negotiating some sort of deal. Would you earn enough from hosting a dinner?"

"We would run a silent auction as well. That's where you could help in approaching people to donate items or services to be auctioned."

While they were talking, Lily kept her eye on Harley in case he looked lost. He caught her eye and smiled. She saw him say something to Dimitri and clap him on the shoulder in a friendly gesture. He then left the other man and made his way over to her. She introduced him to Anh, and to include him in the conversation, gave him a brief explanation of her request.

"Anh is looking for help in securing items for a silent auction. I'm not sure how much use I'll be. Some of the local wineries might donate a case of wine."

"This is for the neonatal unit? It's a worthwhile cause. When are you staging this event?"

"Not for a while yet—probably the autumn equinox. It always helps to have an additional theme for these dinners."

Harley rubbed his chin pensively. "If it would be of any interest, I could paint a picture of a local scene while I'm here. I'd get it framed, of course."

"But you won't even be here." Lily was surprised at the offer.

"That doesn't matter. I can leave the painting with you for safekeeping until then."

Anh grinned with glee. "See… I knew you would have some good contacts. Keep up the good work."

She swung off to tackle another prospect, obviously using the barbecue to solicit as much support as she could. Lily spoke quietly to Harley. "Don't think you have to do this. It's a very generous offer, but it's not expected."

He shrugged. "I might as well do something useful while I'm here. I might not finish it immediately, but I can do the preliminary work on it now. I can send it when it's finished, or even drop it back to you, depending on where I am."

He raised his glass in wordless toast. "Everyone here has been so friendly. That's what I like about small towns; so different from the culture in big cities. Thank you for inviting me."

❧

Harley dropped Lily back to her cottage shortly before ten. Given that Lily had to be out on Sea Witch early the following morning, they left before most people. He pulled up in her driveway with the engine still running.

"You'll be tired tomorrow, given your early start. I enjoyed meeting your friends, though. Dimitri has my contact details, and I said I would show him some of my work tomorrow. Christos is a great bloke also—very down-to-earth. Not what I expected at all."

"He wouldn't be anything else. Nico and Mimi wouldn't put up with any airs and graces. Nor would Eleni and Dimitri. He's just one of the family."

"I can see that. Thank you again for including me. I enjoyed the evening." He leaned across from his seat and kissed Lily on the cheek. She looked startled, but didn't respond until she had slid out of the car and shut the door. He activated the control button to slide down the passenger window. Lily leaned in through the open window.

"Hope you get some news about Ocean Dream soon. I'll see you around the marina."

With that, she was gone. The drive back to Seaspray Cottage gave him time to review the evening. The biggest surprise had been the invitation. After Lily's initial obvious distrust of him, he was gratified to note the thawing in demeanour. Mimi had pulled him aside at one time when Lily was talking elsewhere, and gave him a grilling.

"How long have you known Lily? She is a good girl. She doesn't need someone in her life who messes her around."

"No, I would never do that, I mean… we're just friends, you know? I like Lily, but we've only just met."

"Mama, what are you doing? Leave the man alone."

Harley turned to find Christos at his shoulder. "Sorry, Mama would have all of us married off by now if she could, Lily included. She and Eleni were always hanging around together as kids. Come and tell me about this boat of yours."

Christos had winked and dragged him away to where others clustered around the charcoal fire. "I'm not in Sandy Bay for long, but if you're going sailing one day and need some crew, let me know. I'd love to get out on the water again, and not on a trawler." An eye-roll had accompanied the last comment.

"Sure. The electronics are a problem at the moment, but we can still take the boat out in local waters. Give me your number and I'll call you. There's another bloke, Adam Grant, I promised a day on the water as well, so we can make it a combined event."

Christos had clapped him on the shoulder, muttering that it was a deal, before being snaffled by a cousin to answer questions about his previous film. Havey left them to it and looked around for where Lily was. He wasn't looking for romantic complications while stuck in Sandy Bay, but perhaps he should invite her to dinner one evening.

He was still debating that issue with himself as he unlocked the door of the cottage. Already the place felt like home, and he had only been there a few days. It was quiet after Bryan and Meredith had left. He wasn't one to brag, but Meredith would be both impressed and jealous if he told her about who he had met that evening. It was too late to ring, anyway. Harley threw his phone on the bench top while setting about making himself a cup of tea before retiring.

He had switched the phone to silent early in the evening, not wanting to disrupt a social occasion with private phone calls. He changed the setting and saw that the screen flashed with a slew of missed calls and messages. He checked, and they all came from Ralph, the General Manager with Logistic Solutions.

<Call me. Urgent. We're in strife.>

9 – The Hack

HARLEY CHECKED THE time. It would be even later in Sydney, but if the matter was urgent, he should ring anyway. The call was answered after the third ring.

"Harley… I've been trying to contact you for ages."

"I'm here now. What's up?"

"We've been hacked. All operations are frozen. We've received a ransom request. You have to come back and deal with this."

The news stunned Harley. He had thought their systems were water tight. "I can log on from here and try to plug the hole. I'll do that now."

"This needs to be a team approach. It will be a PR disaster once the word gets out. As the person who developed the software, you should be readily available. Get your arse back to Sydney pronto."

What Ralph said made sense. Much as he didn't want to, he would have to drive to Adelaide and catch a flight in the morning. He could leave the car with Bryan and Meredith. He glanced at his watch. It would take him about an hour and a half to drive to the city so he could do that tonight.

"You're right. I'll get the first flight out in the morning. I'll grab a cab at the airport and should see you in the office mid-morning. I'll want the IT team available for when I arrive, but in the meantime, they should try to isolate compromised systems to prevent further damage. I assume all data backups are safe and intact?"

Ralph was silent for a moment. "I believe so. It's not my area of expertise."

Harley's heart sank. He would have preferred a more positive response. The sooner he was in the office and could check on procedures, the better. He rang off and immediately dialled the number for Bryan, advising that he would arrive towards midnight, and could he have a bed for the night.

"Of course, mate. Trouble in paradise?"

"I don't have time to go into it now, but there are dramas back in Sydney. I have to get a flight out in the morning. Okay if I leave the ute at your place?"

"Sure. See you soon. The guest room is already made up. I'll wait up for you."

"Thanks. I owe you one."

Harley disconnected the call and logged onto the airline website. A flight leaving at six the following morning had a couple of seats left, but only in business class. At least he should get breakfast during the flight. He didn't know how long he would be away, so quickly packed and threw his bag in the car. He would leave the key for Seascape Cottage in the key-box outside the premises of Professional Coastal Rentals and send Maddie an email in the morning. With that decision made, he locked the cottage and drove away. He would have liked to explain to Lily in person, but wouldn't call her now. Would she even expect an explanation for his absence? Maybe not, but she deserved one.

Harley's cab arrived outside the office shortly after nine-thirty. The receptionist looked up with a polite expression, which dropped as soon as she recognised him. "They're all in the boardroom," she said, nodding towards the door leading to the offices. When he pushed the door open, he found a huddle of people around a laptop, with the monitor connected to a screen at the end of the room. Conversation stopped as he entered.

"You're here!" Ralph gestured towards the others in the room. I've put together a team to address this. Mike is our legal counsel, and Shanti is here to handle the PR aspects of this crisis. We've got calls coming in from around the country with reports of software freezing. To say that there are some very unhappy companies right now is an understatement."

"How did this happen?" Harley asked, shrugging off his jacket and grabbing a chair. "Have people been careless and not following protocols? I can review the design and functionality of the software, but cybersecurity professionals will need to conduct a thorough forensic investigation to understand the breach and who is responsible. That sort of analysis is beyond my professional expertise."

A coffee pot sat on a sideboard at one end of the room and he poured himself a cup, aware that the IT team were muttering in a huddle. With only a few hours of sleep the previous night, he needed a boost to cope with the current situation. Nobody had answered his initial questions.

Ralph cleared his throat. "We don't know who the malicious party is, but we suspect it is an offshore operation. That makes it harder to find them."

"What are they asking for?"

"Ten million US dollars."

"They haven't done their research then. The company can't access that sort of money. What have you done to isolate the compromised systems?"

Roscoe, the IT manager, spoke up for the first time. "We've been working through the night to identify that and plug the gap. I'm in contact with a cybersecurity specialist, and he's working with us remotely. We don't have a timeline for solving this issue."

"Back-ups?" Harley asked, trying to keep an even tone to his voice. Back-ups were scheduled to occur automatically.

"We tried to restore the last back-up as soon as we discovered the problem. That operation is frozen also. Neither we, nor our customers, can access the data collected over the last week."

"What message do I put out?" Shanti hovered over her laptop. We must decide how much company employees can know, and what they can to say if questioned. Then, we have to work on a public statement. The phones are ringing hot from our clients and the media is onto it as well."

Harley walked back and forwards, thinking on his feet. "We can't pretend nothing has happened, but we must get the message across that we are not without resources. We do not capitulate to ransom demands. Emphasise that the authorities are involved, and already we are on the trail of those responsible. When we find them, and we will, we'll smash their operations."

"Yeah, right." Ralph didn't sound convinced. "How are we going to do that?"

"I don't know, but the message needs to get back to the hackers that we are not a pushover. The best form of defence is attack, and that's what we need to do." Harley stopped his pacing by Roscoe. "What advice are we getting from this cybersecurity person?"

"He's looking for digital footprints. People think they're clever, but they often leave clues behind. I've got someone reviewing network logs to see if we can spot any irregularities there."

Harley nodded towards Mike. "After the communications have been drafted, run them past Mike. We have to keep the legal consequences in mind. We regret the impact on our client companies. We are doing all we can and as quickly as possible. That's the underlying message."

Mike agreed. "We need to advise the relevant authorities and the cybercrime unit. There might be a familiar pattern that they recognise, and they will have intelligence information not readily available to us. I'll take charge of that."

Roscoe was called out of the room by one of his team, with the request to join an online meeting with the cybersecurity specialist. They watched him go, hoping he would return shortly with good news.

"Have you contacted the police?" Harley asked Ralph. "If we're going to nail these guys, we have to get law enforcement involved. We should offer a reward for information leading to the apprehension of these lowlifes. Let it be known via hacker networks. We might hear if the relevant coding blocks are being sold on the dark web, or if there has been talk in any of the chatrooms."

Ralph glanced at his watch. "I'm expecting the cybercrime unit from the NSW police to arrive at any moment. In the meantime, can you review the coding to see if you can identify any obvious changes? You know it better than anyone."

Shanti rose from where she had been sitting. "I'll get on with drafting communications to our clients, and will put together something for the media stating we have a team working to resolve the situation. I'll run it past the executive before anyone outside this room sees it."

Everyone left the room with a sense of purpose, leaving Ralph and Harley behind. Ralph looked as though he hadn't slept the previous evening. "Thank you for coming so quickly. I know that technically, once you left, the problem was no longer yours, but we need all the help we can get. If we don't fix this soon, Logistical Solutions will never recover."

"I put too much into the company to see it go under. Find me a desk and a current login authority, and I'll start work straight away. I'll join you when the police arrive. I suggest we speak to all staff about the possibility of any phishing emails or other suspicious contact."

The atmosphere in the office was fraught, but with a sense of urgency. As Harley sat at the desk to which he had been assigned, he looked out the window at the cityscape surrounding him. So different to the sand dunes and the surging sea that he'd looked out over this time yesterday. Life could change in an instant. He knew where he would rather be. He hoped Lily had received his message. By now, she should know he had gone.

❧

Monday. Lily felt uncharacteristically tired as she readied Sea Witch for departure. For once, Davey's chirpy but inane comments really irritated. Well, they often did, but she couldn't ignore them as successfully this morning.

"Got out of bed the wrong side today, did we Princess?"

"Fuck off, Davey", she muttered to herself. Lily would not say that out loud. Her father wouldn't approve. Despite the environment in which they worked, where language was often colourful, he didn't tolerate it from his daughter.

Once they had cast off, and were established on course, she retreated to the cabin for the customary hot drink, chocolate this time. She was in the mood for something nurturing and a hot chocolate would hit the spot. She sat down with a book that she kept on board for this part of the day, but found it difficult to concentrate. Her thoughts returned to the previous evening. She had enjoyed catching up with the Antoniou family, plus the various cousins and family friends. When she and Eleni were together, they always picked up from where they left off. Dion seemed a nice man and Eleni looked to be on cloud nine. She was happy for her friend.

Harley had fitted in well, making conversation and showing a genuine interest in other people. Mimi had quietly pulled her aside before they left, saying that he seemed a suitable young man, and that she approved. It would have been better if he had been Greek, but as a second choice, he passed muster. That was high praise indeed from Mimi, who was critical in her assessments of any partners for her children, and she included Lily in that category as well.

It had been useless to protest that they were just acquaintances, and there were no long-term intentions for either of them.

"You young girls know nothing," Mimi had replied emphatically. "You need someone to watch out and choose a good man for you."

"That sounds like matchmaking," Lily had said. "We don't do things like that these days."

"My parents chose Nico for me, and we have been very happy together. Think about that."

Lily escaped the conversation when she could, but it played on her mind. She wasn't looking for a long-term partner, but if ever she did, she would hope it might be with someone like Harley. He was pleasing on the eye, but that wasn't her only criteria. He sailed and understood the sea; he was willing to try new things; and was an excellent communicator. He even got on with her father.

She had become rather insular in the last couple of years. No dates, and comfortable with her own company, but there was more to life. Even she knew that. Harley would leave Sandy Bay as soon as Ocean Dream was seaworthy again, but perhaps she could make an effort to socialise while he was in town. It would be good practice.

Davey flopped down at the table, nursing his cup of coffee. "Get up to anything interesting over the weekend beyond mooching around in your garden?"

She sighed at the interruption and placed her book face down on the table. "I did, actually. I drove down to Pt Reilly with Harley and a couple of his friends. The seafood festival was happening, and we visited the new art gallery on Gordon Street. I hadn't realised, but as part of their opening celebrations, they were holding a launch event for Dimitri Antoniou. His work is rather good."

"Better than your mate, Harley?"

"I didn't say that. They each have their own styles, and he's not *my mate*, as you put it."

"I should think not. An outsider would never understand your lifestyle. You need a local man in your life, not some flash blow-in from the eastern states."

Not another person with relationship advice! "I can choose for myself, thank you very much."

"You haven't been doing much choosing lately. Perhaps you haven't seen what's right under your nose."

Lily glanced at him, trying to read his expression. Was he suggesting what she thought he was?

"Anytime you need a bit of company, someone who understands the lifestyle and has your interests at heart, you can always call me. We could go to the pub for a counter-meal, or even to the flicks in Pt Reilly."

"That's very kind of you, Davey. I'll keep that in mind. In the meantime, I'm happy mooching around my garden, as you put it. I'll slip up to Dad and see how long before we reach today's grounds."

If Davey thought she was avoiding him, he was right. He was a good worker, and probably well set up financially, but she had no interest in him on a personal level. She had to manage that situation carefully in the interest of harmony on the boat. She asked her father about supplying fish for the hospital fundraiser.

"No problems from me, but I would need to run it past the co-op first. You know our catch is contracted to them."

"Sure, but this is for a good cause. I promised Anh that I would help with the organising."

"That's very noble of you, promising something that wasn't yours, but I'll check. How much do you think they'll require?

"They estimate about one hundred and fifty attending, so enough fish to provide that many fillets. "

"I'll see what I can do. Your mother would never forgive me if I didn't. You were born in that hospital."

"Thanks Dad." Spontaneously, she reached up and gave him a hug. He wasn't a man given to demonstrative behaviour and looked surprised at first, but she noted he blushed with pleasure.

When they returned to the marina that afternoon, she half expected to see Harley working on Ocean Dream. There was no sign of activity on the boat. He could be at the cottage, perhaps working on a painting. Dennis strolled along the pontoon as she and Davey hauled the trolley towards the van.

"Nice day for it," he said conversationally. This was his usual greeting, no matter what the weather. "I see you had the skipper of Ocean Dream out with you last week. That must have been an interesting experience for him."

"He seemed to enjoy it," Davey responded, "except for when I nearly scalded him with a kettle of hot water."

"Is that so? Perhaps that's why he's left."

Lily glanced to where Ocean Dream was still moored. "Left? What do you mean? He was here yesterday evening."

"I had a text message early this morning. He was about to get on a plane to Sydney. He wasn't sure when he'd be back. Asked that I give Roger Marriot access whenever he needs it."

Davey gave a scornful snort. "Couldn't wait to get out of the place, sounds like. Why else would he sneak out of town in the middle of the night? He seemed a nice sorta bloke, but perhaps he was on the run from something."

"You've got a vivid imagination. If he left that quickly, he must have had a good reason. I'm sure he'll be back. He'll have to pick up Ocean Dream."

She wouldn't let anyone else see it, but privately, she was blindsided. So much for thinking she might see more of him over the coming week. She slid her phone out of her backpack, intending to call Maddie Masters… she could know more, given he had been renting Seaspray Cottage. She noticed she had a text message from Harley.

<Business emergency in Sydney. Had to leave ASAP, but I will be back. Thank you again for a pleasant evening with the Antoniou family. Harley.>

She shoved her phone away, not wanting to discuss with Davey what she'd learned, but once in the van on the way to the co-op, called Maddie. Her friend had also received a message, and the keys to the cottage had been returned to the office overnight.

"I checked the cottage today, and his personal effects were gone, except for the food in the fridge. He said that if it's still available on his return, he would like to rent it again. No promises, but if it's free, he's welcome to stay there again."

His emergency must have been major for him to take off like that. That sort of drama contrasted with her simple life. There was much to recommend about the way she lived. As

111

her father drove, she looked out over the bay with the late afternoon sun glinting on the water, and a couple of boats heading towards the marina. She wouldn't swap that view for city life, much less life in Sydney, although she wouldn't mind visiting.

Mavis was uncharacteristically grumpy when Lily and Stan arrived at the co-op.

"What's the matter, Mavis? Has Evan been giving you a hard time?"

"Him! Not likely. I've got him under control. No, the software that we use for managing our operations has crashed. We've lost records of our orders and a heap of other stuff as well. I don't really understand that side of things, but it's left me with a headache and a ton of fish that has nowhere to go. It's not good enough. Heads should roll over this."

Lily looked at the tubs of fish they were delivering. "Are you telling me you can't handle today's catch? Surely it will be sorted soon?"

They'll go into the cool rooms for now. The office staff are ringing customers and confirming orders for a manual operation. There will be some overtime for us today. It had better be fixed by tomorrow, though."

I won't email the details of the catch through to you then. I'll print out the paperwork at home and drop it back tomorrow."

"Good idea."

"Hey, Mavis," one of the admin staff called. "We've just heard from the software company in Sydney. They've been hacked and everything's frozen. The company is working around the clock to find and delete the malware. No promises about timing. We have to do the best we can until then."

112

"Great… just great. They can't maintain internet safety and we're the ones who suffer. Who knows what data of ours is now floating around in cyberspace?"

Lily and Stan hauled the tubs inside the facility and beat a hasty retreat. Even Stan knew better than to hang around when Mavis was in a bad mood.

10 – Impact on the Town

HARLEY COULDN'T FIND anything obvious. He had his own copy of the program and checked the coding line-by-line on his laptop. He was reluctant to log onto the company server in case he picked up an infection. Everything looked in order to him, but then he wasn't skilled in detecting cybercrime.

Ralph called him back into the boardroom when the cyber unit from the NSW police department arrived. Roscoe and Mike joined them, wearing expressions that were suitably serious and concerned. The visitors were not encouraging. Finding the culprits would not be easy and would take time, if it were possible. They advised against paying the ransom, and suggested that the best option would be to discover the access point, and to address that vulnerability. The hackers would exploit it until that happened. In the meantime, they wanted copies of all communications received from the hackers.

"Sometimes there are familiar patterns in the approach, and identifying that helps us to narrow down the range of suspects," the head of the unit explained. "If they are based within Australia, we have a better chance of finding them, but we have good relationships with our international counterparts."

"Do you ever find them when they are based overseas?" Mike asked.

"Sometimes. It depends how sophisticated they are. It's such a growth industry that dealing with the players is like a game of Wack-a-Mole. You remove the bad player, and a handful spring up in his place. How were you contacted?"

"It wasn't a direct contact," Ralph said. "Suddenly everything froze. The screen went blank and then it displayed a message saying we'd been hacked and that a payment would be required to release the system. I took a photo… we couldn't even do a print screen."

The police officer looked at Ralph's phone. "Swordfish. That's who's behind it. See the image here? That's their signature. This happened on a Sunday. Were you at work?"

"No, I was called in by one of our IT staff. He was on call, and was contacted by one of our customers when their operations also froze. He investigated the cause and then called me in."

There was a knock on the door, and one of the IT team poked his head around the frame. He looked around the room, with his eyes alighting on Roscoe. "There's another screen message. We've taken too long to respond, so the ransom has just increased by another million."

Ralph stared at the man wide-eyed, as though not understanding what he had just heard. "That's ridiculous. If we can't pay ten million, how are we going to pay eleven?"

Harley wondered if he would have to sell Ocean Dream. The damage to the company would be horrendous if they couldn't solve this problem quickly, and the company's customers would clamour for compensation. He might have reduced his share-holding, but his name was synonymous with the company. His reputation would be mud if they didn't solve this issue quickly and look after their customers.

Their visitors left after recording the relevant detail and promising to contact their networks both in Australia and overseas. Shanti provided the draft documents she had prepared, and after bickering about some of the wording and getting Mike's legal perspective, they agreed the documents would be forwarded. Rather than send a press release out widely, that document would only be provided to media outlets that contacted them. Harley had a faint hope that before the world at large learned of their disaster, it might be solved, and they could give a favourable report.

Roscoe spun around in his chair, rotating a full three-sixty before slapping his hands on the table to stop the turn. "Why us? That's what I keep asking myself. Why have they targeted us? We're a successful company, but still a small fish in a big pond."

A swirl of clouds moved across the sky, dimming the light in the room. Harley stood and paced again. "Perhaps we're an easier target that some of the bigger companies. They would have more dedicated staff and procedures related to security. Within Logistical Solutions, people have to do a bit of everything. That's our strength because it ensures employees are multi-skilled, but it also means those same people are spread thinly. That's a vulnerability."

Roscoe's phone buzzed. He glanced first at the screen, and then apologetically at the others in the room. "Sorry, I had better take this." He withdrew to the side of the room and faced out the window, but they could clearly hear his side of the conversation.

"You have? ... How? ... When did that happen? ... Are you sure? ... There's some hope then. Thank you. I'll investigate at this end."

He disconnected the call and stood looking at his phone for a second before slowly shaking his head and turned to address them. "That's one step forward. We know the name of the malware, and it must have come in via a link or attachment in an email. What we don't know yet is how to delete it, but that information is probably available. We just have to find it."

Ralph dropped his face into his hands. "So, someone here gave this hacker an opening into the company. Someone clicked on something they shouldn't have and invited a malicious actor to hold us to ransom. They might as well have opened the front door and welcomed them in."

"These guys are increasingly clever," Mike said. "You know it's getting harder to decide what is a spam email and what is genuine, especially if you're tired or distracted."

Roscoe stood, leaving his chair spinning behind him. "I know the approximate date on which it happened. I'll go through email logs, but I'll call a staff meeting first. I'll explain what we're looking for and ask everyone to review their emails received during that time period. The trojan must be new if the anti-virus software didn't detect it."

"We're not off the hook, but at least we know there weren't loopholes in our software. More coffee, anyone?" Harley poured a fresh cup for Ralph, Mike, and himself. "Now, we should hit the phones and start ringing our customers. I know the email Shanti drafted has been sent to them, but in this situation, I think the personal approach is needed. At least we now have something to report. Agreed?"

There were nods all round. Contact lists were divided between Harley and Ralph, and they retreated to their individual desks to start on the calls. Roscoe had summoned all staff to the boardroom to brief them on what he had learned, and request that they review their email history, plus any phone calls received that may have sought confirmation of their login details.

Harley had to psyche himself up before making the first call. Customers would be distressed and angry, and rightly so. Their business operations were adversely affected. By the time lunch arrived, ordered in by a member of staff, he felt drained. He had repeated the story so many times, and sat and listened while people on the other end vented at the impact to their operations. Some were understanding, but the question was asked repeatedly; *How did this happen?*

They had barely finished their sandwiches when Roscoe appeared, followed by a tearful young woman. Celia had only been with the company a short time, having not long graduated. She worked in the finance department and prepared the salaries each fortnight. She had received an email from the Australian Taxation Office advising of changes to the individual tax schedules, which had an attached file with the new rates. She had thought that because the email looked legitimate, and had been addressed to her, that it was okay to click on the link."

"I'm sorry," Celia wailed. "I thought it was a valid email. How did they know to reach out to me? I haven't told many people I work here."

"Did you update your LinkedIn account, saying where you worked and what your new role would be?"

"Yes, but I didn't give out my email address."

"It wouldn't be difficult to find out company email protocols. You were an easy target."

The young woman began weeping, with tears coursing down her cheeks. Worse than that, she also began to sniff. Harley ripped a tissue out of the box sitting on the sideboard and passed it to her.

"Thank you for bringing the email to our attention. We'll discuss it further once we have resolved this situation."

The woman turned and fled, much to their relief. He told himself it was a rookie mistake, and anyone could have been targeted. In reality, he wished she had checked the sender address more carefully, or at least queried the email contents with a manager. If she had been better informed, she would have known that changes to the tax schedules happened at the beginning of the financial year, and were well publicised.

"I'll get back to Cyber Guy," Roscoe said, using the name he had dubbed the cyber security specialist. "He's confident now that he can break into our system via the back door and isolate the malicious code. He can't tell me when, though."

"Can he unmask the culprit?"

"He may identify an IP address, but they'll be using a VPN. You can pass that onto the police team and perhaps they can liaise with their counterparts, assuming it's someone from overseas. He says that as soon as they realise we're on their trail, they simply shut down operations and fire up again elsewhere."

Harley had the beginnings of a headache. "Let's hope he does. I need some fresh air. I'm going for a walk around the block. Back soon."

He stepped outside the front door and was startled when a woman rushed up to him, followed by a man hefting a video camera on his shoulder.

"Mr Mendelson—can you tell us how your company fell victim to hackers? Shouldn't you have had protective systems in place? What is the impact on your customers?"

The media… why hadn't anyone warned him they were outside? "I can't tell you anymore than was in our press release. We have a specialist team working with us, and have made encouraging progress. I can confirm that we will not be paying a ransom."

"Does that mean you're willing to sacrifice the operations of your customers by taking a stand?"

"Of course not. I have nothing further to say." He turned and slipped back inside, locking the front door behind him. The last thing he needed was to be on the evening news.

❧

Lily looked forward to an early night. She had gone to bed after returning home from the Antoniou barbecue, but then had tossed and turned. Sleep seemed determined to elude her. She finally dropped off, but then the alarm wrenched her from a deep sleep and it was time to get up. This evening, she would have a hot shower, read for a while, and then have an early night. She pulled a frozen meal from her freezer and placed it in the microwave. When she prepared a slow-cooker casserole on a weekend, she froze individual portions, specifically for nights like this, when she had no inclination to cook.

The evening went according to plan. She stood under the shower until the water turned tepid, and after towelling herself dry, dressed in her pyjamas and a fluffy robe. With her feet jammed in a pair of Ugg boots, she felt warm and incredibly snug. The kitchen seemed cold and uninviting, so she brought her dinner into the lounge room on a tray, and turned on the television just in time for the evening news.

The affairs of the nation always seemed so far removed from Sandy Bay, but watching the news was part interest and part obligation, not necessarily in equal portions. It depended on her mood, and if any events of significance were occurring. They weren't today. She turned the volume down to low, and focussed on her dinner, a bowl of chicken stroganoff, with a slice of sour dough on the side. She had a block of Lindt dark chocolate in the cupboard, and was thinking about whether she would indulge in one or two squares, when movement on the television screen caught her attention. The camera zoomed in on a face, and it looked like Harley. It *was* Harley. She grabbed the remote and turned up the volume. The reporter shoved a microphone in his face, throwing her questions at him.

"Mr Mendelson, can you tell us how your company fell victim to hackers? Shouldn't you have had protective systems in place? What is the impact on your customers?"

Lily put her meal aside and leaned forward, wanting to hear what was being said. Harley looked harried, as though the reporter had ambushed him. He said something about not paying a ransom and then retreated to the building behind him. The reporter turned and addressed the camera.

"Yet another company falls victim to hackers, with not only Logistical Solutions but also their customers being severely affected. Who knows what confidential data has been stolen? Will it then be sold on the dark web? Why didn't the company have stronger antivirus procedures in place? These are questions that still need to be answered."

The news broadcast moved onto a new item. Lily sat back again, thinking over her conversation earlier that afternoon with Mavis. She had mentioned that there was a problem with the operating software, before someone else said that the company providing the software was based in Sydney. They had been hacked. Harley's company had to be the one supplying the software to the co-op, resulting in disruption to fish processing and distribution. If it wasn't fixed soon, it may have a detrimental effect on fish processing in the town. His boat was still in the marina, so he had to return. For now, she would keep this information to herself. Surely no one else would recognise him from that brief film clip? Better to see what happened, rather than stir up trouble, because trouble would certainly come looking for him if the word got out.

It might have seemed a strategic decision, but as she discovered the following morning, secrecy was pointless. When she arrived at the marina, a huddle of boaties was already talking, Davey among them. As she pulled up in the carpark, she could see them gathered under a security light, close to the marina office.

"Hey Lily," Davey called as she made her way along the pontoon, "I saw your mate on TV last night. It seems he isn't so squeaky clean. He's on the run from some corporate disaster, and the software he sold the co-op has stalled. Makes you wonder if he really does have electronic trouble on the boat, or if he just thought Sandy Bay a convenient place to hide out."

"Davey, did you actually listen to what was said in the news report? The company was hacked; it's not his fault. He sold out his major holding in the company some time ago, so he isn't working there anymore."

Her father wandered up to the group huddled under one of the lights as well. "That bloke was a bit of a surprise. I thought I was a good judge of character. I didn't expect him to sell our data to offshore interests. He'd better watch out for that boat of his. Where did he get the money to buy that?"

Lily hesitated. She didn't want to draw attention to her friendship with Harley, especially after she had just emphatically distanced herself from him to Davey the day before. There were parts of her life she preferred to keep private. She couldn't let him take the brunt of the blame, though.

"There's no justification for jumping to conclusions. He only has a small stake in the company. He sold out of his majority holding some time ago."

"And you know this because…? One man raised his eyebrows, his tone indicating a level of scorn.

"Because he told me! He's probably trying to help the company out of a difficult situation."

"I heard he called the CEO of the co-op yesterday. If he did that, then he's heavily involved in company operations, and he bears responsibility for the financial and operational impact to this town."

Sandy Bay survived on more than just fishing. As Lily drew breath to respond, her father grasped her by the elbow. "Gas bagging here won't change the situation." He addressed Lily and Davey. "Shouldn't you two be loading the trawler?"

He was right. Lily fetched the trolley from the enclosure while Davey unloaded empty tubs from the van. The topic wasn't raised again until they were underway and morning coffees had been made. Lily left Davey to his motorcycle magazine down in the cabin and carried the hot drink up to her father in the wheelhouse.

"Will this software issue have an impact on us? I can't see that it will. We just catch fish as we've always done. The co-op will just be slower in their processing."

Stan grunted his assent. "People get soft with all this technological automation. Processing things manually is no different to how things used to be done, and we managed quite well. There are always scaremongers who want to shout that the sky is about to fall in."

Lily smiled at the analogy. Looking outside now, the sky certainly wasn't about to fall in. Dawn crept over the hills bordering the shore they had left behind, and when she looked in that direction, those same hills appeared to be outlined in a soft golden glow, focussed in the area where the sun would soon appear. It faded to a dusky violet at the northern and southern edges. She loved this time of day. Any overnight wind had usually settled, and the sea was mostly calm.

Pinprick lights of the town could be seen in the distance, providing a visual anchor to the current phase of their journey. Further along the coast, she could see the lights of Pt Reilly. Closeted in the wheelhouse with her father, she had the sense that they were enclosed in their own protected world, and no matter what happened onshore, they would always be safe and secure.

Whatever had happened with Harley's company, she hoped he could resolve the threat. It must be a stressful time for him. She debated sending him a text of support, but hesitated. It was none of her business, and if the situation really blew up, perhaps she wouldn't see him again. Someone else could always pick up Ocean Dream. Unexpectedly, that thought left her feeling sad.

11- Harley's Back

BY LATE AFTERNOON, Cyber Guy had traced the source of the hack, but not the identifying information relating to the perpetrator. The overseas location made that more difficult, but all information was provided to the police cyber unit. By unanimous agreement, Roscoe and Cyber Guy mounted a counter offensive, making it known via hacker networks that not only would they not be paying a ransom, but that they had tracked down the hacker and the authorities were coming after them. The message repeated everywhere that counted was, *We're coming to get you!*

There was a bluff in that message, in that they hadn't identified the responsible party, but hopefully the message reached them. By late afternoon, Harley felt he had done all he could for the day. Tiredness from his early flight that morning overwhelmed him. He still had his apartment in Balmain East, overlooking the water. He took the ferry from Circular Quay, and even though the ride was short, enjoyed the sights and sounds of the Harbour again. It was one of the pleasures of living in central Sydney. He could forget the city buildings behind him and focus on life as it happened on the water.

The apartment smelled stuffy from being shut up for so long. Harley threw open the sliding door leading out to the balcony. He never tired of the view. The contrast with the dunes outside Seaspray Cottage was extreme. That coast was wild and untamed. Here, the shores of the harbour were fully developed, and the surface of the water was disturbed by the wash from passing yachts and the ferries, rather than crashing waves. Each had its own attractions, but as he looked at the scene below, he missed the other more primal experience.

He checked his phone in case there had been a response from Lily to his text early that morning. Nothing. There was no reason she should have replied, but an irrational part of him wished she had. He returned inside, sliding the door shut behind him. After a cursory look in the cupboard at what tins of food he might open, he opted to walk down to the local Italian bistro and order a lasagna and a glass of red instead. That would fill the hole in his belly, though not the hole in his soul.

A different mood greeted him when he entered the office of Logistic Solutions the following morning. He arrived early, but the scattering of empty coffee cups and pizza boxes indicated others had been there much earlier, or perhaps had never left. Ralph sat at his desk, munching his way through a giant muffin.

"What news?" he asked of everyone, and no one in particular. Roscoe looked up out of eyes that were red and bleary. He had a rumpled, slept-in look. He gave a yawn that displayed his tonsils, followed by a thumbs up. "We've done it. Working in tandem with Cyber Guy, we've debugged the code and the door that gave them control has been slammed shut."

"Were you here all night?"

Roscoe shrugged. "It was daylight where Cyber Guy and his mates were working, so it made sense to keep going. We seized a bit of kip during quiet times. I'll sleep well tonight, though."

"You need to go home now—all of you."

"There's still some cleaning up to do. We couldn't have done this without Cyber Guy. I hope you realise there's a hefty fee to be paid for the services of these people. They could just as easily be working on the other side of the fence, earning big bikkies. They have a conscience, but it doesn't come cheap."

"I never imagined that it would," Ralph remarked wryly. "At this stage, I'm almost prepared to sell my first born to raise any funds to pay them."

"But you don't have any children," Roscoe objected.

"That's probably a good thing. Someone else will have to sell their first-born instead."

Eyes swivelled towards Harley. He held up his hands defensively. "Hey, don't look at me! I don't have any kids either. At least it will be much less than the ransom demand, and we have the satisfaction of knowing we don't have to cough up for that. Cyber insurance should take care of the rest."

He turned to Shanti. "How soon before we can send out another email to all affected companies and a new press release to the media?"

"I'm one step ahead of you. I've started drafting both. I'll run it past you and Ralph, plus Mike, to ensure that the wording is appropriate, then I'll send them out. There are a couple of companies I recommend you call personally."

"Okay. We've all got a bit to do, but I'm ordering in lunch for all staff, and not just the sandwiches we had yesterday either. After that, some of the team should piss off home for a well-deserved sleep."

"Give my PA your budget and I'll get her to take care of the ordering. She'll know the best local cafés and if there are any dietary issues, etc." Ralph aimed his take-away coffee cup at the wastepaper basket, and gave a fist-pump when it dropped in. "How long are you staying in Sydney? We can catch up over dinner tonight. I owe you one for dropping everything and coming over so quickly."

Harley thought for a while. This was a life he'd left behind, and he wasn't inclined to revisit it longer than he needed to. "Thanks, but I'll grab a flight back to Adelaide after lunch. A better option might be for you to visit me in Sandy Bay. The break would do you good. Believe me, I've learned to appreciate the quieter life."

The rest of the morning was spent in discussion with Mike on their legal situation, and calls to customers. The media were on their doorstep again, wanting updates and interviews, but Harley insisted Ralph handle those. He was the head of the company now, so it was his responsibility. By the time Harley flopped into a chair in the airport terminal, waiting for his flight to be called, he felt as though he had been through the wringer, even though he'd had some sleep the night before. Emotionally, it had been draining.

Bryan picked him up from the airport, and he stayed the night with him and Meredith in their Walkerville villa, rather than drive back to Sandy Bay. He didn't fancy the long drive at night, then having to sleep on the boat moored in the marina. They lived close to the city centre in one of the suburb's more prestigious streets. Bryan showed obvious pride as Harley took time in examining the various paintings displayed on the interior walls. One of Harley's paintings of the view of the Harbour from his balcony also hung in the dining room.

Meredith was delighted to see him, even more so when he mentioned over breakfast the following morning that he had met Christos Antoniou. He opted not to mention he had offered to take Christos sailing. She would desperately attempt to wrangle herself onto Ocean Dream as well. He had a feeling that fandom did not sit easily with Christos, particularly when it intruded on his private life.

"How long is he staying in Sandy Bay? You know you can always invite him to dinner with us. We'd be very discrete, wouldn't we Bryan?"

"Yes, my love, of course we would. However, I hardly think we could invite someone we don't know, particularly when it's his brother with whom I have a connection."

"We could invite both of them… perhaps for Sunday brunch. That wouldn't be so formal."

Bryan sent a panicked look at Harley, who promptly changed the subject to discussion about his own painting, and the work that he had in progress. When Ocean Dream was seaworthy again, he had thoughts about stopping off on Kangaroo Island, both because he wanted to explore the attractions and because he thought there might be some spectacular scenery to paint.

"Great idea. You could have a themed exhibition. I might even join you there for a while. You can paint, and I'll explore the scenery and culinary treats for which the Island is known."

Harley left them to their plans relating to what might, could, and wouldn't happen, and drove the ute back to Sandy Bay. As he crested the hill on the road leading into town, the village appeared laid out in front of him, with the sea and coast behind. It felt like coming home. He stopped off at Professional Coastal Rentals first to check if Seaspray Cottage was still available.

"You're in luck. It hasn't been snapped up in the meantime, so it's all yours. Welcome back. The cleaner has the key at the moment, but she'll drop it back to me mid-afternoon. If you come back then, you can pick it up. I'll call her and tell her not to clear the fridge out."

Harley thanked her profusely. That took immediate pressure off his return. On impulse, he stopped by Maisie's Café for a coffee. Jordan nodded as he entered, pausing in the doorway to consider where he wanted to sit.

"You're still here then?" the young man called from behind the coffee machine.

"You haven't been able to get rid of me," Harley jibed in return. "I might be here for a few days yet. That reminds me… I promised to take your father sailing. I might call him and see if he's still interested."

"Is the Pope a Catholic? Of course he'll be interested. He's totally bored, stuck at home as he is. What can I get you?"

Harley sat a table outside in the sun as he sipped his coffee. The contrast with the pressures of Sydney couldn't be stronger. He needed to check on Ocean Dream though. He drained his coffee and gave Jordan a farewell wave through the open doorway. When he bolted to Adelaide a couple of nights before, he had transferred belongings he didn't take with him to the boat. He now had to collect them and take them back to Seaspray Cottage.

Dennis sat at his messy desk, eating a Cornish pasty for lunch, and dropping flakes of pastry everywhere.

"You're back already. I thought from what I saw on the telly that you'd be gone for a while."

"On the telly? You saw me on TV?"

"Sure did. Probably the whole town did. Caused a bit of chatter around the place, what with the impact on the co-op and everything. Didn't realise it was you at first, but someone else mentioned it."

"Great, just great. That's a notoriety I didn't want. Has Roger Marriott been working on Ocean Dream?"

"Nope. Hasn't been near the place."

Bad news on both counts. Harley thanked Dennis and hurried along the pontoon to the boat. There would likely be a few questions to answer around town. He would be out of sight and hopefully out of mind if he spent a day at sea. Harley rang Christos first and then Adam, suggesting that they might like to join him the following day, if they were available.

"You were serious?" Christos asked. "I'd love to. I thought it was one of those offers that people make and then never follow through."

"I never say what I don't mean. I thought we could leave around nine. We won't go far, because as I explained before, the electronics are shot. We'll be navigating visually and referring to the paper charts."

Christos laughed. "Proper sailing, you mean. I'll speak to Mama. She'll put some food together for us."

"She doesn't have to do that."

"Try to stop her!"

"Okay, I won't. Do you have a life jacket? I have a spare, but Adam Grant will probably come with us, and he definitely won't have one."

"Sure. I'll bring one. See you in the morning."

Adam was just as enthusiastic, and Harley arranged to pick him up in the morning. That just left Harley with checking the battery charge and fuel level, and digging out a life jacket for Adam. According to the weather forecast, it would be a good day out on the water. He looked forward to it. He spread out his charts to plot their course.

&

Lily's phone pinged with a message from Maddie.

<He's back>

No need to ask who. <And I need to know because…?>

<Don't be like that. I knew you would be interested, and if not, you should be. He's an interesting character.>

She declined to comment further, except for sending a laughing emoji back. He might want to steer clear of Mavis. When they last spoke, she was still cranky about the disruption to her day and the extra work she'd been lumped with. Presumably, he was back in residence at Seaspray Cottage if Maddie had seen him.

She joined her father in the wheelhouse as they nosed in towards the marina, awaiting the moment she would need to leap ashore to secure the mooring ropes. As they travelled the last hundred metres, she chatted with Stan about the proposed fundraiser for the hospital.

"We're looking for donations for the silent auction. Harley said that he would donate a painting."

"That's the least he could do after this recent fiasco. It had better be a good one."

Her father's comments made it apparent that Harley would receive a frosty reception back in town. She didn't know how much responsibility for the hacking situation could be attributed to him, but as far as the locals were concerned, it was close to one hundred percent.

When Sea Witch docked, she surreptitiously eyed Ocean Dream in case Harley was onboard. The boat was still moored in the same place, but looked deserted. She busied herself with unloading and reminded her father to speak to someone at the co-op about allowing them to donate fish for the planned dinner.

She and Davey were hauling the trolley along the pontoon when someone called her name.

"Lily… hey, Lily!"

She stopped, surprised at recognising the voice. She wasn't the only one.

"Here's trouble," Davey muttered. "You'd think he'd be smart enough to stay away."

"How can he? His boat's here."

Davey just shrugged with a scornful expression and an eye-roll that said it all.

"You go ahead with the trolley. I'll catch you up shortly."

Lily walked back to Ocean Dream, where Harley now stood on the deck, shading his eyes with his hand as he peered towards her. She hadn't expected to see him back so soon, but was ridiculously pleased that he was. Not that she would admit that.

Harley was not so reserved. His face lit up with a genuine smile of welcome. "You got my message? As you can see, I'm back. The dramas that dragged me away have been resolved, so I could make my escape. Nothing's happened with Ocean Dream in my absence, so I'll be here for a while yet."

He dropped his hand when she drew close to the side of the boat. With the sun falling on his face, Lily was struck by the flecks of gold that now showed up in his eyes. Previously, she had thought them chocolaty-brown, but now they took on an almost tawny hue with an expression that was both open and beguiling.

"I can't tell you how glad I am to be back here, away from the hustle and bustle. Want to join me for dinner this evening? I'm planning on a pub meal at the Regal."

Lily looked towards the van where Davey was unloading the tubs. She shouldn't dally, though the temptation was there. He could transfer the tubs to the van without her. He liked to flex his muscles and show off his ability.

"Sure. You can tell me about your trip over your choice of schnitzel or whatever the special of the day is. Any news from Roger Marriott?"

"I've left a message on his phone, but still waiting for a response. Shall I pick you up?"

"No need. I'll see you there about six-thirty. I need to help Davey. See you tonight."

Lily's usual outfit of choice was trousers, and whatever top best suited the season. Even when not working on the boat, she dressed for convenience and comfort. For a change, she

135

slipped on a shirt dress of the softest blue chambray. Unusually, her hair was pulled back into a ponytail, and tucked under a cap if the weather on the boat dictated that. She left it down, but swept one side back clear of her face and held secure with a tortoiseshell comb.

She added a flick of mascara and outlined her lips in a soft coral lipstick. Her usual concession to skin care and appearance was to apply generous lashings of sunscreen lotion. Make-up seemed un-necessary, but today she felt like a change. Gold hoop earrings slipped into the lobes of her ears, completed her preparations.

Harley already sat at a table when Lily pushed her way through the door leading to the dining room at the Regal Hotel. He had evidently been watching for her, and waved to attract attention. He stood as she approached, impressing her with the gentlemanly gesture. The men she knew rarely observed such niceties.

He kissed her cheek in greeting. "Good that you could come. Some low-stress company is just what I need after the last couple of days. Can I get you a drink?"

"Thank you—a glass of house white will be fine. Sauvignon Blanc if they have it."

"Back soon."

He disappeared toward the bar, returned a few minutes later with two glasses of wine. They clinked glasses in toast, and as she took the first sip, Lily noticed the tiredness around his eyes. Either he hadn't slept well lately, or the stress of the previous days was catching up with him. Possibly both.

"I'm taking Christos sailing tomorrow," he said by way of opening conversation. "Adam Grant too. I owe him a favour after he was so kind to me last week."

136

"Where will you go?"

"Not far. Down the coast and back again. Christos is keen to get back to his water-bound roots. He could even do a spot of fishing. Until the electronics are fixed, I don't want to go far."

"But can you still use the motor?"

"Sure can. That's not affected. We could also sail under canvas."

"You should have a wonderful day. I'll watch out for you." She paused, debating whether to mention what she knew. If she didn't, others would. "I saw you on telly, by the way."

Harley briefly covered his eyes with his hand and sighs. "I gather that surprisingly for a stranger in this town, my face was recognised remarkably quickly. I was only on screen for a few seconds, and really, it shouldn't have been me. I'm no longer CEO of the company."

"If it weren't for the problems that beset the co-op, it would have slipped by un-noticed. Fishing is an important industry in this town, and if the co-op hiccups, that affects many people."

"I understand that. I was mortified by the impact that the assault on the company had, and as a result, on all our customers. Fortunately, we've removed the threat and we're back in business, a few dollars poorer and infinitely wiser. Keeping ahead of these mongrels is a constant battle. It was the software that I developed initially that was hacked, which is why I flew over to Sydney to help when the crisis arose."

"It must have been a nightmare for you. Lucky it's all resolved now. What about your customers? Won't there be claims from them for disruption to business and financial loss?"

"That's still being sorted, and no doubt, the business will call on their cyber insurance. No company can afford to be without it today."

"You've got a nerve showing your face around here." Lily's heart sank. She knew that voice and that tone only too well. Harley looked a mixture of startled and as though he'd been caught in the cross-lights.

"Mavis! This is a surprise."

She stood with hands on her hips. "How would you like to have shit dumped on your working day from a great height? Your half-arsed operational program threw my day into total disarray and caused no end of problems."

Harley stood and extended his hand. "Pleased to see you again, Mavis. I remember meeting you in Pt Reilly. I can't tell you how much I regret the problems this attack on the program created for all the customers of Logistical Solutions, but of course especially so for the co-op. I assure you that the hacker has been locked out and operations are back to normal. They haven't been caught yet, but the police are on their tail, and hopefully it's only a matter of time."

Her glare didn't waver. Harley gestured to a spare chair. "Can I buy you a drink? Would you like to join us?"

"If you think you can buy me off with a drink, you're mistaken. You've outstayed your welcome in this town."

12 – Sailing Day

BIRDS CIRCLED OVER the marina, flying in slow circuits. Moonlight picked out the silvery bodies. Unlike in the daytime, their flight was silent, even eerie. Lily watched them for a moment, marvelling at the sight as she did on many mornings. Ocean Dream bobbed gently at its mooring as she passed. She knew Harley was back at Seaspray Cottage, but he would be here in a few hours. She had the impression from their discussion the previous evening that he looked forward to setting out to sea again. He felt he and the boat had been separated for too long.

Christos would enjoy the trip. They'd spent a lot of time in and around boats as kids. The Antoniou kids had a small sailboat, and she often joined them when they often took it out on weekends, learning to read the waves and the weather. Thinking back on it, she marvelled at the fact they never came to grief, despite the precarious adventures that, by agreement, they never told their parents about. Perhaps she would see Ocean Dream on the water later in the day.

She checked the forecast and examined the sky. The weather man predicted a mild day, with no chance of rain, but the possibility of winds increasing later in the day. If that was the case, she hoped Ocean Dream carried a good supply of sea-sick pills. The winds that blew up from the south could be rough.

❧

Harley knocked on Adam's door at eight thirty. Adam greeted him with a delighted grin, and carrying a small insulated pack.

"Maisie packed some food from the café. She insisted I couldn't go empty-handed."

"That's very kind. Between you and Christos, we'll be set in case we get shipwrecked on a desert island. At least we won't starve. I think Christos wants to try his luck fishing, so perhaps you can bring home a fish in return."

By the time he had settled Adam and his moon boot on the boat, organised his charts and undertaken his pre-sailing checks, Christos appeared, lugging an esky and small fishing box. The two locals knew each other, and exchanged welcome handshakes before Harley gave them a tour of the boat and a safety briefing on the boat operations, warning them to keep their life-jackets on at all times. He started the motor, and a gentle rumble vibrated through the flooring of the deck. Christos jumped ashore to loosen the mooring ropes before clambering back on board. Dennis had wandered out from his office, and gave them a wave as they pulled away from the pontoon and, after reversing, slowly chugged through the navigation channel towards the open water.

A fresh breeze whipped around their ears, and all three men pulled on their beanies and zipped up their jackets. Their cheeks already looked flushed.

"Smell that water," Christos murmurs in delight, lifting his face to the sky and inhaling deeply. "I've missed this. I don't spend enough time back in the Bay. I must do something about that."

"Why don't you make a movie here?" Adam suggested helpfully. "There could be some good stories… Pirates of Sandy Bay?"

"I don't think so, mate. Anyway, I just act in them. I need someone else to write the story, finance it and produce it. I don't have that sort of skill or clout."

"You don't know until you try. You could put the area on the map."

"Is that what you really want, Sandy Bay over-run with tourists all wanting to see where the film was made?"

"Ah, no… You've got a point. Better that you make your movies elsewhere and negotiate more time off."

Having Christos on board was like having a navigator. After poring over the charts, he pointed out areas of both interest plus sections of the coast to avoid. While he and Harley were busy chatting, Adam settled down on the bench seat in the cockpit, leaning back to watch the view ahead. He alerted the others with a shout. "Dolphins… a whole pod of them."

Harley and Christos followed the point of his finger to see the animals skimming through the water beside the boat. Adam rose and lurched unsteadily with his compromised leg as he shuffled around the side of the boat towards the bow, to get a closer look. He clutched his phone in one hand.

Harley looked up in alarm. "Adam, keep a grip on the side rail."

Adam gave him a thumbs-up and kept shuffling until he reached the front, where he aimed his phone camera toward the pod. Harley puffed out his cheeks and exhaled slowly as he watched. Adam wasn't an accomplished sailor, and he was unsteady on his feet. He didn't know how quickly an unexpected surge could throw you off balance.

Christos clapped him on the shoulder. "He'll be right, mate. He's got his jacket on if he goes overboard."

"And are you going to dive in and get him? That moon boot isn't the best for swimming. He'll sink like a brick."

"You're probably right."

They both watched as Adam edged his way back towards them, dropping into the cockpit with a hoot of glee. "Did you see that? I got them on video. Beautiful watching them swim like that."

Leaving Christos to take charge of the wheel, Harley ducked into the cabin to make them all a cup of coffee. He pulled up the collapsible table in the cockpit and brought out the hot drinks, plus the cinnamon scrolls provided by Maisie.

Christos took a bite and sighed with obvious satisfaction. "I've always liked these, even when they're not heated. I hope you two are hungry, because Mama packed a heap of food for our lunch."

"Sea air is always good for the appetite," Adam replied, licking sticky icing from his fingers. "Where are we heading?"

"We're not venturing too far, given we don't have the benefit of our electronic systems. Down past Pt Reilly, then towards Pelican Cove, and over to Batton Island. We can stop there for lunch. Perhaps Christos can throw out his fishing line as well."

"Sounds good to me. Of course, I'm happy to go wherever you take me."

The three men sat back, while Christos and Adam pointed out places of interest on the passing coastline, and chatted about local people and events. A trio of shearwaters followed them for a while, wheeling in the updrafts above the boat before disappearing. The boat rose with the crest of the swell, then smacked down again, causing Adam to spill his coffee, but not otherwise causing any discomfort.

The swell remained, but not strong enough to cause any concern. Harley kept his eye on the weather, thankful that the day had turned out as mild as it had.

"So, Harley… how long have you and Lily known each other?"

Harley was jerked out of his thoughts to see Christos regarding him intently.

"Only since I lobbed up in Sandy Bay a week ago. I ran into her and Stan at the marina shortly after I limped in, and a couple of days later, Stan took me out on the trawler."

"Yeah, I heard about that. She's a strong woman; growing up with Stan as a father, she would have to be. I hope you're not playing with her emotions though."

"Playing with her emotions? What do you mean?"

Christos looked embarrassed. "Leading her on when you're going to sail off into the sunset once your electronics are fixed. Sorry, it's none of my business, I know, but I'd hate her to be hurt. She and my kid sister were always close."

Harley fixed him with what he hoped was a sincere expression. "Your brotherly concern is understandable, but Lily and I are friends only. There are no expectations on either side."

Christos didn't comment further, but still looked at him speculatively. Adam broke into the conversation.

"She's a hard worker, that one. She had a part-time job in Maisie's Café when she was still in school."

The conversation moved on, but it rammed home to Harley that your business became everyone's business in a small town. Mavis had emphasised that the previous night. If Lily hadn't been with him, Mavis might have picked up a steak knife and rammed it through his heart. Were all the women in Sandy Bay so feisty?

Harley assessed the wind speed and direction. It looked good.

"Christos… I reckon we can sail under canvas for a while… if you're up to it."

"Absolutely. I haven't forgotten everything."

Under Harley's direction, Christos hoisted the headsail and the mainsail, winding the winch to unfurl the canvas. The yacht listed slightly to one side, but they skimmed over the surface at an acceptable rate, now with a slight flapping of canvas replacing the rumble of the motor. The stress of the previous couple of days dissolved as Harley stood at the wheel, braced against the breeze. This was the life his grandfather had wanted him to have.

Pelican Cove lived up to its name, with a pod of pelicans occupying the beach. There were more of those birds in one place than Harley had seen before.

"Do we stop here for lunch?" he asked Christos as they neared the beach.

"The Island will be better. Sheltered mooring, and I don't have to compete with that lot for some fish."

"Sounds good to me. Batton Island, here we come."

They adjusted the sails for the change of direction and tracked a course for the island. Christos directed them to a sheltered cove which he had visited many times in the past. Harley reefed the sails and turned into the wind, slowing down before dropping the anchor. The boat swung around gently with the movement of the tide, but the anchor secured them in position.

Christos spread out the contents of the packages he'd brought on board—pickled octopus, stuffed vine leaves, spanakopita, cheeses, olives, and his mother's home-made bread. In case they were still hungry, another package contained kourbiedes and bunches of grapes.

"Is this all for us?" Adam asked as he eyed the spread. "It will keep us going for a week."

"Never let it be said that a Greek mother doesn't feed her family enough, and that goes for friends as well. If there are any left-overs, Harley can take them home. It will make my mother happy to think we've eaten it all."

Christos opened his box of fishing tackle. "You two make a start on lunch. I'm going to throw a line over first in case there are fish biting here."

"Good luck with that," Adam said, casting a curious glance at the contents of the tackle box. "I see people fishing off the jetty all the time, but I know more about eating fish than catching it. I'll happily watch, though."

A musical sound intruded on their lunch, causing them each to pause, heads perked, and listening.

"Is that your phone?" Adam asked.

Harley leapt to his feet and jumped down the few steps into the cabin. He hadn't expected to have coverage out here, let alone receive any calls.

"Are you three enjoying yourselves? Has Christos forgotten how to hoist the mainsail?"

"Lily… I didn't expect you to call. We're moored off Batton Island, having lunch, kindly supplied by Mimi, and no, he hasn't forgotten."

"That's good. I was concerned after the altercation with Mavis last night. I just wanted to check that nobody had scuppered Ocean Dream or anything like that."

"No. Hopefully, that will soon blow over. Everything's fine. Christos is trying his luck with fishing. I'll call you this evening."

"Okay. Keep your eye on the weather. We're on the other side of the island, but the wind has picked up out here. We might swing past you on the way home. Speak to you tonight."

He threw the phone back on the table and joined the others. "Just a check-up call from Lily to see we haven't capsized or drowned. Anyone for another drink?"

In the end, all Christos caught was a tiddler, which he threw back. He didn't seem perturbed, explaining that he enjoyed the process of fishing as much as actually catching any. By the time Harley decided it was time to move again, they had eaten a surprising amount of food. Mimi knew more about the appetites of three men in the fresh air on a boat than they had initially assumed. Even so, there was still some cheese and some of the sweet treats left over, plus half a loaf of bread.

"If you two aren't too bloated to move, we'd better make tracks. Christos, can you do the honours with the sails again?" Keeping in mind Lily's comments about the weather, Harley checked the skies. There were some dark clouds to the south. Time to head for home.

"Aye, aye, Cap'n. I'll pull up the anchor first. I feel as though I should have a parrot sitting on my shoulder."

As soon as the anchor was back on board, they drifted away from the Island. The sea was choppier than before and the wind had picked up.

Adam shuffled himself off the bench and stood upright, clinging onto the cabin roof. "Anything I can do? I feel useless sitting around while you two do all the work. I can help raise the sails."

He grabbed the traveller line, holding the boom in position, and before Harley realised what he was doing, Adam had released the line. As the boat pitched, the boom swung wildly over to one side, collecting Christos as he made his way back from the bow. He never saw it coming. His head jerked back, and he was thrown against the side railing, with his arms windmilling. In the next instant, he was gone, over the rail and swallowed by the sea.

"Keep your eye on him" Harley screamed. He leapt to secure the boom before returning to the wheel, spinning it hard. He scanned the surface of the water, looking for the yellow jacket. Panic threatened to choke his throat. What if Christos had a head injury? What if he couldn't find him? With the electronics out of action, he couldn't even radio for help. The tide was moving fast and would sweep him away.

"Can you see him? Where is he? Grab the lifebuoy."

Adam had a firm grip on the side rails as he stared intently towards where they had last seen Christos. Both men knew it was easy to lose sight of someone in the swell, and the danger of sharks in these waters was ever present.

Harley started the engine and motored back towards where they'd moored. Surely, they would spot him. He had to be floating there somewhere.

Adam cupped his hands around his mouth. "Christos! Christos!" Calling against the wind had reduced effect.

"There he is… I've got him!" Adam pointed

To their relief, the man in the water raised a hand. Harley motored towards him and then cut the motor, while Adam stood poised with a length of rope, ready to throw it when they were close enough. Christos grasped the line, and Adam dragged him around to the platform at the stern. A small ladder lead from there onto the deck. Adam had to lean down and grab Christos by the hand, hauling him upwards. They both collapsed onto the bench in the cockpit.

"I'm sorry, mate," Adam jabbered. "I didn't mean to clobber you like that."

Christos rubbed his head and winced "Usually, I have a stunt man to do the dangerous stuff. It's in my contract." He stood unsteadily on his feet, with his eyes reflecting the shock of his unexpected dunking.

"I'll get you a towel. I've got some dry clothes in my cabin. Come down below. Adam, can you take the wheel and keep us pointed at the bluff in the distance? I'll be back in a minute."

Harley led Christos down into the cabin and found him a towel. "Strip those wet clothes off. How is your head? It's not bleeding, but you might grow a hefty bruise."

Christos undid his life jacket and stepped out of his sodden trousers, leaving a puddle on the floor. "I'm fine. I was stunned, but hitting the water took care of that. Damn, it was cold. Thanks for coming back to get me."

"Can you imagine me leaving Australia's favourite film star to float around the ocean as shark bait? That's if the hypothermia didn't get you first."

Christos attempted a smile, but it looked more of a grimace.

"I'm so sorry you got hit. I should have been more on the ball. Adam loosened the boom before I realised what was happening. That was lax of me."

"Don't worry about it. I'm fine. I'm equally to blame. I should have kept my wits about me. I just won't tell my mother or I'll never hear the end of it"

"You're not the only one."

At this rate, he would have the entire town baying for his blood. Harley's phone rang again.

"What's happened? Was that Christos?"

Still holding the phone, Harley mounted the stairs back to the cockpit and saw that Sea Witch was off to their port side. Lily stood at the railing, peering through a pair of binoculars.

"It was a minor mishap with the boom. He's fine… warming up down below."

"Dammit, Harley! You can't lose people overboard like that. Where did you learn to sail?"

∾

Ocean Dream appeared to be sailing in circles. What were they doing? Lily picked out two figures, but the third must be below deck. She raised the binoculars and adjusted the focus, then watched in horror as a figure was dragged from the water. She was about to ask her father to slow down, then thought better of it. Now three men stood on the deck, and the one who had been dragged on board looked to be Christos. This was not the weather for swimming.

Christos and Harley disappeared into the cabin, leaving Adam at the wheel. Contacting Harley by radio wasn't possible, plus anyone on that channel could listen in on their conversation. She reached for her phone.

"What happened? Was that Christos?"

She saw Harley appear on deck again, looking toward Sea Witch.

"It was a minor mishap with the boom. He's fine… warming up down below."

"Dammit, Harley! You can't lose people overboard like that. Where did you learn to sail?" She snapped her phone shut. She had no patience for not following safe practices out on the water.

Stan poked his head out of the wheelhouse. "Anything the matter?"

"No. Christos seems to have gone for a brief swim, but they're heading for home."

"Swimming! That's an odd thing to do out here. It's not the weather for that. The lad must have lost his smarts."

Lily wasn't about to tell Stan what had really happened. Harley was in enough trouble as it was. She saw him take over at the wheel from Adam, who promptly disappeared down below. Hopefully, they'd had a good time, aside from their mishap. The trawler overtook the smaller vessel and arrived back at the marina first. The tubs were loaded into the van before she saw Ocean Dream coming through the channel.

She stood with a hand shielding her eyes as she watched the boat approach. Christos leapt off at the berth to secure the mooring ropes, so presumably he wasn't suffering after-effects from being walloped and shoved into the water.

"Lily, are you standing there all day? I want to get home, even if you don't." Stan opened the driver's door of the van and jumped in.

He was right. There was no point in hanging around. Harley would call her later—unless he was too embarrassed. Operations at the co-op were completely back to normal when they dropped off the day's catch. So was Mavis. That didn't equate to cheerful, but as close to normal as could reasonably be expected.

"We've almost caught up," she said in response to Lily's query. "This episode has been a learning experience for all of us. Never rely entirely on automated systems, make sure the processes are understood, and be prepared for disasters. If we had a power cut for instance, we'd be in the same boat."

"Sounds sensible to me. I'm glad you have it under control."

"Lily, I always have things under control."

"So, you weren't out of control at the pub yesterday evening when you tore into Harley?"

"Of course not. Someone's got to tell things as they are."

Lily rolled her eyes but didn't comment further. Mavis had a point.

13- Changes for Lily

AS THEY DOCKED, the sky was a turbulent mix of dark clouds and shifting shades of grey, casting a sombre tone over the marina. The wind whipped along the coast, causing the boats to rock gently at their moorings. It created an atmosphere of unease.

Christos didn't hang around. He wanted to get home, have a hot shower, and change.

Adam regarded him ruefully. "Didn't mean to dunk you, mate. I should have waited for instructions."

"No worries. I thought you were just getting me back for all the grief I gave you at school."

The older man gave a bark of laughter. "Your behaviour wasn't too bad, compared to some. Considering the lip you get from today's kids, it was mild."

Harley raised his eyebrows. "School?"

"I never told you what I did. I was the principal at the local high school. I probably gave Christos detention a couple of times… I don't really remember, so it can't have been too bad. He didn't set fire to anything, that much I do know."

"I seem to recall setting off the fire alarm. Mostly, it was mundane stuff, though we thought it funny at the time. I've still enjoyed today, even with an unexpected dip. I'll drop your trousers back to you," Christos added, nodding in Harley's direction.

He gave them a wave and sauntered towards the carpark. Harley grabbed the day's rubbish to put in the bins onshore and helped Adam climb off Ocean Dream.

"Thanks. I'm hoping this boot comes off next week. You've no idea how tired I am of the restriction."

"I can guess," Harley said as they walked towards his ute. "You're retired now?"

"Not quite. I've retired from active teaching, but do freelance work in curriculum development. I can do that despite mobility issues, and it's flexible, so I can go sailing if I want, or tour the local gourmet establishments with visitors."

"Sounds ideal. I've been considering my future. I don't have to work currently, as long as I manage current finances carefully, but I'm too young to do nothing. Painting is an interest, but I need more in my life. I just don't know what it is."

Adam shook his head. "Don't dwell on it too much. The more you worry about it, the more elusive an answer will seem. One day, the stars will align and the solution will be obvious. There may be options with your technology skills. On the other hand, you could stay in Sandy Bay and become a fisherman."

"As if. I'll leave that to the people who know what they're doing."

"Probably a good idea. Thanks for the invitation today. Stay in touch, and let me know how you get on with the boat. Hope that Marriot fella gets it fixed soon."

The drive back to Seaspray Cottage was contemplative. After dropping Adam at his home, Harley thought about what the other man had said. Wait until the stars are aligned, but how would anyone know when that was? He had no answers to that puzzle. Once inside, he showered and changed into comfortable clothes. He poured himself a glass of whiskey, savouring the warmth it brought, before calling Lily.

"Hey… we're back, all in one piece. As you saw today, Christos was knocked into the water when Adam loosened the boom, but he's fine… probably a bump on the head, but otherwise fine."

"I'm pleased to hear that, but shouldn't you have supervised Adam? That's a rookie mistake."

"You're right. It shouldn't have happened on my watch, and I'm grateful no actual harm was done. He was wearing a life jacket, and we picked him up quickly."

"Okay. I'm sure Mimi, Nico, and the whole fan club in Australia will be pleased to hear that."

"I don't think Christos was going to tell his parents. He seemed to think the ensuing drama wouldn't be worth it."

"He's probably right. I have things to do, so I have to go."

She disconnected the call, leaving Harley staring at the phone. He was no longer in Lily's good books. The weight of her disappointment settled over him, blending with the melancholy of the storm outside. The rain began falling, a steady patter against the windows, mirroring his mood as he pondered the day's events and his uncertain future.

It was too early for an evening meal, but he laid out some cheese and biscuits to accompany his drink. Sitting at the dining table, Harley pulled his sketch pad towards him. He had told Bryan that he wasn't a portrait painter, but now he found himself sketching an outline, moving with swift strokes to capture the image in his mind. When he needed to refresh his memory, he opened his phone and searched for the photos he took the day that he spent on Sea Witch. He studied them before returning to the pad and continuing the work, erasing some lines and expanding on others.

He had finished his second glass of whiskey before he put his pencil down, satisfied with his preliminary attempt. He put it aside, unsure if he would work on a watercolour version, but was still satisfied with what he had produced. He propped the drawing up on the mantelpiece above the fireplace, and when he looked back at it, he could have sworn the eyes not only looked at him, but followed him around the room. It could reflect his skill in capturing the essence of his subject, or perhaps the drawing had taken on her personality.

He opened the door to the front veranda and wandered outside, inhaling the salty seaweed tang. Dusk had fallen. The sea surged beyond his line of vision, though as his eyes adapted, he could make out white caps as they flung themselves against the shore, flattening and then merging into a thin froth. Pinprick stars were visible. Being able to see those pinpricks of light in a dark velvet sky was one pleasure of being at sea at night and away from city lights. He took comfort from still being able to see them, now he was ashore.

The lone cry of a night bird hung on the night, half mournful, half a cry to others of its kind.

"Don't call to me with your problems," Harley mutters as he turned to go inside. "I've got enough of my own."

🙰

Lily knew she had been unfair. She couldn't quite put her finger on the reason for her mood. Despite all precautions, accidents could happen. Her first impression of Harley had been of a poor little rich boy in his flash boat, playing at being a sailor. As she got to know him better, her opinion of him had softened, particularly when he pulled his weight during the day he spent on Sea Witch. Allowing the boom to swing free was a rookie mistake. It had made her think that her initial impression had been the right one.

Eleni's words surfaced unbidden. *You push men away.* She didn't mean to repeat history, but maybe the habit was ingrained. It made sure she didn't get hurt again. If she kept Harley at arm's length, he couldn't cause her grief. She enjoyed his company. She would be lying to herself if she denied the attraction, but she couldn't allow him to get too close if he was about to sail off into the sunset. Roger would have Ocean Dream fixed soon, and then he would continue to Adelaide, and Meredith would introduce him to all her women friends.

The ringtone of her phone jolted Lily from her introspective ruminations. She knew who it would be. She had selected a Gladiator theme song as the ringtone for her father.

"What's up, Dad?"

"Lil, we need to talk. Family talk. Can you come over here?"

"Isn't it late? Can't it wait until tomorrow?"

"No, it can't. We're all busy, and then there's no time."

"Sounds serious. What's it about?"

"Quit wasting time and just get over here."

He disconnected the call, leaving her perplexed, verging on annoyed. It was a demand, rather than a request, and what could he possibly have to discuss that couldn't wait until tomorrow? Family talk… surely he wasn't ill? Her mother, perhaps? She was the one who usually imparted family news.

Her parents lived on the other side of town, too far to walk at this hour of night. She considered riding her push bike, telling herself that she didn't ride it often enough. It gathered spider webs where it was stored in the garage. In the end, she caved in and jumped in the car. The outside light was on when she pulled up in the driveway of her parent's house. The front door opened as she approached, and her mother opened the screen door for her.

"Hello, love. Your dad's in the dining room. Do you want a cup of tea?"

Cup of tea… that was her mother's solution to everything. "That would be lovely, mum." She didn't really want one, but found it easier to accept the usual pattern of behaviour instead of challenging the status quo.

Lily walked through the house to where her father sat, with paperwork spread out over the table in front of him. To her surprise, she could also see glossy travel brochures.

"Sorry to drag you out at short notice, but I wanted to discuss this with you now. Long story short, I've decided to sell Sea Witch and our fishing licence."

"But… what's prompted this? Why haven't you discussed it with me?" The news stunned her, almost to the point of incoherence.

"I'm getting on, and I've looked around at some of my mates. They're all developing various ailments and aren't as fit or mobile as they used to be. It made me think. All this work is not of benefit to me and your mother if we can't enjoy the rewards."

Her mother entered carrying a tray with the teacups and a plate of biscuits. As she lowered the tray to the dining table, her hands shook, causing the crockery to rattle. That didn't used to happen. Lily tried not to think of the implications. She used the moments in which the cups were distributed and tea poured from the teapot her mother always used to gather her thoughts.

"I have a bit saved up, and can speak to the bank about a loan. I can use my cottage as equity. I should be able to confirm that in a day or so."

She saw her parents exchange a glance. The wordless message she intercepted gave her a queasy feeling.

"The thing is, Lil, I've already found a buyer. I'm selling to Davey."

"Davey! But why him? He's not family. I've worked on Sea Witch longer than he has. Why haven't you discussed this with me! I should be the one to take over from you."

Her mother reached out to lay a hand on her arm. "We're just thinking of you. I know you're upset, but this decision will be for the best, you'll see."

"How can it be, when you're taking away my livelihood and selling it from under my feet? What am I supposed to do?"

Her father bit a biscuit, wiping crumbs from around his mouth. "The thing is, Lil, I had to think about what was best for everyone, you included. I know you like working on the boat, but is this the best lifestyle for you long-term? Working on Sea Witch takes you away from the usual social connections. You wouldn't want to get to my age, and still be a woman on your own, going to sea every day."

"The thing is, Dad," Lily parroted, speaking slowly to emphasise her words, "what I do with my life and where I work is my decision to make. I'm not a kid."

Her mother pursed her lips as she took a sip of tea with her eyes fixed on a brochure. She hadn't said much, but Lily knew enough to realise that her mother would have been a joint conspirator in this plan of theirs. She'd never made a secret of her wish that Lily formed a steady relationship and hopefully produced grandchildren one day. She had never supported Lily's decision to go to sea, although she had never voiced that opinion. Her father was the one delivering the news, but her mother would have been persuasive behind the scenes.

"Lily, you will thank me for this later." Stan said. "You have a lot of opportunities available to you; you just haven't understood that. I know you have had a vested stake in Sea Witch, supporting me and sometimes working long hours and in conditions that weren't always comfortable. When the sale is completed, your mother and I have agreed that you should be compensated for that. A percentage of funds will come to you, which will help to set you up in a new business, if that is what you decide."

"Are you telling me that this is a done deal?"

He gestured to the papers sitting on the table in front of him. "It is. Davey signed the paperwork late today. He takes over at the end of the month."

"You've been planning this behind my back for a while, then." It was a statement of fact, not a question.

"Not behind your back. When I broached the subject with Davey, he jumped at it. Negotiations happened quickly, and were only finalised today."

"And you think that a male, who is a non-family member, is more entitled to take over Sea Witch than your daughter." Even her tea tasted bitter.

"In this situation, yes, I do. Call me old-fashioned if you like, but the sea is a demanding mistress, and it can take over your life. A young woman should look at other options. Also, I can see the writing on the wall; larger companies will take over small operators like myself, and as fishing stocks are depleted, the government will restrict the number of licences that are available. Fishing has been good to us and our lifestyle, but now is a good time to get out."

Lily gestured to the pile of brochures on the table. "You're planning on cruising instead? Is that what you want… sitting on one of those germ-infested, floating palaces that circle the globe in a form of hedonistic self-indulgence?"

Her mother winced. "It won't be like that. We may do a cruise—that's one option, but I want to travel, to see Italy and the Northern Lights, and perhaps to explore my ancestral roots in England. I've never had the opportunity before, and if I don't do it soon, I never will."

Lily ran her fingers through her hair, massaging her scalp. Her mother was right–the holidays that she and Stan had taken were limited and never overseas. If they were to go, sooner was better than later, but she and Davey could have managed Sea Witch on their own, or else with hired help for the duration. From what they had just said, this wasn't an option. The papers were signed and Davey would be the new master of Sea Witch. The only certainty she now had was that she wouldn't work for Davey. She had more pride than that.

She rose, leaving her half-drunk cup of tea on the table. "I note that you made no mention of this to me until it was a fait accompli. I'm not happy, and I won't forget this."

"I'll see you in the morning, then."

Stan acted as though she hadn't spoken. Lily knew that for him, the matter was now closed. Her mother followed her to the front door.

"I know you're disappointed, love, but think about it—the economics of this decision makes sense. I'd hate for you to be lumbered with an asset that was declining in value. Then there's the lifestyle… you could never have a family with living the life that you do. You would miss out on so much."

"Says who? I'm getting a cat… perhaps two. They won't let me down."

Her mother closed her eyes briefly, shaking her head. "Don't be like that. It doesn't become you."

As Lily backed out of the driveway, the outside light was switched off. The irony of that action made her snort. The life she had known for so many years had just been switched off, and ruthlessly at that.

Lily could hardly bear to look at Davey the following morning. His smug air of entitlement made her want to either puke or push him overboard. She noticed him running his hands over the side of Sea Witch as though imagining that the boat was his already. She blinked rapidly to hold back the tears of rage that were close to the surface. Concentrating on checking the weather forecast for the day and slow breathing helped her gain control of her emotions.

"Hey Lily, you know your dad is selling Sea Witch to me? It's a logical move really, because who else would know the boat better than me? I've wanted to be master of my own boat for so long. Today, I'm one very happy chappy."

"Congratulations. I'm sure you'll do well."

He grinned, entirely misreading her tone. "Hey, I'll be happy for you to keep working on Sea Witch. Together, we'll make a good team. You'd just be working for me instead of your dad, so not much would change."

How could you even think that? "No, Davey, I won't keep working on Sea Witch. I'm considering my options, but my days working on this boat are limited."

Incomprehension showed on his face. "But I thought you loved this work. That's what you told that yachtie who came out with us. You said you loved the sea."

"Loving the sea is one thing. Having Sea Witch sold from underneath me by my own father is something else again. After a betrayal like that, how can anyone expect me to stay?"

"But, it makes sense that Stan would sell to a bloke. Running a business like this, and it is a business," he added earnestly, "it takes a lot of time and devotion. A woman will have other interests in her life, you know, kids and things. You can't expect to do this sort of work forever."

"I'd quit while I was ahead if I were you, Davey. You'd better start thinking about who's going to sail with you because I'm telling you now, it won't be me."

෨

Lily didn't go straight home after work that day, feeling the need for some down time to help clear her head before she did. Once she was home, she would start fuming. Not that she wouldn't fume anywhere, but she needed a neutral space. She had checked out Ocean Dream after docking that afternoon in case Harley was on board. He wasn't, but Roger Marriott was. That meant work was happening on the electronics, and if that was the case, Harley would leave soon. His focus would be over the horizon. No point in talking to him.

She contemplated the front bar of the Regal Hotel, but in driving past Maisie's, noticed that the café was still open. An iced coffee might soothe the conundrum in her brain. The person she didn't expect to see was Adam, sitting at a table in the corner.

"Hi Adam. Good to see you getting out and about again. Did you enjoy yourself yesterday?"

It had taken her years to get used to calling him Adam instead of Mr. Grant, as he had been when she attended the local high school. After he resigned from his principal role, he dropped the formality with his former students.

"Lily—I did indeed. It was good of Harley to take us out. Unfortunately, I gave Christos a bit of a ducking, but I hope he's forgiven me for that. I should have waited for directions from the skipper."

"The skipper should have been more on the ball. He should have made sure you knew what to do, or more importantly, what not to do."

"Be fair. It's a bit like being a teacher. You think you've covered all bases in giving your class specific directions, but there's always that one student who reacts in a way you never considered. Some things are difficult to anticipate."

"Yeah, I guess… I'm just in an off-mood today. That probably influences my attitude."

"Want to talk about it? Why don't you sit down?" He shoved a chair out from the table with his good foot. "Jordy," he called to his son, "get Lily a drink."

Lily surprised herself by sitting down. She respected Adam's opinion. He had always been fair-minded in his previous role, and anyone who could wrangle a school full of free-spirited adolescents had to have some smarts about him. She gave her order to Jordy and waited until it arrived before outlining her discussion with her father and the consequences for herself.

"There were never any promises, Adam, but he's cut my future off at the knees. I've worked on Sea Witch for years now, and always assumed that when Dad was ready to retire, that I'd take it over. I didn't think it mattered that I was his daughter, not his son."

"So, what are your plans now?"

"I've no idea. Dad says that some proceeds from the sale will come my way, but I don't know how much. My life is here in the Bay. I don't want to leave, but I may have to if I can't find suitable work here. I don't know what else I can do."

"If you want my advice, don't decide in a hurry. You still have a job until the contract is settled. I know you're upset, but suck it up for now. It means you still have an income while you do some research. There are a few options. You can work on another boat. You can look for a different job in town or start your own business. Failing that, you can make a clean break, and look for a job in the city. A change might do you good."

What Adam said made sense. Lily sipped her drink, taking time to let the options sink in. "I wish I knew what I wanted to do."

"That's why you need to take your time. I am sure there are options you haven't considered. Have you ever travelled? Now might be a time to do that. It's a good way of putting things at home in perspective."

"Mum and Dad are doing the travel thing, but I hadn't considered it."

"At least take a break. I can forward some websites that I used with students who were considering work and career options. They help you work through your values, skills, interests, etc. and come up with a range of potential careers, based on the information you provided. Would that be useful?"

"Thank you, Adam. I'm a late starter in making these decisions, but I need some objectivity. Any help you can provide will be gratefully received."

By the time she left the café, her dark mood hadn't entirely lifted, but was certainly lighter. Speaking to Adam was more productive than speaking to Harley would have been. There was no point in discussing her affairs with him.

14 – Diagnosing the Problem

HARLEY ROSE EARLY, after it became apparent that further sleep would be elusive. His mind had slipped into overdrive in the interrupted moments when he lay awake. He could leave Sandy Bay in the next day or so, based on the work that Roger Marriott was about to do. The parts had been returned from the supplier and needed to be installed and tested. After that, he and Ocean Dream could go. The option of spending time on Kangaroo Island needed researching, but it had appeal. Alternatively, he could bypass the island and head straight for Adelaide. He lacked justification for staying longer in Sandy Bay. He was no closer to resolving his options when he opened the front door to test the temperature of the coming day.

In the half-light, the promise of the day to come was elusive. Harley pulled on some warm clothes and his walking shoes, and ventured out onto the beach in front of the cottage. A loose carpet of small shells crunched underfoot. Waves threw themselves against the shore, thumping on the sand assertively. Threatening grey clouds hung heavily in the sky. The coming day looked as mixed as his muddled thoughts.

He had the beach to himself. Most early morning walkers ventured out closer to the town and the jetty. The relative isolation of Seascape Cottage meant that at this time of day at least, nobody was likely to disturb his solitude. That suited him and his contemplative mood just fine.

By the time he had tramped a distance along the beach, and then traced his footsteps back to the cottage, he had mentally shuffled his current options. Assuming Marriott fixed the electronics, he would be free to go and he should visit Kangaroo Island while he had the opportunity. He would search online for potential mooring facilities. Bryan could join him if he wished, either flying over or putting his car on the ferry. Before he left Sandy Bay, he would finish the painting he had promised to donate. If he reneged on that promise, his name would be muddier than it already was.

Daylight had well and truly cracked by the time he shook the sand from his shoes at the door to the cottage. He threw open the curtains to the front window, letting the morning light flood the room. As he turned, the eyes on the mantelpiece met his. Even in a rough, sketched state, the drawing captured the essence of the subject. Harley paused, studying his work. He didn't know when, but he had to finish the portrait.

After breakfast, he searched online for available mooring locations on Kangaroo Island and bookmarked a couple before calling Bryan.

"Mate, just letting you know I might be on the move soon. I'm still thinking of spending some time on KI, so if you want to visit for a few days, that's fine by me. I'll let you know when I have more precise detail."

"Is the boat sea-worthy again?"

"Not yet, but should be by the end of today."

"That's encouraging. I could do with a break, so I'll take you up on that offer. Not sure that it's Meredith's thing. Bit too close to nature for her."

"She doesn't know what she's missing."

Bryan snorted. "If I know her, she'll probably use it as an excuse to indulge in a series of spa days, or even take herself off for a bit of R&R in Melbourne."

"Sounds like everyone will be happy then."

"I'll drive down to Cape Jervis, where the ferry docks. If I take the car over, we'll have transport on the island. It's a big place, bigger than you might think. We'll need wheels. How's Lily, by the way?"

Harley glanced at the portrait. "Not happy with me, since you ask. I took Christos sailing, and because of a minor mishap, he was knocked overboard. Nearly drowning the town's favourite son did not earn me any brownie points. She was on her father's trawler and saw Christos clambering on board again."

"Meredith would have conniptions if she knew."

"Don't tell her… please." The thought of the drama that gossip would cause was enough to give anyone a headache.

"I hope you smooth things over before you leave. I like Lily."

So do I. Harley wasn't about to admit that. "I'll call you when I know more."

He disconnected the call and gathered his painting materials and the unfinished picture for the fund-raiser. He

168

could work aboard Ocean Dream while waiting for Marriott. That way, he could monitor progress with the repairs. Perhaps Adam Grant would get the painting framed for him if he left enough funds to cover that.

Instinctively, he looked to the Sea Witch berth on arriving at the marina, but all the trawlers were out. A couple of new boats were in, and Dennis stood chatting with the crew, wearing his trademark cap. Harley waved in Dennis' direction, but made a bee-line straight for Ocean Dream, not wanting to be caught up in idle chat. He needed to talk to Ralph in Sydney to make sure that the dramas were under control, and customer relationships were being managed. He checked the time on his phone. There was a slight time difference between their locations, but Ralph should be at his desk.

"Hallo, sailor." Ralph sounded chirpier than on their last conversation.

"Hallo to you too. What news? Has everything settled down? Have those mongrels been found?"

"It's with the police at the moment. I don't believe they've nabbed the culprits, but that hacking cell has been busted. The key players have vanished. No doubt they'll start up again from somewhere else."

"Bastards."

"That's putting it mildly."

"What about the customers? Did you know that the fishing co-op here in Sandy Bay was affected by the hack? My name is mud in this town."

"Ouch. Sorry to hear that.

"There is something you could do to make it better. A fund-raising dinner is being held for the babies' ward at the local hospital. If Logistical Solutions were to make a donation, all might be forgiven. The co-op is a significant employer in this town."

"Are you suggesting that I save your hide by making a donation to the town?" Harley could hear the eye-roll.

"No. I'm suggesting that given the impact of the disruption to operations at the co-op, Logistical Solutions giving a donation to a worthy cause, i.e. the neonatal unit at the hospital might be a responsible thing to do. Up to you, of course. You're the boss now."

"Are you suggesting that we make a donation to every company that was affected by the disruption? That could set a dangerous precedent."

"Not at all. I've got to know a few people in this town and they've been good to me. I think it would be an appropriate thing to do."

"I'll discuss it with those who control the company purse. I don't want to make any promises we're not in a position to keep."

"Sounds good to me. Let me know what you decide."

After disconnecting the call, Harley opened his box of paints and took a moment to consider the work he'd already completed. He'd chosen a harbour view as his subject, though from a different angle to the picture he'd given to Adam. He checked outside to compare his work against the quality of the light and the local features before picking up his brush. This was more emotionally rewarding than combatting cyber hackers.

"Coming aboard!"

Harley looked up at the call to see Roger Marriott about to make the leap from the pontoon onto the deck. He dropped his brush into the jar of water and peered up the steps at the man, who now stood waiting to descend into the cabin.

"Glad to see you. How long do you think this will take?"

"As long as it takes. Maybe an hour… maybe two. Have you got the manuals handy?"

Informative as ever, I see. "Come on down and make yourself at home. I'll keep out of your way. I've left the manuals on the chart table. Can I make you a tea or coffee?"

"No thanks. Just had one. I'll need to disconnect the power, so if you're relying on that, you're in strife."

Harley nodded with a deadpan face and moved his painting gear to the far side of the table. Marriott dumped his kitbag on the floor and removed the tools he required. As he began unscrewing the panel behind the navigation console, giving him access to the electronic system, Harley nudged him for more information.

"What was the problem?"

"Nothing major. Just a faulty connection. That part has been replaced. The impact that it had was the major issue. Small part, big impact."

Marriott didn't engage any further, but focused on the work he needed to do, which suited Harley. He also wanted to finish his work, and with minimal disruption. He would normally play some music while painting, but the taciturn man made him feel that music would be an annoyance. By late morning, the errant part had been replaced and systems had been tested. Harley checked as much as he could whilst docked in the marina and declared himself to be provisionally happy with the job.

"Take her out for a spin and put her through her paces. Let me know if you have any problems. I'll email you the invoice."

Marriott packed away his tools and picked up his kitbag. "You can switch the power back on now. Nice boat."

That was the first friendly comment Harley had heard the other man make. The two men shook hands, and Marriott departed, still without having cracked a smile. From what he had seen, Marriott knew what he was doing, and that concerned him more than a friendly nature. The rest of the town made up for that.

Harley glanced at his watch. Lunchtime. His stomach had already told him that, but he'd wanted to check that the feeling was valid. Rather than try to put a meal together from the pantry on the boat, he wandered up to the seafood café at the edge of the marina carpark. He wasn't the only one. A flock of seagulls collected expectantly on the periphery of the outside tables, watching for anyone who was silly enough to sit there. A family group sat at one table. A small boy threw them a chip, and the birds rose as one, screeching indignantly when one of their kind snatched the chip mid-air and hastily gobbled it. A second later, they had all settled again, only this time closer to the family and squawking loudly.

He took his serving of crumbed fish with chips and a wedge of lemon back to the boat. If the kid kept throwing chips into the air by the café, the marauding gulls would stay there instead of following him to Ocean Dream. He sat on a deck chair at the stern, facing the open water. It gave him some quiet thinking time. Not long until he would head in that direction. It made sense to do a small trip first to test the electronics, but that wouldn't be this afternoon. He was close to finishing the painting and wanted to continue with that. If everything performed as expected, he could leave the day after. He looked forward to being on the move again. That's what this trip was all about—sailing, exploring, and new experiences.

He crumpled the cardboard packaging in his fist and left it on the galley sink for disposal later in the bins onshore. The aroma of fried chips permeated through the cabin, making his stomach churn slightly. The thought of chips, well sprinkled with salt and perhaps vinegar, was always better than the reality. The aftertaste called for a cleansing cup of tea.

While the kettle boiled, he reviewed his progress on the painting. There wasn't much more to add. There came a point when you had to put down the brush and declare it to be finished. More than once he had continued, only to realise that he had gone too far. In this instance, some last details were still required. With his cup of tea at a safe distance from his work, Harley washed his brushes, freshened his glass of water, and sat again to complete the details.

By the time he heard the first of the trawlers heading into the marina, he declared himself finished. He pushed the painting to one side to finish drying. Later, he would spray it lightly with a sealant to protect the surface. It didn't take him long to wash the brushes again and to tidy up. While he did that, he kept an eye out for Sea Witch. He wanted to speak to Lily, assuming that she was still speaking to him. The trawler nosed into the marina some twenty minutes later. Now was his chance.

&

Lily saw Harley standing on the deck of Ocean Dream as she secured the mooring rope around the cleat. He stood with one hand on his hip and the other shielding his eyes. He waved when he saw her glance in his direction. She waved back. It would be churlish not to.

Harley disappeared below, but when she and Davey wheeled the trolley drew level with Ocean Dream, she saw him sitting in one of the deck chairs. This time he wore a brimmed hat protecting his eyes. Smart move. Davey stopped pushing.

"Some people have it easy. It's a good life if you can get it. Got the boat fixed yet?"

"I have actually." His eyes slid in her direction. "I need to test the equipment, but I can leave after that."

"Good for you," Davey replied cheerily. "Why would you want to hang around here when you could travel where wind and sea take you?" He began pushing again.

Harley called out to her. "Lily, when you've finished unloading, you might like to look at the painting I finished today. It's for the fund-raiser."

"Sure. Give me five, and I'll be back."

It was more like 15 minutes, but she couldn't help that. Davey seemed to be deliberately obstructionist, asking silly questions and then wanting to re-organise the load in the van.

"You know, Lil, I've been thinking about the contract we have with the co-op. They control the price we receive and the volumes they accept. If we sold directly to the markets in Adelaide, we could negotiate a better deal. What do you think?"

"Davey, if you want to try that, it's up to you. I just recommend you do your research before making any changes. If it was easy or profitable, I'm sure others would have done it before. I think we're done here. I'll leave you to put the trolley away."

That man gave her a tension headache. He hadn't let up with his chat about taking over Sea Witch and trying to solicit her involvement. Why didn't he get the message? Harley was in the cabin when she arrived back at Ocean Dream.

"Hello… coming aboard."

She leapt onto the deck as Harley peered out from the cabin. He stood back from the steps, gesturing to her to come on down.

"I won't keep you long. You're probably keen to get home, but I wanted to show you the painting before I drop it off to get framed."

The painting sat on the galley table, propped against a mug for better viewing. It depicted a familiar scene and was sure to attract attention, and hopefully a good price. She examined the detail carefully before turning to him. "You've done a fantastic job. It's kind of you to do this. I'm sure Anh will be thrilled." She couldn't stay annoyed with him when he did something like this.

He shrugged in a half-embarrassed way. "It's all for a good cause. Only too pleased to help."

"So… Roger Marriott has fixed things for you. When are you leaving?"

"Probably the day after tomorrow. I'll take her out on the water tomorrow and test all the systems before I leave the town. I'll report back to Roger Marriott after that, and if it's all good, I'll be free to go."

"Well… that will be good for you." She wasn't sure what else to say. It was as she had already told herself. He wouldn't be staying long, so there was no point in getting involved, even if a small part of her wished it had been different. She had enjoyed his company in the short time they had known each other. Even though she had been abrupt with him over Christos, he didn't even seem to be intimidated by her. Perhaps they made men differently in the eastern states.

"Would you like to join me for a last dinner before I sail off over the horizon? I'd like it if you would, but will understand if you're busy." He sounded hopeful.

"I'd love to. Why don't I cook for you? You've fed me on a couple of occasions. I can cook for you instead. You know where I live. Seven o'clock, if that's not too late for you?"

He smiled with a delighted expression that crept up to the crinkles at the corners of his eyes. "Seven is fine. I'll take the painting over to Pt Reilly to the framer before they close, and grab a bottle of wine while I'm there. Look forward to it. Anything else you want me to bring?"

"Just yourself. See you tonight."

By the time she had dropped the day's catch off at the co-op, and retrieved her own vehicle, the panic set in. She never cooked for other people, and didn't know what had possessed her to offer that invitation. Maddie might be her salvation. She would have more experience in the kitchen. Lily crossed her fingers that she would find her friend in the office, and not out inspecting properties.

She was in luck. Maddie looked up in response to the buzzer when Lily pushed open the door.

"Lily! Do you have another handsome sailor who needs accommodation? Isn't one enough for you?"

Lily ignored the jibes. "I need help. He'll be gone in a couple of days, but I've invited him to dinner. I don't know what to cook. What shall I do?"

"You could always order in take-away and pretend you cooked it."

176

"That's an idea. I hadn't thought of that."

"No! I was joking. You cannot invite a man to dinner and then not cook… unless you have access to a gourmet home delivery service and that is a definite no in Sandy Bay."

"You're no help. I should never have made the offer, not with my lack of skills in the kitchen."

"Just keep it simple. You'll have to anyway, given the limited time. Do a cheat's chicken with roast potatoes and a green salad, followed by a desert of mixed berries and cream. That won't take you long to whip up."

"Cheat's chicken?" Lily had never heard of it.

"Buy a roast chicken, remove the skin before tearing the meat into chunks and put aside while you make the sauce. You can even buy jars of different sauces that you'll find on the supermarket shelves, but I recommend you whip up something like a green curry and coconut cream sauce, or a lemon sauce, or perhaps a zingy tomato sauce. Raid your spice and herb products—flavour with some coriander, or a bit of tamarind juice or grated ginger. If you have any sherry, add a dash of that for a sophisticated taste. Bring the sauce to a simmer, then drop in the pieces of chicken meat. Easy."

Lily shook her head slightly. "Sounds complicated to me, but I'll give it a go. I'd better dash to the supermarket, if I'm going to get these ingredients organised. The potatoes will take a while to roast."

Maddie grinned with the appearance of someone who has a solution for everything. "Buy the roast potatoes as well. When you get home, chop them into smaller pieces, mix with chopped rosemary and salt, scatter them in a well-oiled baking tray and pop them into the oven. Not for too long, mind. You'll have quick and easy rosemary potatoes."

"Is all your cooking like this? I thought you always slaved for hours over food prep with carefully designed meals."

Maddie laughs. "Who has time for that? While you're shopping, buy some sprigs of herbs or edible flowers, unless you have some in your garden. Scatter those artistically on the plate. It will give the impression that you're a five-star chef."

Lily screwed up her face. "That's stretching the imagination, but I'll give it a go. I'll get that shopping done. Thanks for your help. You're a lifesaver."

The two women hugged before Lily pulled open the door, heading back to her car.

Maddie poked her head out the door, calling after her. "Good luck! Let me know how you get on. Don't let this one get away. I'll be waiting for the next instalment."

Lily wanted to call back that it was nothing like Maddie's assumption, but she also didn't want to broadcast her business to all and sundry. She had invited Harley to a farewell dinner, nothing more.

15 – Lily Cooks a Meal

HARLEY CAREFULLY LAID his painting on the passenger seat of the ute, and drove down the coast to Pt Reilly. He knew from Adam that a picture framer had a showroom in town, and he wanted to choose an appropriate frame for the painting. It would be finished after he had left Sandy Bay, but perhaps Adam could pick it up for him.

The road between the two towns had become familiar. The climate was drier than that of Sydney, and the vegetation reflected that difference. He still admired the low undulating hills to the east, and the rugged coastline to the west. The local council had implemented a program of protecting and re-vegetating the sand dunes with native plants after early shack development had caused some of the local ecosystem to be destroyed. He could see the benefits. It was so different to the sub-tropical greenery along the shores of Sydney Harbour, but it had its own attraction.

He found the picture framer and left the ute parked outside the store while he wandered down to the local bottle shop. There, he chose a bottle of locally produced sparkling wine. He passed a florist on the way back to the ute, and on impulse brought a bunch of yellow and purple Dutch Irises. He couldn't remember the last time he bought flowers. Probably for his mother on Mother's Day.

Back at Seaview Cottage, he rummaged in the cupboards looking for a vase for the flowers to sit in before it was time to leave. He had to settle for a pitcher, more commonly used for iced tea or similar. He put the wine in the freezer to cool quickly, before retreating to the bathroom and throwing himself under the shower to freshen up. He hadn't been on a date for longer than he cared to remember, though it wasn't a date really… just a catch up between two friends.

At least Lily was talking civilly to him again. That thought reminded him to call Christos. She was bound to ask him if he'd suffered after-effects following his ducking. Harley checked his watch. Still time to do that.

"Take more than a dunk in the sea to incapacitate me," Christos said in response to Harley's query.

"I was more worried about your head. That was a nasty crack on the skull before you went over the side."

"It's tender in that spot, but otherwise, I'm fine. You should see what happens on set sometimes. We all get a few bumps and bruises."

"I thought you had an understudy for the dangerous parts."

"We do, but sometimes some action is unavoidable. Happens all the time, but it's not publicised."

"I'm glad to hear you're okay. Lily would never forgive me if you weren't, plus the whole town, I suspect. I'm seeing her this evening, so I can give an encouraging report."

"What's happening with the boat?"

"All fixed. I'm taking her out tomorrow to test everything on the water, and then I'll be off the day after."

"Well, it's good to have met you. Watch out for my little brother in the galleries. Your mate seems to think he can sell a bit of Dimitri's work."

"I'm sure he will. You've got my number. Call me any time you want to go sailing again."

He disconnected the call and grabbed the wine from the freezer and the flowers from the makeshift vase. It would be poor form to be late.

Harley knocked on the door of Lily's cottage at seven o'clock sharp. He heard footsteps approaching before the door was opened. He fixed his face into a smile.

"Not too early, am I? I know that's the height of bad manners." He thrust the flowers in Lily's direction, and feeling brave, leaned forward and kissed her cheek. "I thought you might like these. The colours are beautiful." An aroma had followed her from the kitchen. "Something smells good."

She blushed, but looked pleased. The reaction astonished Harley. He hadn't thought she was the blushing type. Actually, she looked stunning. Instead of caught in the usual plait, or tucked under a cap, her hair hung loose about her shoulders, and the colours in the silky-looking top she wore accentuated the blue of her eyes.

"Thank you, they're lovely. Come on through."

She led him into the dining room, beside the kitchen. It overlooked the rear garden. The land sloped away from the house. A sliding door opened out onto a deck that extended out over the garden below, with a set of timber stairs leading down.

I didn't realise your property was so big. The front appearance is deceptive."

"This place is my refuge. I love the sea, but I need my garden as well. Working out here is my counter activity to a day on the water."

"I guess we all need something like that. Painting is my escape." Harley still held the bottle of wine. He lifted it to draw her attention. "Shall I open this?"

"Good idea. I've already put glasses out on the kitchen bench. While you open that, I'll put the flowers in water. Dinner is almost ready. We can have a drink while we wait."

He poured the wine, and after handing her a glass, Lily led him out onto the deck. They clinked their glasses in a toast."

"Cheers."

Twilight settled outside, with the muted sky colours sending the reaches of garden into semi-gloom. The trees against the back fence stood out in silhouetted relief against the fading sky. The silence was broken by the call of night birds and a growing chorus of crickets.

"I can see why this is your refuge. It's calming out here."

Lily shrugged. "I like it. You must be relieved that Ocean Dream is seaworthy again. It would have been frustrating to be stuck here."

"Not at all. I've met some great people, and I did some painting. I dropped that latest work over to the framer in Pt Reilly. I'll ask Adam Grant if he can pick it up and drop it off to you. I've paid the framer already."

"I can pick it up. I'm often in Pt Reilly, so it won't be any trouble. The potatoes should be done now. We'd better go inside."

Lily directed where he should sit while she plated the meal and brought it to the table. The promise delivered by the smell when he arrived was followed by a truly delicious meal.

"You're a superb cook," Harley said, as he placed his knife and fork together on the empty plate and topped up her wine. "Tastier that I would have made."

Lily looked at him over the rim of her glass as she sipped. "Thank you—it's an old family recipe."

She coughed. Perhaps she had something stuck in her throat. "Have you sorted out the issues associated with the hacking on your company?"

"Yes, and no." He paused, choosing his words carefully. "We know how the trojan was introduced, and that has been fixed. The location of the bad actor has been identified, but not the person or group. They are slippery characters. It's in the hands of the police and their international colleagues. The CEO, that's my old partner, Ralph, is still addressing the impact on clients of the company. That's his problem now."

"Is he liaising with the co-op?"

"I assume so. That is part of his responsibility, either him or Shanti, who is in charge of PR and corporate communications."

"Speaking of PR, that reminds me. I need to make a list of people to approach for donations to the auction. I mustn't leave that until the last minute. I'm thinking of asking Christos if he'll be the MC, but he might not be available on that date."

"That will certainly bump up the attendance. You'll be kept busy if you're door-knocking after work each day seeking donations."

Lily put her glass down with a resounding clunk. "That won't be a problem. I won't be working for much longer."

This was puzzling news. "Why not? What's happening?"

She pushed a piece of potato around her plate with a fork before abandoning it with a sigh. "My father has just announced that he is selling Sea Witch to Davey. I'd thought I would take over the business when he wanted to retire, but that is not happening."

"That's out of the blue, isn't it? Couldn't you keep working with Davey?"

"I could, but I won't. It's complicated, for various reasons. No way am I working for Davey."

Harley gave a wry smile. He could understand that. During the day he had spent on Sea Witch, it had always been Lily calling the shots. Having the tables turned would not be an appealing proposition. "What are you going to do instead?"

"I don't know. My father thinks I'm going to get married and have a heap of children, and then I won't be able to work on the boat. He could have talked to me first about this instead of making assumptions, or projecting his and Mum's dreams on me." Her voice displayed the bitterness she felt.

Harley wasn't sure how to handle this turn in the conversation. "What would you *really* like to do? You're young enough to try different things. You have a few options, starting with staying in town or leaving. If you stay, are you going to work for someone else, or start your own business? That could be something to explore."

"I left town some years back when I studied in the city. I don't think it's for me."

"That's one decision. You don't have to make a choice right away, do you? You probably need some time to let the ideas percolate. Even doing nothing for a while can be a good option. Ideas present themselves when you least expect them."

"You're right, and that's more or less what Adam said when I chatted to him recently. I'm still feeling very raw about it all, and it's preying on my mind. I always thought I would be involved with the sea, not necessarily fishing—that was a family thing—but that I would build my own business around sailing."

"See? You're already focussed on a particular direction. You just need time to tease out the options."

"I know. It's good to discuss it with someone objective, and who's not involved in my decision. Enough about me. There's desert still to come and then you can tell me about the rest of your plans."

Lily cleared away their plates and fetched the bowls of mixed berries she had prepared in advance. She had sprinkled the berries with powdered sugar, and then lightly drizzled them with Cointreau, leaving them to soak. They looked and smelled divine.

Harley remained silent for a while, seemingly absorbed in the taste of the berries. "You're not the only one considering options. When I left Sydney, my intentions were clear, to me at least. I needed a break from the pressures of my corporate career and wanted to re-calibrate my life. I'm proud of what I achieved in a relatively young age, but there has to be more.

He ate another strawberry and waved his spoon in the air to emphasise his point. "I've appreciated having more time to paint. Even spending this time in Sandy Bay, unexpected as it was, has been an exercise in de-stressing. It emphasised to me that I need to be more flexible and open to the opportunities that the universe delivers. That's different to the disciplined life I've led to date."

"I know you were heading to Adelaide before you anchored here. Where were you going after that?"

"My plan was to visit Bryan and Meredith, and then head further west. There's some stunning coastline to explore, and towns I'd never visited. I thought I would keep going until I reached Perth, and then meander up the coast towards Broome. That town has a mystique that has always fascinated me."

"You can still do that, can't you? What's changed?"

You, he wanted to say. *You're what's changed*, but that would be ridiculous. He'd only known Lily for such a short time, but he'd never quite met a woman like her. She was gutsy, opinionated, and passionate about what she wanted, even though she'd hit a road-bump in her plans. Ralph would say she had balls. He'd had relationships in the past, but none that had lasted the distance. That was because of his obsession with work, as much as anything, and the women involved had wanted more of him and his time. Lily didn't rely on any man to complete her life. He'd like to get to know her better, but now that the boat was fixed, he had no reason to remain in Sandy Bay.

"Stopping to draw breathe has made me understand I can take my time. I'm planning to stop at Kangaroo Island for a while. I hear there's lots to explore on the island, and lots of painting opportunities. It's been on my bucket list for a while, so I'd be mad not to stop off there. Bryan might join me for a few days. He would put his car on the ferry, so we would have transport on the island. The boat is big enough to accommodate us both."

"You'll enjoy it. I haven't been there for years, but besides the scenery, there are various cottage industries. I still remember the honey ice cream at the honey farm. Yum." She screwed up her face at the memory. "The sea can be rough on the southern side, but it has some great beaches."

"Are you working tomorrow?" Harley asked tentatively, turning an idea over in his mind.

"Sure. The deal with the boat won't settle until the end of the month. Davey has to get his finance organised. Why?"

"I need to take Ocean Dream out, as I explained, but that doesn't have to be very far. I thought you might like to come with me. You took me out on Sea Witch, so I can return the favour and take you out on Ocean Dream before I go. I can defer departure until you dock in the afternoon."

Lily sat back, looking surprised at the suggestion. Harley couldn't tell if that was good surprised, or bad surprised.

"Sure. I could do that. I'd love to come."

∾

Lily couldn't think why she'd never entertained like this before. In part, she'd had no interest, and in part, the concept had seemed too difficult. Okay, if she were honest, there wasn't anyone she would have wanted to entertain. Certainly not Davey, nor any of the other men who had sniffed around on occasions. None of them had been Harley Mendelson. And now he was leaving.

What to cook hadn't been her only decision of the evening. There had also been what to wear. She rarely put on anything other than jeans and practical protective clothing. She had a wardrobe of lighter trousers for summer, and shorts if she was working in the garden. She had a dress that she wore to weddings and similar festive occasions, and another for less formal events. Other than that, her wardrobe consisted of skirts teamed with a couple of different tops, which she cycled through according to her mood.

Accepting that the meal was a casual occasion, after showering off the day's sea-spray, Lily had donned a pair of white trousers with a top of blue-green jersey. To add the glamour touch, she added gold hoops to her ears and a light touch of eye make-up.

Initially, she had thought she couldn't possibly have enough time to buy the ingredients, prepare the meal according to Maddie's instructions, and then get herself ready before Harley arrived, but she had timed it perfectly. The telltale bag in which the chicken was sold was in the bin, and the kitchen tidied all before the doorbell rang.

Harley was easy to talk to. She hadn't meant to discuss her future, or confusion regarding what she would do next, but he seemed genuinely interested. He was moving on soon, so there was no harm in telling him about the recent events. Any objective advice would be appreciated.

"These berries are delicious," Harley said. There's an underlying flavour I can't quite identify. What have you soaked them in?"

"Chef's secret. If I told you that, I'd have to kill you."

His eyebrows shot skywards in surprise. "That sounds serious. I had no idea you kept closely guarded culinary secrets."

"I don't have many. It was an experiment, actually. I sprinkled them with powdered sugar and then followed up with Cointreau. I nearly added some orange zest, but thought that might be too strong. Some things are better left subtle, don't you think?"

She rose from the table to make a pot of coffee. She had also purchased some Cointreau-flavoured truffles during her frantic shopping trip. A local artisan chocolatier made them and their cost relegated the treats to an occasional indulgence. An evening like this warranted it. While she moved between the cupboard and the bench in the kitchen, boiling the kettle and setting out the cups and saucers, she was conscious of Harley watching with a curious expression. A couple of times he looked as though about to speak, before apparently changing his mind.

She carried the cups to the table, followed by the coffee pot and the milk, and then the plate of truffles. She sat again, indicating that he should help himself to the coffee. Harley slid one of the truffles from the plate and tentatively bit one edge. That intrigued her. She had expected him to devour the chocolate in one bite. It suggested a cautious personality, one who didn't take any actions without assessing the risks. A smudge of chocolate remained on the corner of his mouth, and she was tempted to reach out and wipe it away with a finger. What would it be like if he were nibbling her instead of the truffle? Lily quickly banished the thought and fixed a polite expression on her face in case he could read her mind.

When he finally spoke, it had been to extend his invitation to join him on Ocean Dream. He sounded hesitant, as though sussing out the boundaries of a risk. She was quietly thrilled at the offer and Harley actually looked pleased at her response.

Their conversation drifted into more mundane topics, such as some of their favourite sailing experiences, and who else she was approaching for donations for the fund-raising dinner. That topic pricked her conscience. She needed to get her arse into gear and start asking people and local businesses.

Approaching ten, Harley looked at his watch. "I've enjoyed the dinner—much better than I would have had cooking for myself or at the pub—but you have an early start tomorrow. I should get out of your hair."

He wasn't in it, exactly, but she wished he was. Perhaps that was the Cointreau talking.

Harley stood. "I'll be ready when you dock tomorrow. I can wait for you to offload at the Co-op, and we'll cast off after you get back."

She followed him to the front door. As she reached past him to open it, he turned to face her. Tilting his head to one side, he looked as though assessing another of those risks before reaching out to rest one hand against the side of her face and kissing her. As kisses went, it was more of a light buss, a promise perhaps, rather than one that was loaded with passion and emotion. Lily stared at him in surprise as he stepped outside the door, turning to deliver a quick smile that was caught in the glow of the outside light before climbing into the ute and driving off.

She watched the car disappearing down the street with her fingers resting on her cheek where his hand had only just touched her. Sometimes life delivered cruel blows. Just when a man arrived in town who awoke her senses in a way no other man had, he was about to sail away. The universe would be cruel.

16 – Sailing with Lily

HARLEY DREW TO a halt outside the cottage and cut the engine. The car lights illuminated the surrounding low-lying scrub before extinguishing. The dark closed around him, with the sound of the distant waves intruding on his thoughts. He sat for a few moments, listening to the ticking of the engine as it cooled. The close confines of the cabin afforded him the luxury of processing the evening.

Inviting Lily to sail with him the next day was an impulsive move. Kissing her even more so. Not that he was sorry on either count. He had intended to leave the marina early, in case there were any problems. That would give Roger Marriott time to fix it, but then Lily couldn't come with him. Instead, he would run a few errands and stock the boat with provisions. If he was delayed yet another day, that wouldn't be a major problem.

Once inside the cottage, he turned on the lights. Instinctively, he looked at where the portrait sat on the mantelpiece, still needing to be finished. As before, the eyes watched him, this time with a knowing look.

First task in the morning was to call Bryan. "Didn't wake you up, did I?"

"Be nice. I go for a run most mornings. What's got you so chirpy today?"

"I should depart for Kangaroo Island tomorrow. I have to arrange for the ute to be returned to the car hire place in Pt Reilly, but after that, I'm free to go. I'm heading for Penneshaw, because if you come over on the ferry, that's where you'll disembark. I can pick you up there."

"And your electronics?"

"Fixed. I'm taking Ocean Dream out this afternoon to test her on the water, but I'm not expecting any problems." Self-preservation prevented him from mentioning that Lily was coming with him. Bryan would give him a ribbing. He might also tell Meredith, and he didn't need any grief from that quarter.

"I'm looking forward to this. Meredith understands this is a boys' only jaunt. I'm not sure what she is planning instead, but no doubt I'll find out when the credit card bill falls on my desk. I'll drive down to Cape Jervois the following day and then put the car on the ferry. Give me a list of anything I need to bring. I'll put a bottle of my best Scotch in my kit, or should that be rum if we're going to be sailing?"

Bryan had his priorities sorted. "Either is fine. Warm clothing, a rain-proof jacket and a beanie should be on your list. Bring a book if you want to read in the evenings. I'll have everything else."

"Great. I'll book the ferry and let you know what time to expect me."

Harley disconnected the call and loaded the ute with his belongings. It would make sense to spend the coming night sleeping on Ocean Dream. He could make an early start in the morning. On the way to the marina, he dropped the key to Maddie at Professional Coastal Rentals. She greeted him with a twinkle in her eye that he found vaguely suspicious. "I hope you enjoyed your stay at Seascape. I have fond memories of that cottage." He smiled politely. She had alluded to as much to Lily when he first picked up the key.

"Thank you. It's been very comfortable. If I come back this way again, I'll contact you."

The marina was quiet when he pulled up in the carpark. Now that he was preparing to leave, he would miss the place. A handful of children shrieked and played on the play equipment, while their mothers chatted nearby.

The trawlers were all out, and only a couple of cabin cruisers bobbed at their moorings. A catamaran eased its way through the entrance and pulled up close to the main office. He waved to the skipper as he carried the first load to Ocean Dream. Dennis wandered out of the office and greeted the newcomer enthusiastically. Presumably, the catamaran was a frequent visitor.

After stowing everything away in its designated place, Harley delivered the ute back to the car rental company in Pt Reilly. He grabbed a taxi ride back to the marina. All that remained then was to wait for Sea Witch to return. He was down in the cabin when he heard the rumble of the trawlers. He knew it would be a while before Sea Witch was tied up and unloaded, and settled down with a book to wait. Some fifteen minutes later, he heard the telltale squeal of the trolley wheels. Another dose of oil was required.

"This is as far as I'm going. You'll have to unload at the co-op by yourself today." The satisfaction in Lily's voice was evident.

"What do you mean?" Harley stepped out on deck in time to see Davey's eyebrows raised and then lowered again, reflecting his displeasure.

"I'm going sailing. Think on it as good practice for when you're handling this on your own." She glanced at Harley. "Ready to cast off?"

"Ready and waiting."

She unwound the mooring ropes and flung them onto the deck, following herself with a leap from the pontoon. Davey stood for a moment, watching with eyebrows lowered before turning to push the trolley towards the carpark. Harley couldn't make out the words, but knew Davey was muttering to himself. Probably not complimentary, whatever it was.

As he started the motor and edged away from the mooring, Lily busied herself with winding up the ropes and securing them. Sailing with someone who knew what they were doing was always easier. She joined him in the cockpit, flopping onto the bench beside the wheel.

"Good day?"

Lily removed her beanie and ran her fingers through her hair as though easing some tension. "As good as can be expected. This should be better."

"Not that bad, was it?"

She shook her head and blew out her cheeks before replying. "No, it wasn't. I'm the problem. Now that I know my time on Sea Witch is limited, I just want it to be over."

Harley nodded his understanding, but he needed to focus on navigating through the channel leading out of the marina. He cast an eye over the screens available to him at the controls. So far, so good. Everything was responding as he expected.

"Any preferences on where we go?" he asked.

"Not really. Can I take over at the wheel at some point? I'd like to see how she handles."

"You can do that now. I'd like to slip inside and check the navigation console and verify the information that's available there. If we can put her through her paces first, we can then relax a bit. Hold her on a heading of 274."

Working together, they checked the read-outs, and the veracity of the data provided. Everything functioned as it should. Harley declared himself happy.

"We've still got some daylight left. Unless you have any preferences, we can head down the coast to Pelican Cove, and then back again."

"Sounds good to me. It's a relaxing end to the day. I'm enjoying the contrast to being at the helm of Sea Witch. This is easy."

"Not always. Have you thought about other sea-based options, other than fishing? That's a hard life. I can understand why your father feels it's time for a change."

Lily sighed theatrically, still keeping her eyes on the horizon. "It is hard, I know. It's just that I had built my assumptions around that boat. Sometimes... sometimes I've thought about other options, never seriously though."

"What sort of options?"

"Charter operations. Taking people out on fishing expeditions, or researchers, marine biologists, day trippers...

that sort of things. Whale watching. Coastal tours. There are a few possibilities."

"What's holding you back?"

"A suitable boat, for one thing. The money to buy one is another. Then I need a business plan."

"Can you borrow some funds? Perhaps your father would give you a short-term loan until you get on your feet."

"I know that some money will come my way after the sale, in recognition of my unpaid investment in the business. I'm not sure how much that will be, but perhaps, combined with my savings, I can look for a boat. I doubt I'd find what I need in South Australia, but might find it elsewhere. Then I'd have to sail it back here."

"Sounds to me as though you have the beginnings of a plan. If you like, I can help you sketch out the beginnings of a business strategy."

She turned to him speculatively, with a small frown furrowing her forehead. She didn't speak for a while, but he could almost hear the cogs whirring. "It would help to have an objective sounding board," Lily said finally. "You're not invested in my plans like some other people might be."

Harley wasn't so sure about that, but he wasn't about to say so. What was the point? Tomorrow, he would be sailing out of Sandy Bay and out of her life.

❧

Lily's brain went into overdrive as she thought of the ideas she had just outlined to Harley. She hadn't told anyone else about her thoughts, concerned that they would pour cold water on them. Her father thought she should do something away
196

from the sea; Davey had a personal interest; and even Eleni would raise her eyebrows. Only Maddie, who ran her own successful business, might give her the encouragement she needed.

Harley had the advantage of knowing about boats, understanding some costs involved, and also having a business background. He wouldn't try to influence her one way or the other, but could provide valuable input.

They rounded Pelican Cove, and then swung a wide arc in preparation for the journey back to the Marina.

"I'd offer you a glass of wine," Harley said, "but I have a policy of not drinking alcohol while sailing. I have cold drinks in the fridge or can make you a cup of tea or coffee."

"Sensible. I don't need anything for now. My head is too full of ideas."

"So, you can't think and drink at the same time? When we're back at the marina, I'll open a bottle of the fabulous local Sauvignon Blanc, and we can sit down and start brainstorming. I don't know if the wine will help, but it might stimulate a few more bright thoughts."

Harley nodded at the wheel. "Can you take over here again? I want to do one last check at the nav desk. Then I can call Roger Marriott and give him the all clear. No doubt his invoice will ping into my in-box shortly after."

Lily stepped up to grasp the wheel, imagining how it might feel if this were her boat and she had a charter of fee-paying passengers. To combine her love of the sea with earning an income would be awesome. Wisps of hair had escaped from her plait, and the late afternoon breeze sent them dancing around her face, tickling and teasing. As she swiped at the offending tendrils, she saw a pair of dolphins, mother and calf, swimming beside the boat. The sight filled her with delight. She saw the magnificent creatures often enough, but today it seemed as if they swam in support of her and her dreams.

They tied up Ocean Dream as dusk fell, working in tandem to secure the boat and perform the shut-down tasks.

"You don't have to rush off, do you?" Harley asked. "I'll pour us a drink and organise some nibbles." He thrust a notepad at her. "While I do that, start jotting down some ideas. Who do you think your customers will be; how will you find them; what will be your principal business?"

"But I have so many ideas."

"Write them all down, but then you can prioritise them. Focus on one at a time. Make a success of that and then expand. Walk before you try to run."

"I'm not even at crawling stage," she muttered as Harley busied himself in the galley, filling two glasses of wine on the table, followed by a platter of nibbles, beautifully laid out as he had done before. He must have prepared it earlier in anticipation of her company. Not that she minded. The thought rather pleased her.

"What industry contacts do you have?" Harley asked after he had joined her at the table. "Where will you look for customers? Will it be a seasonal thing, or will the business operate year-round?"

Lily piled a cracker biscuit with a slice of brie and a dried tomato. "That's a good question. I can speak to Maddie about promoting my charters to people who rent her holiday accommodation. Then I can leave brochures in the tourist information centre here and in Pt Reilly. I can commission a website and investigate social media marketing."

"Good ideas. Write them all down. What will you focus on?"

"I would be available for charters at any time of year. Whale watching during the season, mid-winter through to mid-Spring. That's when the mothers arrive in our waters to give birth to the calves."

"I'd love to see those massive creatures up close. I might be your first customer."

Lily bit into a giant strawberry and licked the juice from her fingers. "Don't be silly. You could take yourself out to see them."

"I could, but you would know where to find them. I'd rather see them with you."

"Okay. Looks like I have my first booking." She couldn't conceal her delighted grin as she slid another slice of brie onto her plate and wrote on the notepad 'Online booking for whale-watching tours'. That meant she would need a website as well. She made another note.

"Do you have to be licenced with the National Parks and Wildlife Service to conduct whale tours? Add that to your list of things to do."

"I am sure I do. I think I need a list of bureaucratic tasks, such as investigating what licences or permits I need." She paused, tapping her teeth with the pen. "I wonder how many people I will need to operate a charter. That means employees, and paying tax and GST for them. I don't look forward to that part."

"Unless you're a sole trader, you will have those responsibilities in any business. There will also be workers' compensation insurance, public liability insurance and similar expenses. You can hire a bookkeeper to assist with those tasks."

"I'm beginning to think I need that wine." Lily reached for her glass. "I'd been considering all the fun parts, and not the background administration. That's not what I enjoy at all."

Harley gave a small huff. "Not many of us do. You also need to think about what size and design of vessel is going to suit your purposes. I don't suppose you know how much you'll receive from the sale of Sea Witch?"

"No. I was so upset when Dad told me what he'd done that I didn't think to ask for that detail. I will, though. The boat that I can afford will influence what type of operations I can offer."

Lily looked at the notes she'd scrawled all over the pad. It didn't give the impression that she knew what she was doing, and if she was honest, she was floundering. At least with Harley's help, she had identified the issues she needed to focus on. Later, she would sort them into categories and number them in order of priority, but this was his last night. It would be selfish to take it up with her business plans. She ripped off the page of notes, folding it carefully and pushed the pad aside.

"We've talked enough about my plans. What about yours? Kangaroo Island tomorrow, and where after that?"

Harley filled her glass again. His pensive expression told her he was thinking about his answer. She was surprised to realise that she had finished the first glass of wine. She rarely drank on a work night.

After placing the bottle back on the table, Harley folded his arms and sat back in his seat. "The beauty of this trip is that I can be flexible, and I'm fortunate in that I have the finance that allows me to do that. I mean, staying in Sandy Bay was not on my itinerary, but perhaps it should have been. I've enjoyed my time here, and I've met some great people." Here he looked directly at her. "I wouldn't have done that if I'd kept sailing through to Adelaide, as was my initial intention."

He gestured towards the night sky, which could be seen through the open door. "Look at that view. It's not as clear now with the lights of the marina, but when I'm out on the water, I can see the Milky Way. I can identify the visible planets and watch out for the Southern Cross or other constellations. How lucky am I? Come and look."

Harley grasped her hand and pulled her from her seat, up the stairs and onto the deck. "Come down to the bow, where we can look out to sea. Isn't it magical?"

They stood against the low railing at the bow. A soft breeze danced around them without being too cold. It took a while for their eyes to adjust, but after a few moments, the starry pinpricks in the sky became more defined. The stars weren't in such strong relief as they would have been away from the town, but still made quite an impression. Standing there made Lily think of Rose on the bow of the Titanic. She nearly threw her arms out in imitation and empathy with the emotion of the scene.

She threw her head back instead to better absorb the view, shivering slightly. "Makes you feel small, doesn't it?"

"Are you cold?" Harley said. "I'll keep you warm. Lean on me."

She leaned back into his chest and he wrapped his arms around her. She drew comfort from that steady warmth, feeling his heart beating against her back.

"I'm following the stars," he murmured softly against her hair. "I will get to Adelaide, but after that, who knows?

Initially, I thought I would circumnavigate Australia, but I realise now I don't have to do that, not in one trip, anyway. I don't have to be bound to any route or schedule, whether real or imagined."

If that is the case, why doesn't he stay here longer? The thought surprised her. She hadn't allowed herself to verbalise her feelings, even to herself. "You could even stay in Sandy Bay." She kept her voice deliberately light.

"And that's an option, too." He tightened his hold marginally. "I've promised Bryan and Meredith that I would see them in Adelaide, and now I have this commitment with Bryan on Kangaroo Island. I feel obligated to keep those promises, but after that, who knows?"

A contemplative silence fell upon them. Ocean Dream bobbed gently at her moorings, generating an almost soporific sensation. Or was that because of the two glasses of wine she had drunk? Lily couldn't be sure. The lights of the sky were reflected on the uneven surface of the water, looking like shoals of silvery-gold fish engaged in a moonlit dance. She sighed with contentment. Wasn't this just the perfect place to live?

"I should be going," she murmured, not really wanting to do that, but feeling she ought to make a move. "Work tomorrow, and you'll want to make an early start."

"I don't have to... make an early start, I mean." He grasped her shoulders and turned her around to face him. "Lily... I want you to know how much your company has meant to me during my time in Sandy Bay. You were the one who made it a time to remember."

Perhaps I should give you one more time to remember. Looking up at him, his eyes were hooded in shadows, making it harder to judge what he was thinking. Lily focussed instead on his lips, lips that were incredibly well-defined for a man, the sort of lips that, after a couple of glasses of wine, begged to be kissed. She was aware of her own heartbeat. Reaching up to cup the side of his face with her hand, she leaned forward and brushed his lips with hers. She pulled back, intending to look for his reaction, when he slid an arm up to the back of her head to hold her close and brought his mouth down on her lips that had parted in anticipation.

Lily closed her eyes and sank into the embrace, savouring every nuance of the encounter that left her feeling both bruised, but wanting more. "Do you realise," she said in a strained voice when she managed to disengage, "that we're standing on the deck of your boat in clear view of anyone who wanders by?"

His answer was a slow, seductive smile. He reached for her hand, and with deliberation, led her back to the cabin below. As Lily followed, a jumble of thoughts flashed through her mind. *Is this what you want? You might never see this man again.* The emphatic answer was *Yes. I'm not going to live with regrets. This night is mine.*

17 – Time to Go

THE RUMBLE OF the trawler engines faded into the distance. Harley rolled over, aware that he had the bed to himself. He debated with himself about rising now, or snatching more sleep. With the way his thoughts already raced, that was unlikely to happen. He rolled onto his side so that he could peer through the porthole next to his bed. It offered a limited view unless he contorted himself to either side, but there wasn't much to see. Aside from the trawlers, most of the activity happened after daybreak.

He flopped back into his original position, thinking about the previous night, idly scratchy his belly. He hadn't expected the evening to develop as it did, but had no regrets. He would be devastated if Lily did. Would she think that this was his usual practice, to charm and seduce and then move on with a girl in every port? He'd lived like a monk for longer than he cared to admit.

They hadn't talked about what the evening meant to either of them. Talking had been the last thing on their minds when they retreated to the cabin. He still needed to clarify for himself how he felt, so couldn't expect any feedback from her. Perhaps she was happy with the thought that she might not see him again.

Harley gave into the siren call of the day and slid his feet over the edge of the bed. He found these pre-dawn moments to be magical. There is promise in the stillness, and only the night birds are awake. If the sky is relatively clear of clouds, the celestial bodies are still visible. Occasionally, a sea creature would break the surface, only to plop back again. Anything could happen at this time of day.

Harley scratched the skin on his chest where the night air played across it, creating a soft and almost sensuous itch. While showering in the ablution block, he decided to treat himself to one last breakfast at Maisie's Cafe. Still wrapped in his towel, he padded into the galley to make a morning cup of coffee, setting himself up for the day. A sheet of notepaper lay on the table, torn out of his notebook.

"May you have winds at your back. Safe travels. Thank you for last night. No regrets. L"

Reading it brought a smile to his lips, with a pang of regret. It didn't seem right to be leaving now, but what right did he have to stay? He had his apartment in Sydney whenever he and Ocean Dream returned, and in the meantime, he had his own future to unravel. He didn't feel old enough for a mid-life crisis, but this trip was all about pressing his reset button. He couldn't impose his disruptive influence on her.

He wandered up on deck with his coffee between his hands. A playful breeze ruffled what it could find of his hair, still damp from the shower. Soft bands of light streaked across the sky to the east. The soft, cotton-wool clouds on the horizon were outlined with tinges of coral, promising a spectacular sunrise. He glanced at his watch. By the time he wandered up the main street, Maisie's should be open. Time to get dressed.

Jordan looked up with a nod of recognition as he erected an umbrella over an outside table. "You're up early today, mate. Couldn't you sleep?"

"Not really. I stayed on Ocean Dream last night, so heard the trawlers leave early. I'm leaving today, so there's a bit of nervous energy in the mix."

"Leaving! Does the old man know about this? I saw that painting you gave him. You and Dimitri could put this place on the map as artist central."

"Very kind of you to say so, but this is Dimitri's territory. It's time I continued the trip I was on before fate sent me this way. Now that I know Sandy Bay, I'll probably be back, even if it's for one of your breakfasts."

"Yeah, people travel miles for a feed like this." He spoke with smug assurance. "What about Lily? What does she think about you leaving?"

Harley regarded him with astonishment. Was nothing private in this town? "You'll have to ask her about that." He wasn't about to discuss his feelings for Lily, nor to comment on their relationship.

"Yeah, righto. Do you want the menu, or will you just go with the Big Breakfast?"

"I'll have the works. It will set me up for the day."

"Grab a seat. Give us five minutes for the chef to work his magic."

Jordan whistled as he sauntered towards the kitchen door. Being chirpy so early in the morning was almost indecent, but that's what youth and sea air did for you. Harley was relieved that Jordan hadn't pursued the topic of Lily. He grabbed a copy of yesterday's paper from the rack and seated himself at his favourite table near the window. He'd reached the crossword page before the plate laden with eggs, hash browns, tomatoes, mushrooms, bacon and toast appeared before him. Harley was hungry, but by the time he'd cleaned up the plate, he felt as though he wouldn't need to eat again for a week.

He pushed his chair back and stood. Hearing the noise, Jordan hurried over.

"Thanks for looking after Dad and taking him out on the water. He enjoyed that day." He extended his hand and grasped Harley's with a firm shake. "Safe travels." Jordan then followed Harley to the front door of the café, giving him a wave as he walked along the footpath back towards the marina.

Recreational fishermen were busy at the boat ramp when he got back to the boat. Harley wandered into the office, surprised to see that Dennis was already there.

"I'm leaving Dennis. Thanks for your help while I've been moored in the marina."

He handed over the key to the marina ablution block. Dennis lifted his feet from his desk and stood, giving a sloppy salute.

"My pleasure. Drop by anytime."

"Maybe."

As the door of the office slammed behind him, Harley found an unexpected figure standing outside.

"Adam… this is a surprise!"

"Jordy rang me… said you were going. I've got the all-clear to drive again, so thought I'd drop by and wave you off."

"That's very kind of you. I've had more farewells this morning than Nellie Melba." He nodded towards the boat, tied at its mooring. I'm about to cast off, so you arrived just in time."

"I'll wander down and untie you then."

As the two men wandered down to Ocean Dream, Harley filled Adam in on the route he planned for that day, and how he would spend the coming week.

"I'm jealous. It's an ideal life, you lead, mate… sailing where the whim takes you." Adam paused for a moment. "Heard you took Lily out yesterday afternoon."

The eyes of the whole town must have been watching. "I did. I needed to do a test run, checking on all the repairs. After the day I spent on Sea Witch, I'd promised to take her out on Ocean Dream as well."

"I notice you didn't take Davey or Stan."

"I hadn't promised them, had I?"

"I guess not. You haven't broken that girl's heart, have you?"

"Adam…" Harley turned to face the other man. 'That is the last thing I'd do. Lily's life is here, and I'm not sure where mine lies. We get on well, and yes, I'm fond of her, but… I'm not sure that I'm who she needs at the moment."

"None of my business, anyway. I'm sure you both know what you're doing."

Harley smiled weakly, but didn't feel the need to respond. It wasn't something he wanted to discuss further. He leapt onto the deck of Ocean Dream.

"I'll do the honours, if you like." Adam stood by the cleat on the pontoon, ready to unwind the rope and throw it on deck. "Makes me wish I was leaving on an adventure, too."

"Thanks. You're welcome to join me on different legs. A friend from Adelaide is joining me on Kangaroo Island, but there are lots of other opportunities. You have my number. Give me a call, or send me an email. Mobile coverage isn't always good, but I'll eventually get internet access."

"I'll keep that in mind. Bon voyage, and all that. I hope the weather is kind to you."

Harley turned the key in the ignition and pressed the starter motor. The engine rumbled into life. Now that he was actually going, he felt the hint of nervous excitement. It always grabbed him like this. Sailing into the unknown brought with it a host of challenges. Anything could happen, as he already knew. He gave Adam the nod, and the other man unwound the ropes and tossed them on deck, then stood back with his hands on his hips to watch the departure. Knowing that someone cared enough to come down and see him off was a comforting feeling. It wasn't that he felt lonely, he enjoyed his own company, but… perhaps he needed a cat. Lots of boats had a ship's cat, supposedly to keep down the mice and rats, but no doubt for company too. He had a vague idea that there was even a statue somewhere to Matthew Flinders' cat, Trim. Amazing what useless facts he recalled from school geography lessons.

He motored slowly out through the navigation channel, then set course for Cape Willoughby at the eastern end of Kangaroo Island. From there, he sailed along the northern coast until reaching Christmas Cove, adjacent to the Penneshaw township. The strait between the mainland and the island was known as Backstairs Passage, and Harley knew it could be a rough trip. With that in mind, he had plotted the route that exposed him to the shortest section at the mercy of the waves. The sea gods smiled on him, for the journey was relatively smooth sailing.

By early afternoon, he had moored at the Cove marina. Three other yachts occupied berths, and the owners on one nodded as he manoeuvred past. The others were unoccupied. No doubt the owners were settled in their holiday accommodation, either owned or rented. It was a popular destination for yachties. Harley went for a stroll around the small town and sat down on a park bench in Thorn Park overlooking the sea to call Bryan.

"I'm safely moored at Penneshaw. What time will you arrive tomorrow?"

"I'll get the ferry departing Cape Jervis at ten, so expect me to arrive forty-five minutes after that. It may take a while for vehicles to be unloaded."

"I'll be waiting on the wharf as you dock. Give my love to Meredith."

After he disconnected the call, Harley realised how much he looked forward to this sojourn with Bryan. Exploring the island with a mate would be a suitable distraction from the events of the last week, and all it meant to him.

❧

Lily looked back at Harley as she crept out of the cabin. He snuffled softly, and one arm was flung out as though still reaching for someone. She had used the light from her phone to find her shoes on the floor and softly padded upstairs onto the deck before putting them on. The night air was still, but the security lighting showed the outlines of the marina, and the other boats tied at mooring. Sea Witch was one of them.

She couldn't see anyone else stirring, which wasn't surprising, given the hour. Only those with nefarious intentions or those sneaking home under the cover of darkness like her would be out and about. Not that it mattered if anyone saw her. She wasn't ashamed of spending the night with Harley. She hadn't fully investigated her feelings, but it had been a deliberate and conscious choice. At a time of such indecision in other parts of her life, it was an element of control that she could exercise. The other reason that she didn't want to acknowledge was that she was attracted to Harley. In the short time she'd known him, she'd developed feelings which she'd tried hard to suppress. What was the point when he was moving on? They lived in different cities and came from different backgrounds. She refused to lay her heart open for the inevitable distress when he left and never contacted her again. She knew what that felt like.

Lily arrived home with enough time to crawl into her own bed, snatching a couple of hours of fractured sleep before crawling out and heading back to the marina again. As she wheeled the trolley past Ocean Dream, still tied at its mooring, she almost blew him a kiss, except that Davey walked alongside her. She steadfastly looked ahead.

"I heard that he's leaving tomorrow," Davey said. No need to ask who he meant.

"I believe so. The problem with the electronics is fixed, so there's no reason for him to stay."

"Sandy Bay would be too quiet for him. He'd always be looking for the bright lights, and fine wining and dining. We don't have sophistication on offer here."

Lily risked a side glance. Was Davey trying to tell her something? "The day he spent on Sea Witch wasn't exactly sophisticated, particularly when you tried to scald him with boiling water."

"That was an accident, and he wasn't seriously burned. Coming out with us relieved a day's boredom for him. I'm sure he prefers the comfort of his la-di-da yacht."

There was no point in responding to that comment, so she let it slide. Now that Harley was going, she needed to turn her mind to other things. Like refining the notes she had made the night before, and following up on her tasks for the fund-raising dinner. Her discussion with Harley had given her clarity on her options, but she had time in which to do some research. First step was to find out from her father how much money she would receive because of the sale of Sea Witch. Knowing how much money she had to play with would dictate the size of the boat she could purchase. She looked forward to starting the investigations. It would take her mind off other things.

Lily knew she would be headed for an early night. She needed to make up for lost sleep the night before. As soon as deliveries were finished at the co-op, she headed for home and the luxury of a hot shower. She stood longer than normal, letting the water course over her body, with the hot spray massaging her shoulders. Sometimes they ached so much. It reminded her that the work she did was intensely physical. Maybe it was time for a change.

She had only just changed into the tracksuit pants and sloppy joe she wore around the house in the evenings, when her phone vibrated on the kitchen bench top, doing a slow dance sideways. She picked it up and checked the screen. Rather than the suspected scam call, Lily was relieved to see Eleni's name. She thought her friend had already returned to the city. "Hey, girlfriend, what are you still doing in town?"

"And, hello to you, too. I stayed a few extra days. It's not often that we're all together. I am going tomorrow though. It's chaotic at home tonight, but I wanted to say goodbye, and invite you to drop in to see me in Adelaide any time. You don't have to wait for me to come back to Sandy Bay. We have a spare room, and you're always welcome."

"Thank you. You never know, I might even take you up on that. I'll have some free time in the coming weeks."

"Why's that?"

"It's a long story, but Dad is selling Sea Witch to Davey, and my job has gone with it. I'll be taking a break while I sort out the rest of my life."

"Bloody hell… that's sudden, isn't it?"

"For me, yes, but he must have been thinking about this for some time. Mum's been egging him on behind the scenes. She wants him to retire and spend more time with her, probably travelling and doing all those sorts of things. They both think I shouldn't be working at sea."

"It wouldn't be my choice, but then, I'm not you. What are you going to do?"

"I've got some ideas that I'm working through. When I've got more clarity, I'll let you know." She wasn't prepared to disclose her plans, not until she had researched them further and worked out the costings. That way, she wouldn't look stupid or naïve if it wasn't viable.

"If you need a sounding board, I'll be all ears." She spoke in a wheedling tone. "What about Harley, mister cool dude himself? What's happening between you two?"

"Nothing. He's gone. Left today."

"When's he coming back?"

"He's not. The problem with the yacht is fixed, so he's on his way."

"I thought there was a connection between you two. I'm disappointed for you. I thought… I thought from what I saw of you both together that he might hang around." Eleni was saddened, and it showed. Lily was glad they were talking over the phone and not face-to-face. If she had to confront the obvious disappointment on her behalf, she'd probably get emotional herself.

"Get real, girlfriend. Harley's from Sydney, the city of bright lights and fast living. What is there for him in Sandy Bay?" Davey's words from that morning played again in her head. If she repeated them often enough, she would come to believe them.

"There's you for a start," Eleni responded staunchly. "He got on well with Christos, and obviously he and Dimitri had a bit in common. If Christos can make the world his stage, but still call Sandy Bay home, anyone can."

"Your brothers grew up here and have long-standing connections. It's different for them."

"I suppose you're right. I'm still disappointed for you."

"Hey, don't be. I wasn't under any illusions. You know me… I value my independence."

214

"Yeah, I know. That's fine until it's not. Anyway, I have to go because Mama's calling us all for dinner. Don't forget; come and see Dion and me in Adelaide. A break will do you good."

That break was only two weeks away. Her father had confirmed during the afternoon that Davey's finance had been confirmed, and ownership of Sea Witch would take place in two weeks' time.

"I know you were disappointed about this decision, but your mother and I feel it's for the best. It's a hard life... I should know... and it's time you did something more conducive to relationships and better health."

Lily opened her mouth to protest, but Stan had raised his hand to cut her off. "Hear me out. There would come a time when this lifestyle didn't suit, and then you might be stuck with a body that's worn out and nobody to help ease the pressure. I know you've worked with the expectation of taking over the business one day, and it's only fair that you're compensated for that. Your mother and I have discussed it. You'll be able to set yourself up in some little business on land. Take your time; think about it. You'll come to see that it's the best outcome for you."

Her hand-written notes lay on the bench top with the phone. They were her salvation. Now that she knew how much money would come her way from the sale of Sea Witch, she could plan in earnest. Whatever she did, it wouldn't be some nice little business on land.

18 – Lily finds a Boat

AFTER WANDERING UP from the marina to the Penneshaw Hotel for a counter meal that evening, Harley retreated to Ocean Dream and worked on Lily's portrait. It took him a while to be confident that he had captured her eyes correctly, but he used the photos he had taken of her for comparison. One of them showed her standing at the bow. She had stared ahead at where patterns on the surface of the water indicated a shoal of fish, when Stan had called out from the wheelhouse. Lily had turned in response, just as he took the photo. The early morning sun highlighted her face, showing the colour and shape of her eyes.

Those same eyes now stared back at him, challenging him. They dared him to finish the painting, and to do her justice. By the time he rinsed his brush for the last time that evening, he knew he had. He put the painting aside to dry, cleaned his brushes and packed away the painting gear. It deserved a celebration. He reached for a glass and a bottle of single malt whiskey. Pouring himself a nip, he took it on deck to sit in the night air. The crew of a neighbouring boat were also sitting and chatting on-deck, and they enjoyed a cross-boat conversation about yachts, specifications, and sailing adventures until he decided it was time to turn in. The events of the last twenty-four hours had caught up with him.

The ferry appeared on time on the horizon. Harley sat in front of the window in the lounge area of the ferry terminal, watching as the vessel drew closer and then docked. Passengers streamed off, many them climbing onto waiting coaches, and vehicles began emerging from the hold. He recognised Bryan's BMW and wandered outside the terminal building to stand at a point where he could hail Bryan as he drove up the ramp. Once in the car, he provided directions to Christmas Cove, and parked near Ocean Dream. Bryan dumped his luggage in the spare bunk and Harley set up the makings of a welcoming coffee.

"How was the trip over?"

"Smooth as glass, mate. Make mine a double shot," he added as Harley spooned coffee into the machine. "I left early this morning to drive down to Cape Jervis, and I'm still waking up." He glanced at the painting on the table, still lying where Harley had left it the night before. "Hey, what's this? I thought you said you didn't do portraits. No guesses as to the subject. This is good, Harley. I'm impressed."

"I forgot I had left it there. I'll just spray it with sealer and put it away. I'm sticking with landscapes; this was an experiment."

"Looks like you were painting from the heart. You've captured the essence of Lily. That's not easy. You should reconsider the portraiture. There might be a different career evolving for you."

"I could use that after the recent debacle with Logistical Solutions, but I'll stick with what I know I do best."

Bryan let the topic slide as the two men debated on how they would spend their time over the coming days. They planned a trip to the major town of Kingscote, sailing around the island to the acclaimed beach at Vivonne Bay, stopping off at Seal Bay, and on another day driving down to Cape Willoughby and climbing the historic lighthouse.

"We could follow Farm Gate Trail. We'll need to stock up on some of the local produce. There's even a gin distillery" Bryan seemed to remember that Harley had done a similar trek with Adam near Sandy Bay.

"Sure, but don't forget, this is a painting expedition I've invited you on. I didn't think we were going to eat and drink our way around the island."

"Can't we do both?"

"Perhaps painting in the morning and then touring in the afternoon—or vice versa."

In the end, Harley took lots of photos, and carried his sketchbook with him. Bryan had to take a walk or just chill while Harley made a quick sketch of a scene that potentially he would later paint. Their evenings on the boat were spent chatting with their neighbours, and they shared a barbecue on the second night.

"I can understand this sailing venture of yours," Bryan remarked on the third morning as they sat on the deck with their coffee. "I haven't felt this relaxed in ages. Having some time-out from the daily grind was just what I needed."

"Aren't you missing Meredith? You usually take holidays with her."

"Sure, but you know… absence makes the heart grow fonder. I'm sure she's having a fabulous time without me, indulging herself in a way that would drive me silly." His voice took on more of a deliberate tone, as though he was importing advice of infinite wisdom. "That's what marriage is all about… giving each other the freedom to be the people we need to be. What was it that fellow Gibran said? *Love one another, but make not a bond of love. Let it rather be a moving sea between the shores of your souls.* That's how we treat each other and so far, it's worked just fine."

Harley turned to look at his friend with a new sense of respect. "I'm impressed. I knew you two were tight, but I didn't expect you to be quoting poetry about it."

Bryan raised his mug in a toast. "When you find the one, mate, you'll understand. I know Meredith puts on airs and is a drama queen, but underneath that veneer, she's a wonderful partner in life. She has my back, and I have hers. You should try it some time."

Harley kept his gaze fixed on the horizon. "You know me—once bitten, twice shy. I'm not in the mood for settling down, and my track record in the romance department isn't great. I'm happy as I am."

"Who are you kidding? I saw the way you looked at Lily. You're mad to let that opportunity go. Listen to your Uncle Bryan. Life can get awfully lonely on your own. You two have got the sea in common, and there looked to be chemistry. Life may have taken you in different directions to date, but that doesn't mean you can't make constructive plans for the future."

Harley forced a laugh. "You're making a lot of assumptions. Lily has her life back in Sandy Bay, and I don't know where I would fit into that, not that she would even want me to. I think you should stick to your art business, and leave the matchmaking to others. Better still, forget about it completely."

Bryan stood and collected both coffee mugs to carry back inside. "that's fine with me, but don't expect Meredith to give up anytime soon. I think you're her next project. You'll find out when you get to Adelaide next week."

Harley rolled his eyes. "You'll have to talk to her." He was sailing onto Adelaide after these few days on the island, and of course he was staying with them. One thing he was sure of. Meredith wouldn't be trying to set him up with Lily. The polite frostiness between the two women would see to that.

Now that the sale of Sea Witch was almost upon them, Lily directed most of her spare time to refining her business plans. She searched through various websites selling water craft to find what boats were currently on the market around the country. She could look further afield, of course, but that would mean sailing the boat back from Singapore or wherever. She would have more confidence in getting the condition and credentials checked if the boat were already in Australia. She had flags registered on some sites so that she would be notified whenever new stock was listed.

Aside from that, Lily threw herself into helping organise the fund-raising dinner as a diversionary tactic. It took her mind off her uncertain future, plus her anger at the way her father had pulled the rug from beneath her. She accepted responsibility for finding sponsors and donations for the silent auction. Harley's painting was the first donation, but she needed a few more if they were going to raise significant funds. Delia Kennet, from South Coastal Native Plants had offered a voucher for a garden make-over, and Rachel Thompson had promised to donate a six-pack collection of her alcoholic cordials made using flavours from indigenous plants.

She remembered her brainwave of asking Christos to be the MC.

She still hadn't contacted him. He would be a fantastic draw card. He had left town, but she had his mobile number. He was in film studios on the Gold Coast, but she connected with him late afternoon after Sea Witch docked for the day.

"Lily! This is a pleasant surprise. Are you in town?"

"No, still in Sandy Bay. I've got a big favour to ask. You know we're organising a fund-raising dinner for the neonatal ward at the Pt Reilly hospital? I want you to be the MC. You can say no, but of course I would have to let Eleni and your mother know that you didn't want to help the babies in town, in that same hospital where you were born."

"Are you trying to strong-arm me?"

"Absolutely. The town needs a draw card for this event, and like it or not, you're it. Please say you'll do it."

His sigh came down the phone, then put on a truculent voice, that she knew was all hype. "What's in it for me?"

"Lots of warm fuzzies, and I'm sure your PR team will make the most of it. It will make your mama very proud."

"No promises, but I'll think about it. What's the date? I'll have to consult my schedule. If we're in the middle of filming, it probably won't be possible."

Lily gave him the date. "You can fly to Adelaide that afternoon and then back again in the morning. I can organise transport to and from the airport."

"I'll let you know."

"Don't go yet. There's one more thing."

"Lily, you're straining the friendship. What now?"

I want to auction the right for a couple to sit at your table during the dinner. When people buy their tickets, they'll be offered the opportunity to place a bid. It will be hugely popular."

"And I'd have to make polite conversation with people I don't know and probably have nothing in common with. I'd feel like a prize chook in a raffle down at the pub on a Friday night."

"Hmm, we could always organise a chook outfit for you if you liked. It could look rather cute. Think what that would do for your TikTok views."

"Lily! I am not dressing up as a chook!"

"But you'll do it? I promise I'll only let interesting people place a bid. It will do wonders for your public profile."

He gave a dramatic huff. "If it fits with my schedule, I'll do it. You owe me for this, Lily Jardine. I won't forget."

"Fine. You've earned yourself a few brownie points. You need them to make up for all the teasing you gave me and Eleni when we were kids. Let me know your availability as soon as you can."

Anh squealed with excitement as soon as Lily gave her the news. "I'll add that to our social media campaign straight away. That will really give our numbers a boost."

"Hold on, he hasn't confirmed yet."

"I'll just hint that a super-star will be present. Watch this space, that sort of thing. It'll create a buzz."

"As long as you realise if he doesn't commit, you'll need to find someone else. Don't dump that task on me."

"Of course he'll come. Eleni will be on our side. She'll make him turn up."

Lily felt as though she'd had two wins when later that day, she found an interesting boat online, and amazingly, it was moored in Adelaide. It was different to what she initially had in mind, as it was a catamaran, but it was only a few years old, and could accommodate up to 8 passengers overnight, or else forty-five passengers and two crew for day trips.

She hadn't planned on a boat this big, and would have to pull some financial strings if she were to purchase it, but first step was to inspect it. She could drive up to the city and inspect it in the next day or so. Maybe she could stay overnight with Eleni, seeing as the invitation had been extended. No time like the present. She reached for her phone. Her friend was effusive in response to Lily's tentative enquiry.

"Of course you can stay. The timing's perfect. Dimitri is driving up to the city as well. He has a meeting lined up with that art dealer fellow. You two could drive together."

"But do you have room for both of us? It won't be convenient if Dimitri's already staying with you."

"Don't be silly. There's plenty of room. I wouldn't have made the offer if that wasn't the case. I'd love you to see the changes I've made to the house. We can go shopping too and do some girly things. Stay for a couple of days."

"Me? Girly things? If buying a boat is girly, then I'm all for it. Don't forget the purpose of this trip."

"You're no fun at all. Whatever. I'll be pleased to see you. Get here in time for dinner; I'll have a hot meal waiting."

She told her father that she wanted a couple of days off and was staying with Eleni, but not why she was going. She didn't want him to talk her out of her plans. Dimitri was happy to have company on the drive to the city. They took Lily's car, as she needed the transport in the city. He could easily borrow Eleni's car while there. They chatted about local acquaintances and town gossip during the drive, in between singing out of tune to songs on Lily's Spotify playlist. Only as they neared the city did Dimitri raise the reason for his visit to the city.

"How much do you know about this bloke, Lily? Is he trustworthy, or does he take advantage of fledgling artists like me and charge a huge commission? How do I know he's even going to pay me? I've only got his word for it."

"Firstly, don't take his word, get the agreement between you both documented and signed. Alyssa Finchley could look over it for you. Secondly… well, I can only go by my impressions. He seemed genuine when I met him, and he has represented Harley for a couple of years at least. Harley has his business smarts, so he would have checked out the arrangement before he signed anything."

"I guess you're right. A little voice inside me said that the deal is too good to be true. I'll take your advice about getting a legal eye to look over it though."

She was a fine one to be giving Dimitri advice. She was about to look at a boat costing hundreds of thousands of dollars, and doing that on her own. Who would look out for her?

Eleni bounced out the front door when they pulled up in the driveway of the villa in Prospect. She seized them both in a hug before ushering them inside.

"Two of my favourite people. You're just in time. Dinner's nearly ready. We'll have time to sit down and have a chat first. Dion arrived home just before you. He's under the shower, so he'll join us shortly."

Eleni offered them their choice of beer or wine, and they adjourned to the family room, looking out over the recently landscaped garden. She gave them a running commentary on the months it took to get the work done, and then her plans for further tweaks. Dion joined them for one drink before they adjourned to the dining table, where Eleni served up a Green Chicken Curry.

"So, what are you doing in Adelaide?" Dion asked. "Eleni didn't give me all the details. Just said that you were making plans for life after fishing and that involved some research and big-ticket expenses."

"Just looking at this stage. I want to start a charter business, and for that, I need a boat. I've seen something online that interests me, and I'm inspecting it at North Haven tomorrow. It's probably out of my price range," she added.

"Do you have a partner in this venture?"

"No. Just me."

They all stared at her with varying expressions. Dion was dubious. Eleni rolled her eyes in resignation, and Dimitri grinned. Being the youngest, and the one who had never engaged with his father's fishing business, he had little idea of the practicalities or otherwise of what she was suggesting.

"Sounds a great idea, don't you think?" He belched gently before clamping an apologetic hand over his mouth and giving them a rundown on the results of his exhibition. Lily was glad that the topic of conversation moved away from her. Until she had something definite to tell, she didn't want to talk about her plans. Most people would think she was crazy, and what if nothing came of her ideas? Then she would look stupid and naïve as well as crazy. Better to stay vague and minimising the detail.

Besides these three, nobody else knew any of her thoughts. Except for Harley, of course, and he was floating around Kangaroo Island or somewhere along the local coast. On top of that she didn't really know where she would get all the money. The more she thought about it, she was probably punching way above her weight.

19 – Brunch in Adelaide

HARLEY SAILED TO Adelaide from Kangaroo Island and moored at the South Australian Yacht Club. Bryan had made the trip back by ferry and car the previous day, and had obligingly driven down to the marina to pick him up after Ocean Dream had moored. The two men ferried the various treats they had purchased on the Island to the car, plus Harley's luggage. Bryan pointed to the portrait of Lily.

"What are you planning on doing with the portrait? You should get it framed."

Harley shrugged and avoided eye contact. "If I run into Lily again one day, I can give it to her. She can decide if she wants to frame it or chuck it in the bin." It was a private painting, and for now, he wanted to keep it that way.

Meredith kissed him and gave him a bear hug when he finally arrived at the Walkerville villa. "You looked after my man beautifully over the last week. Now I can look after you.

You've got the same bedroom. Drop your gear in there and join us in the lounge. I want to know everything you two got up to on that island."

Harley looked over Meredith's head at Bryan, who made *no way* gestures behind her back. "What happened on the island stays on the island," he said, trying not to chuckle. It had hardly been a few days of revelry and debauchery. Most days, they had collapsed early into bed after touring and hiking over the various nature trails. "Why don't you tell us what you got up to with your women friends instead?"

"Not a chance. You'd find it boring, anyway."

She was right about that. Harley complemented her on how well she was looking and the conversation moved onto other topics. Over dinner that evening at a local Indian restaurant, Bryan mentioned he had a meeting the following morning with the young artist from Sandy Bay.

"You remember him… he was a childhood friend of Lily's. I purchased one of his paintings at his exhibition, and I've placed it in the boardroom of the State Insurance office. I think there will be a steady market for his work, so we're having a chat about future commissions and reviewing his existing portfolio."

"Doing me out of some income, are you?" Harley asked in a jovial tone. He didn't depend on his sales, though he appreciated the recognition.

"Not at all. I'm glad you're here as well. You can cast a professional eye over the paintings he has to show me and give me your opinion.

"Why don't you invite him to brunch on Sunday morning?" Meredith suggested. I thought we might have a few people over to celebrate Harley's eventual arrival, and it would be an opportunity to introduce your new protégé around. A young man from a small town wouldn't have many contacts in the city."

"Don't go to any trouble on my behalf," Harley protested. "As for Dimitri, I think he went to boarding school in the city, so he probably has some mates around. I'm sure he would appreciate the invitation, though."

"No trouble. I'll simply order in supplies from a gourmet service I have on speed dial. They'll even serve it for me." Meredith gave a satisfied smile at what both men knew would be a fait accompli.

Harley rose early the following morning and went for a long walk after leaving a note to that effect on the kitchen bench. In part, he felt as though he needed the exercise, and in part he enjoyed the opportunity to explore the neighbourhood in the crisp morning air. He discovered the linear path along the River Torrens and followed that for a distance before doubling back along Walkerville Terrace.

The cafés bustled with the morning jogging and pre-work crowd, and he grabbed a take-away flat white as he resumed his walk. It took him past colonial villas of luxurious proportions in some streets, and modest cottages in others. Some infill development was occurring, with new houses nestled between neighbours from the turn of the previous century. The ambience was so different from his early morning walks around the coastline of Sandy Bay.

The walk took him longer than he expected. He hadn't received any calls on his phone, so assumed that Bryan and Meredith were not fussed about his absence. He heard voices as he entered through the side door leading into the kitchen area, and after peering into the living room, found Bryan and Dimitri engaged in deep discussion.

"G'day." He nodded a greeting to Dimitri before turning to Bryan. "Just letting you know I'm back. I won't interrupt."

He turned to go but Bryan called him back. "Come and join us. You can re-assure Dimitri about my professional credentials."

Bryan had propped a series of paintings against the wall. Harley dropped his cap on the table and squatted on his heels as he examined each one. "I recognise some of these scenes. I imagine some of the regular visitors to the Bay will do so as well. When did you drive up to the city?"

"Yesterday. Lily and I drove up together, as she has business in the city. We're staying with my sister."

Harley straightened and tried not to sound overly interested. "That's convenient. I enjoyed meeting Eleni and Dion at your parent's barbecue that evening. How long are you staying in the city?"

"We drove up in Lily's car, so I'm depending on her to get back. I think she's happy to spend the weekend here. She and Eleni always have something to talk about."

"No doubt they do," Bryan said smoothly. "Harley, perhaps you can tell Dimitri where your paintings have ended up. I've been representing Harley for a couple of years now," he added to Dimitri.

They sat around the table, discussing the contract and the art world. Meredith knocked on the door to the room and brought in a tray laden with a coffee pot, cups, and plates of chocolate brownies. "I thought you might need sustenance. Darling, did you remember to invite Dimitri to come to brunch tomorrow?"

"I was about to. Dimitri drove up to Adelaide with Lily. We should invite her as well. It would be good to see her again."

"Yes... wouldn't it."

Harley knew Meredith would as happily stick pins in her eyes, but she would never object to Bryan's suggestion, particularly in front of him and Dimitri.

"I don't suppose your brother is in town as well?"

"No, he's back working on the Gold Coast. Some new film. I don't bother keeping track of what he's doing. I know he'll be back in Sandy Bay for a fund-raising dinner supporting the local hospital. Lily has talked him into being the MC."

"How clever of Lily. Perhaps we should support the dinner as well, Bryan. Do come tomorrow morning, Dimitri, and bring Lily. We'll expect you both at ten thirty."

"Okay. She'd love that, I'm sure."

Harley didn't have quite the same level of confidence, but it meant he could see Lily again. He ignored the wink that Bryan gave him and retreated to his room to catch up on some emails and some research. He wasn't sure how long he would stay in Adelaide, but his next port of call would be Port Lincoln, possibly stopping off at Edithburg at the bottom of Yorke Peninsula on the way. He needed to research the options for mooring, and also for refuelling. He wondered what had brought Lily to the city, and whether it had anything to do with her plans. He couldn't ask Dimitri, as she may not have disclosed those to anyone else. He would have to wait until the brunch to find out, assuming that she agreed to come.

&

Lily was still unsure about accepting the invitation when she and Dimitri parked outside Bryan and Meredith's villa. Dimitri had insisted that it had been freely given. He'd also told her that Harley would be there, and that brought on another attack of nerves. Would he be pleased to see her?

Dimitri chatted on the drive there. "You should see their house, Lily. Full of art, of course. Looking at the furnishings, the antiques, and the size of the place, you can see that being an art broker is a lucrative occupation. Better than being an artist."

"Just wait. When you become famous, you'll earn a good income as well. Isn't that what Bryan is doing for you in part— getting you known in all the right places?"

"I hope so. C'mon, we ought to go inside."

Lily picked up the bunch of flowers she had purchased on the way and followed Dimitri to the front door. Bryan threw it open with a welcoming grin.

"Lily! Good to see you." To her surprise, he drew her to him with a hug. "Come through. Harley's here, in case you didn't know."

They followed him down the hall to where Meredith was distributing glasses of mimosa to her guests. Lily thrust the bunch of seasonal blooms at her and received an air kiss in response.

"Lovely to see you, Lily. Are those for me? How lovely. Can I get you a drink?"

She shoved a glass in Lily's hand without waiting for an answer. A warm smell suggested that croissants were heating in the kitchen. French doors opened onto a covered patio, and Lily could see that a table was set up for brunch with platters

232

of fruit, various cheeses, and cold sliced deli meats. Harley sat at one end, chatting to a woman. He looked up and spotted her as she paused uncertainly in the doorway.

"Lily… I'm glad you could come." He jumped up and, seizing her by the shoulders, gave her a greeting kiss. "Dimitri said you were in town. Come and sit down. "Have you met Louisa?" He gestured to the woman sitting on the other side of him.

No, I haven't, given that I haven't been here before. Lily smiled politely and offered her hand. The other woman shook hers with a hand that was adorned with several rings.

"You come from Sandy Bay? Bryan and Meredith have told me about their recent visit."

Before she could sit, another couple arrived. Conversation revolved around greetings and introductions until Meredith carried a heated dish of croissants to the table, and declared they should all sit down and eat. Harley pulled out a chair for her, and Lily was grateful to be sitting beside him. Dimitri sat on her other side, so she didn't feel so out of place. She faced the carefully manicured gardens, and everything she could see, plus the glimpses she'd had of the décor whilst walking through the house, made it obvious that she sat with people who had a more affluent lifestyle than hers. Harley was slumming it during the time he spent in Sandy Bay.

Harley leaned back with his nearest arm resting on the back of his chair so that he partially faced her. This way, he could speak directly to her.

"Dimitri said you had business in town. Tell me to mind my own business if I'm prying, but is this anything to do with your future plans?"

She filled a small plate with slices of melon and some strawberries, then answered quietly. "It's probably crazy, but I came up to check out a catamaran. It's moored at North Haven and I looked over it yesterday."

"Any good?"

"It's fabulous, but…"

He raised his eyebrows in query.

"It's a lot of money and I'm crazy to even think about it."

"Lily, can you pass the fruit platter down the table?" Meredith looked at her pointedly, and Lily had the impression that she didn't like her and Harley having private conversations. She did as asked and focused her attention on the couple opposite, who were describing their recent visit to Japan. Harley engaged in conversation with Louisa on his other side, as she wanted to know more about his trip.

"It sounds wonderful. I'd love to look over your yacht sometime, if that's possible. It may be a romantic dream, but I've always wanted to sail under canvas. Not in international waters, of course—I'd be afraid of pirates or cyclones, but off the coast of Australia would be a fantastic experience."

Meredith had overheard this comment as she brought around a pot of coffee. "Don't you have family in Port Lincoln? Harley is headed that way next. Perhaps you could do a quick trip with him, getting off there and visiting your family. You could catch a flight back to Adelaide."

"I can certainly show you over the boat. The sea in that stretch can be quite rough. For anyone who doesn't have their sea legs, seasickness can be horrible."

"That's what travel pills are for," Meredith said sweetly.

Lily could hardly believe what she heard. Meredith was blatantly trying to foist Louisa onto Harley. She sneaked a look in his direction. Perhaps it wasn't foisting at all. Perhaps he didn't object to the suggestion. It was difficult to tell.

"Tell us what's been happening in your life, Lily." Bryan sat at the head of the table and dropped in and out of the different conversations."

"Much the same as when you visited Sandy Bay." She had no intention of telling him about the changes ahead of her. That would invite questions she didn't want to answer. "I've been helping to organise a fund-raising dinner supporting the neonatal ward at the local hospital."

"Dimitri mentioned that yesterday. He said that his brother has offered to be the MC."

"Offered is not quite the right word. He's working on a film set in the Gold Coast studios, but he'll fly back home for the event. I've also organised an auction in which the winner and a companion can sit at his table during the event. When people buy a ticket for the dinner, they can also place a bid. It will be drawn before the dinner so that the winner knows of their lucky draw ahead of time."

"That should be a good draw card."

"I don't know why," Dimitri broke in. "I've had to sit next to my brother at dinner for most of my life. There's nothing special about it. He'd pinch my food if I wasn't watching and always take the best bits."

He had the interest of the table now. "Who is your brother?" Louisa asked.

"Christos Antoniou."

"You mean *the* Christos Antoniou? The one who recently starred in 'Dark Night'?"

"That's him."

Meredith set down her coffee cup with a thump. "What date is this dinner? Bryan and I would be happy to support such a worthwhile cause, wouldn't we darling We could stay overnight. There are a couple of hotels in town."

Bryan patted her hand. "Of course, we'll go… if it fits with our other commitments." He looked at Harley. "Are you going back for this dinner as well?"

"I hadn't intended doing so. I left a painting with Lily to be used as an entry for the silent auction. Hopefully, someone likes it enough to bid on it."

"I'm sure they will." Lily placed a hand on his arm as a mark of familiarity. Childish perhaps, but Meredith brought out that reaction in her. The scene is recognisable to anyone who knows the area; I'm sure it will be hugely popular. It's being promoted in the local paper. Perhaps a local hotel, restaurant, or even the local council would be interested in submitting a bid."

"So, you're an artist as well? Meredith didn't tell me that." Louisa turned her attention back to Harley.

Lily noticed his ears turn a shade of red. She removed her hand from his arm. He could deal with flirting women on his own. She smiled sweetly at Meredith. "Tickets are available online. You could put together a table. I'll write out the address for you. They are selling fast, so you had better be quick."

"A table… that's an idea. We could make an event out of it. You'll be there, Dimitri?"

"I probably won't be able to get out if it, especially if the family's involved."

"Good. I can organise a ticket for you as well. You can sit at our table. Do you have a 'friend' who is likely to join you?"

Lily knew that was a smart strategy. If Meredith and Bryan sponsored Dimitri, they were bound to be introduced to Christos. At least the neonatal ward should benefit from their interest. The rest of the meal progressed relatively smoothly. Dimitri happily discussed his work and future ambitions with Bryan and the other guests, and mostly Lily listened. Occasionally, she responded when drawn into the conversation, but was happy to let the conversation flow around her.

She wanted to have a second inspection of the catamaran, and had arranged with the vendor that she would arrive at the marina around two that afternoon. She needed to allow enough time for the drive back to Sandy Bay. She gently nudged Dimitri when she could break into his conversation.

"I need to leave shortly. I can drop you back to Eleni's, or pick you up later."

Bryan overheard her comment. "If you need to go, I can drop him back to his sister's later. There's a local gallery I'd like to take him to this afternoon."

"If that's no trouble… that's most kind of you." She stood and took her leave of her hosts. "Thank you so much for inviting me. It's been a lovely morning. I look forward to seeing you at the dinner."

Bryan accompanied her to the front door, but as she walked down the driveway, Lily heard footsteps behind her.

"Lily, wait! We didn't chat properly. Did you want to talk about this boat you've looked at?"

"I haven't made a decision; I'm going back now for a second look. That will probably be enough to convince me it's a crazy idea."

"Would you like me to come with you?"

Yes, I'd love that. "Won't Bryan and Meredith think it's rude if you leave now?"

"I doubt it. Too bad if they do. Wait for me. I'll grab a jacket and let them know I'm going."

He dashed back inside the house, and a moment later ran out the door again, shrugging his arms into his jacket and clutching his phone. When he climbed into the front passenger seat, he leaned across and kissed her lightly on the cheek. "I hope that meal wasn't too painful for you. I know Meredith isn't your favourite person."

"I never said that."

"I know you didn't, but I've learned to read your expressions. Enough about that. Tell me about this catamaran."

As she drove back to the marina at North Haven, Lily outlined the boat specifications and the possibilities for developing a business based on its capabilities. "It's not at all what came to mind when I thought of a charter business. The more I looked at it, the more I started seeing the possibilities. The money is a stumbling block. I have some money, but I might need to ask my father for a loan. I can't see a bank coming to the party."

"I can put you in touch with a good finance broker. Let's look at her first, and then if you're still interested, we can discuss the options."

This marina was busier than the facility at Sandy Bay. It was bordered by residential development, many with frontage to the water. Some of those houses also had boats of varying descriptions floating at their private moorings. Lily led the way past a flotilla of smaller boats towards where a larger vessel sat at the end of the pontoon. The catamaran caught the afternoon sun, showing off her gleaming white hull. The name

238

Serendipity was painted on her bow. A man sat in a chair on deck, his face turned to the sun.

"That's her," Lily said. "What do you think?"

"She's beautiful, that's what I think."

20 – Business Plans

HARLEY WAITED WHILE Lily spoke to the boat owner, before joining her onboard in response to her gesture.

"Harley, this is Frank. He's kindly agreed to me having a second inspection over Serendipity. Harley is here to give me the benefit of his experience."

The two men shook hands. "Know a bit about catamarans, do yer?" Frank said, looking Harley up and down.

"I know more about yachts. Why don't you give us the grand tour? You can point out the features that we might miss."

Frank grunted in reply, but took them over the three levels of the boat, outlining the specifications and highlighting the features that, in his eyes, made it a highly desirable purchase. Harley could see the appeal. The boat could be used for group expeditions, such as whale watching, but could also be used for smaller charters, with the cabins below providing facility for overnight trips. The cabins were small and basic, but that was as expected. The galley could turn out light refreshments, or more complex meals.

Frank started up the motor, and took them out of the marina and executed a few manoeuvres beyond the breakwater, giving each of them the opportunity to experience the handling features before heading back into shore and mooring again.

Lily looked wistful. "Thank you, Frank. I appreciate you coming out here again on a Sunday. I have a few things to consider, and I'll be back in touch. I'll let you know either way."

"Righto. Don't take too long. A boat like this doesn't come on the market often."

As they walked back to her car, Harley was tempted to take Lily's hand. She looked as though she needed the support. Instead, he suggested they have a cup of coffee. "I noticed a café on the foreshore a hundred metres down the road. Why don't we stop off there and have a chat about what we've just seen? You can tell me what you're thinking."

"That would be good. I need to clarify my thoughts on this. You can see why I needed to come back for a second inspection."

They found the café and sat outside in the sun, waiting for their order to be delivered. Lily's face looked flushed with excitement. No doubt she was running numbers in her head. Harley leaned forward with his forearms resting on the table. "I understand why you're taken with the boat. It has so many possibilities."

"As I mentioned before, I hadn't thought about a catamaran, but now that I've seen this one, the rationale is obvious. It's more stable than a mono-hull, travels faster, is manoeuvrable, and has a shallow draft. That's important if I'm going to stop off at different beaches or islands."

"All good points. With that sort of outlay on a boat, you would have to hit the ground running, or perhaps I should say hit the water. You would need your marketing plan in place, and to start taking bookings before the actual launch. Then there's the staffing issue. From both a safety and a practical point of view, that boat needs a minimum of two crew."

"I know. I hadn't thought about becoming an employer so soon. Without the money though, it's pointless even considering it."

"You need to produce a business plan quickly. If you're going to approach anyone for finance, that is what they will want to see. Do you have an accountant or financial adviser?"

"No! I do my own tax return. I've never been involved in anything more complex."

"What about Adam? Didn't he teach Business Studies and Economics? If he can't help you, he might know who can. It's my impression that retirement isn't sitting too comfortably on his shoulders. He'd probably welcome the chance to help you out."

Lily looked at him, chewing her bottom lip. "I did chat to Adam a week ago, but just generalities. You're right; he might help. I know I can approach my father for a loan, but I doubt he could lend me enough, and anyway, he and Mum have plans of their own. If my venture goes belly-up, that would deprive them of their retirement funds. I'd rather do this independently of them."

"You're speaking as though you're going ahead with this."

"I'm going to try. I know other boats may come up, but this one is available locally, and it ticks so many boxes."

"Next step then is to get a mechanical inspection from marine technician, and ask to see the Certificate of Survey. Frank must have one of those. It will specify the vessel's operating conditions. The inspection will take a while. In the meantime, start working on the business plan. You can ask Frank to let you know if there is any other genuine interest."

"You make it sound real and possible. I won't be able to sleep tonight for thinking about it. I had told myself that I was living in fairy land for even thinking about it, but now… now I think I might just be able to make it happen."

Harley hadn't seen Lily look this excited before. It stirred a feeling of conflict. This was such an exciting new venture, and he wanted to be there for her. This was her dream though, and she hadn't expressed any interest in him being involved beyond that of a confidant. At least he could offer her that.

"We'd better get back to Walkerville. You've still got that drive ahead of you."

"It's a familiar route, but I have work tomorrow, so you're right… I shouldn't leave the city too late. I'll give Dimitri a quick call and let him know I'll be back at Eleni's house shortly." She made her call, and they climbed into Lily's Hyundai.

As they pulled up in front of the villa, Meredith and Louisa were strolling down the driveway towards Louisa's car. They stood chatting on the footpath, while Harley opened the car door and place one foot on the ground in preparation for stepping out.

"I hope I was of some help. Call me if you want to discuss anything else. I'll be here for a couple of days before I head off to Port Lincoln." He wanted to say that he could borrow or hire a car and drive down to Sandy Bay if she needed him, but hesitated to sound intrusive. If she wanted him to do that, she would have asked. He looked her directly in the eyes, searching for any message he might read there. "You know you can call me about anything. I'm glad we could catch up today."

He saw her eyes slide towards where Meredith and Louisa were standing, before glancing back at him. "I'm glad too. Thank you for coming with me today. I really appreciate it." She leaned forward and lightly kissed him. "Safe travels."

Harley shut the car door after climbing out and leaned in through the open window. He was about to suggest that he would call her in a day or so, when Meredith came up behind him.

"Harley, when will you take Louisa to look at Ocean Dream? You can make the arrangements now while she's still here. You could also discuss the possibility of that trip to Pt Lincoln."

He saw the expression on Lily's face change. She threw the car into gear, and he took a step back, watching her drive off, before turning to acknowledge the two women. "That was a long brunch. Have you two finished the champagne?"

They both looked a little flushed. Belatedly, Harley realised his joking comment might have been correct. Meredith rolled her eyes before shaking her head slightly. We've had a lot to catch up on. We go back a long way."

Louisa looked at him expectantly. "Only if taking the boat out is convenient. I don't want to put you to any trouble."

"No trouble at all. I can show you over tomorrow morning if Bryan or Meredith will lend me a car."

"You don't need to do that. I can pick you up. Shall we say, ten o'clock?"

He nodded in agreement. He had no problems with showing Louisa over Ocean Dream, or even taking her, Meredith, and Bryan for a twilight trip down the coast and back perhaps, but as a passenger to Pt Lincoln? What was Meredith thinking?

❧

Lily had been about to suggest that she and Harley meet up again, or he could even drive back to Sandy Bay with her now for a couple of days while she liaised with Adam and drafted her plan. Meredith put paid to that. She was dangling Louisa in front of Harley, and if they went sailing together, the inevitable would happen. Hello sailor! She should have realised that a man with his resources would have a girl in every port.

By the time she arrived back at Eleni's, she was in a rotten mood. Dimitri hadn't arrived back, so she had to make small talk until that happened and they could start their return trip.

Eleni sniffed the air and regarded her with suspicion. "Something smells off around here. Could it be your foul mood, perhaps?"

Lily glared at her before relenting. "I'm sorry. I didn't mean to bring my mood back with me. The brunch was fine. Lovely house and garden, like Dimitri said, and everything was very tasteful and civilised."

"What's the problem?"

"Some of the company got up my nose, that's all."

"Who was there?"

"Don't get excited, but Harley was. He's staying with Bryan and Meredith after visiting Kangaroo Island. Next stop is Pt Lincoln. There were also some friends of theirs, people who would be interested in Dimitri's painting."

"So, what was the problem?"

Now Lily felt silly, like a petulant teenager who has her nose out of joint over a juvenile crush. "Another woman was there, an old friend of Meredith's. It's my guess that Meredith invited her to the brunch to set her up with Harley. Louisa, that's her name, has talked her way into Harley taking her sailing, and now I think he's taking her onboard as a passenger on his next leg to Pt Lincoln. You know what happens when people are confined to small places."

"Yeah, they end up hating each other. What does it matter to you, anyway? If Harley meant so much to you, why didn't you do something about it?"

Lily had no answer to that question. That last night she had spent with Harley had been memorable, and meant more to her than she was going to admit, but she hadn't expected a relationship to follow. He hadn't said anything, so neither had she. What was the point? They came from different worlds. That was obvious during the brunch. "I didn't say he meant anything to me," she replied stiffly.

"Sure. For a bright woman, Lily, you can be incredibly stupid. I know you like him. It's as clear as the nose on your face. If you want to be in his life, and not some floozy from the city, it's up to you to do something about it."

"When I need you to organise my love life, I'll let you know."

Dimitri arrived home at that point, cutting off their discussion, though Lily thought she heard Eleni mutter, *What love life?"*

❧

The week that followed was the last week of working on Sea Witch. Davey was the most upbeat member of the crew, with even her father in a sombre mood. It had finally hit him that he was giving up his beloved boat and the life he had loved for decades. The fishing fraternity planned a shindig for the end of the week to commemorate the handing on of the baton, Stan to Davey. Lily stayed out of the organisation, having her own tasks at hand.

She rang Adam to seek his help. "Adam, this is highly confidential at this stage. You know that Dad has sold Sea Witch? That means I'm out of a job, and I'm researching a new business venture. I need to put together a business plan, not only for me but to support an application for finance. Can you help me with that? I'll pay you, of course."

"You've got me intrigued. Of course, I'll help you. No need for payment. When and where would you like to meet?"

"Tonight? My place? I would offer to cook dinner, but wouldn't like to subject you to my cooking."

He laughed. "I'll be around at your place around seven."

Lily laid out all the information she had collected on the dining table, together with her initial spreadsheet workings. His eyes widened when he saw the pictures of Serendipity.

"You don't do things by halves, do you? Explain to me what you're proposing and how you're intending to achieve it. Are there any time constraints?"

"Frank could sell the catamaran to someone else. I've asked him to keep me informed if there is any other serious interest."

"You can take out an option over the sale. If you proceed, then the option fee is discounted from the sale price. If you don't proceed, then you forego that money."

"Ouch. I don't have enough to lose any."

"It's the price you have to pay for protection while you get your act together. First, we'll go over your finances and undertake a preliminary business plan. If that looks good, we can progress to the next stage, which is paying for the mechanical inspection, and subject to that, making an offer."

Lily noticed that Adam said *we*. She didn't mind. For an enterprise like this, it helped to know she had someone she trusted working with her. "So, you don't think the whole idea is a pie in the sky?"

"You won't know until you go through the process. If it is, the work won't go astray. Much of it will be relevant for the next boat that seems suitable. That's assuming you don't change your mind about the sort of business you want to start. He looked up from the picture he was studying. "Did you speak to Harley about your plans? He knows a bit about boats."

"I did, and he looked over Serendipity with me in Adelaide. He's continuing with his travels now though, so I don't expect him to be involved further.

Adam waved the picture in the air to emphasise his point. "The details we put together for step one will be sufficient for running past a finance broker. With an indicative response, we can then prepare a detailed financial application."

"Adam, you make it sound so simple. I can't thank you enough for helping me like this. Harley suggested I approach you, and it was an inspired suggestion."

"My reward will come from seeing you succeed. It will be a great boost for the town and our tourism industry. It won't only be you who benefits.

They worked on it a couple of nights that week. Harley emailed her the address of a finance broker he could recommend, and Adam also knew of one. Harley didn't mention where he was, or if Louisa was with him, and Lily didn't ask. She clarified with her father how much she could expect resulting from the sale from Sea Witch, and combined with her savings, she could put down about half the cost of the boat. That still left her with a huge shortfall, also allowing for marketing and business set-up costs. She woke up in the middle of the night more than once, wondering if she was crazy, and then would have to psyche herself up to continue with the planning process the following day. Throughout it all, Adam remained a staunch supporter.

Preliminary advice from each broker was that she would require a guarantor if finance were to be approved. She didn't have a track record that they could rely on. The other option they suggested was that she mortgage her cottage. Of course, if the business didn't succeed, she would lose the cottage.

"In that case, I would have to live on the boat. Losing the cottage after the time I have spent in paying it off is a frightening thought, but it will spur me on. I have to make this work. If it's what I have to do, I'll do it."

"Think of it as an adventure. We all need adventures in our lives. That's what makes living fun."

Lily told herself she would keep repeating that mantra. Taking out a mortgage meant more paperwork with two separate loan applications, but she felt confident enough to organise the Marine Survey and request a copy of the Certificate of Survey. With Adam's encouragement, she submitted a written offer. Now the nail-biting wait for a response.

Stan's retirement party was a bitter-sweet experience. Davey couldn't stop grinning, and there were a few speeches with reminiscences, plus a lot of food and mostly beer. The crowd took over a function room at the Regal Hotel, and Stan's demeanour ranged from anticipation to maudlin as the night progressed. Mavis sidled up to Lily as she stood to one side, observing the crowd.

"How does all of this affect you, luv? What are you doing next? I hear you're not going to work with Davey."

Mavis was the only one who had expressed concern for how her father's decision affected her and her career. "No, I'm not going to work for Davey. Dad's decision was a shock, although I appreciate the reasons behind it. I'm still working on my future plans. I can't talk about them at the moment, but as soon as they're definite, you'll be one of the first to know."

"Whatever they are, you'll do well, I'm sure. I've got a ticket for that dinner, by the way. Not that I'm bidding for the chance to sit with Christos. I've known that kid since he was in nappies. What would I want to sit next to him for?"

Lily gave a belly laugh, the first one she'd had in ages. "You're right. Who wants to sit next to a snotty-nosed kid who used to pull your hair in the playground?" Mavis was just the tonic she needed on a night like this. It also reminded her that she needed to focus her attention on the preparations for the event. That was one good thing about the coming week. She would be available during the day for those tasks.

She had been dragooned onto the decorating committee, and she had to organise the floral arrangements, other table decorations, place names and menus for each table, and the sign-up forms for each auction item. She was also tasked with liaising with Christos. He wouldn't arrive until the afternoon of the dinner, but he needed to be briefed on the dignitaries who would be present, and the order of events. It would be his job to keep to the program schedule and make sure the crowd was in a donating mood.

She split her time between working on the dinner and preparing the financial paperwork for submission. For once, she was pleased she was no longer working on Sea Witch, and had the time to devote to both activities. She kept in touch with Adam throughout, and they refined her business plan together. Buying her cottage had been a significant transaction, but it paled into insignificance compared to her business concept. In moments of self-reflection, she doubted she could have done it without him.

The day the various documents were emailed to the finance brokers, with a copy sent to Adam, she met with him at Maisie's for a celebratory iced coffee.

"Let me buy, Adam. I at least owe you that."

"Have you forgotten where you are? I don't buy my coffees here, and today, you don't either. This is a celebration. You've worked hard on your submission. Not much else you can do now except forget all about it and wait."

"Forget about it! It's going to be on my mind night and day. Still, the dinner should help divert my mind. I've put you at Christos' table, by the way, you and Maisie. You don't have to take part in the auction for that."

"Have you checked with him? He might not have forgiven me yet for pushing him into the water, and giving him a sore head to boot."

Lily snorted. "If that affected him, the difference isn't noticeable. He's as crazy as he's always been."

Her phone beeped with an incoming email.

"Adam gestured towards her mobile. "It's okay, answer it. I know you've got a lot going on at the moment."

She swiped over the screen and open her messages. It was from Frank. Her offer had been accepted.

21 – Dash Back to Sydney

"BRYAN, I'M HAPPY to take Louisa and any others you suggest out sailing, but this idea that Meredith has of me taking her on as a passenger is not happening." Harley had pulled Bryan aside when he had a quiet opportunity.

"Sorry mate, she gets a bit carried away sometimes. You know how it is. If we can organise that twilight event, that would keep everyone happy. There are a couple of people I'd like to invite from the art world, if that's okay? Meredith will organise some platters to take, something to drink, and anything else we might need."

"That's fine by me. Pick a day and let's do it. I'll probably head off towards the end of the week, so any day before then."

The cruise was organised for late the following Tuesday. Meredith took charge of the catering options, and Bryan invited the friends he had mentioned. They owned a gallery in the city, and the networking opportunity was too good to pass up. Louisa also joined them, dressed in what Harley assumed was an outfit specifically for sailing, featuring lots of white and blue, topped with oversized sunglasses.

The weather was relatively calm, but not long after their departure, a gusty wind sprang up, along with an increasingly choppy sea. His guests were unsteady on their feet, and Harley suggested that if they were too uncomfortable sitting on the deck, that they transfer to the cabin. Louisa was one of the first to disappear inside, and when he checked on his passengers, leaving Bryan at the helm, he found that Louisa was distinctly pale. Her face looked clammy, and she sat with her head back, resting on a bolster.

"Are you okay, Louisa? Can I get you anything? A drink, perhaps?"

"Is it always this rough?" she moaned, with her hand resting on her forehead. "I'm not sure if I could keep anything down."

Harley fetched her some ginger tablets from his bathroom cabinet, and placed them in front of her with a glass of sparkling water. "You're welcome to lie down, if that helps. Best to lay off the champagne when you feel like this." Louisa was the only one who felt so poorly, with the remaining passengers coping well with what, as Harley mentioned to Bryan, was only a slight swell.

Bryan winked at him. "Looks like the question of doing a longer sea trip has been quashed before being seriously raised. Even Meredith can't push this one."

Harley was sorry that Louisa felt so bad, but was still relieved that he didn't have to discuss the matter further. Confrontation was not his style.

Aside from Louisa's reaction, everyone else appeared to enjoy the opportunity to spend a pleasant couple of hours on the water. Bryan impressed the guests he had invited, and Meredith derived satisfaction that she had better sea legs than Louisa. Harley had just tied up at the marina again when his mobile rang. The screen announced the caller was Ralph.

"Hey, Harley, where are you now?"

"Adelaide. What's up?"

"Great. Somewhere civilised with an airport. Can you jump on a plane and come back for a day or so?"

"I can, but why? You haven't been hacked again?"

"No, thank God. We're still dealing with the fallout from the last event. The question of compensation for clients who were adversely affected has arisen. Some things are covered by insurance, but not all. There are significant consequences for the company. As a major shareholder, you might like to be a party to the discussions."

Harley reviewed his plans for the coming days. He didn't have a deadline for moving on. "I can fly over in the morning, assuming I can get an early flight out. I'll let you know."

"Thanks mate. Text me your arrival details. I'd offer to pick you up, but traffic at the airport's a nightmare. You'll get here quicker in a taxi."

He had thought the drama surrounding the hacking was in the past. Evidently not. Harley secured a seat on an early flight and packed an overnight bag in case he had to stay longer than a day. A subdued group waited for him in the boardroom. Ralph, Mark, Roscoe and Shanti—it was a flash-back to a couple of weeks ago.

"What, no pastries?" he quipped. "Standards are dropping around here."

Ralph glared at him in mock anger. "Get your bum on a seat. We've a bit to discuss. You can have your pastries when we've got through the morning's business." He displayed a list of major clients on the boardroom screen, accompanied with details of the losses claimed by each company. Some of those losses had been met by the client's insurer, but some companies did not have adequate cover. Companies were claiming compensation from Logistical Solutions. This was both a legal and ethical dilemma, and debate ranged about the extent of liability that the company held.

"Are we liable for expenses suffered when a company doesn't adequately insure?" Harley asked. "Surely having enough cover is Business Practice 101. Why should they be compensated for their failure to address an increasingly common risk?"

Mark explained in his professional lawyer voice. "The claims we received have argued that Logistical Solutions has a duty of due care towards clients, and that we did not meet that requirement in allowing our systems to be hacked."

"Will that claim stand up in court?"

"It's hard to say, because there isn't precedence on this issue. The legal process will be costly, and the adverse publicity will have a negative impact on our bottom line."

"So, can we meet these companies part way without penalising ourselves with a huge financial impost? I've already experienced the weight of community disapproval. The fishing co-op in Sandy Bay also uses our software and operations ground to a halt for the duration of the crisis. When my role within the company became known, my name became mud. I half expected to be run out of town."

Silence settled around the table as they looked at each other, hoping someone else had a solution.

"Can we give them a discount on their annual subscription, or is there an additional service we can give them? What about contributing to their community benefit program, assuming that they have one?"

Mark frowned. "Don't set a precedence for yourself. This situation shouldn't arise again, given the steps we've taken, but there is always an element of risk as bad actors become more technologically sophisticated."

Shanti spoke up for the first time. "What if we get any recipients to sign a waiver stating that this is not usual practice and won't happen again? You would need to do the legal wording, Mark, but you know what I mean. Isn't it called a disclaimer?"

Serious debate began about the various options. They all agreed that in this instance, the do-nothing approach was not the most appropriate. It also became apparent that solutions were not a one-size-fits-all, and they discussed each application one-by-one. There were two companies that by total consent, they agreed did not warrant any contribution, due to nature of their operations and the fact that they had done nothing to mitigate their losses. The process they applied was unconventional, but one with which they felt comfortable.

Harley looked around the table. "To finish up, there's one request I'd like to follow up on. I mentioned earlier that the co-op in Sandy Bay was hit hard, and that affected many people in the town. Fishing is an important industry there. I've raised this with Ralph as an option, but at the end of the week, there is a fund-raising dinner in town to purchase needed equipment in the neonatal ward at the local hospital. Instead of compensating the co-op, I'd like to make a donation to the event."

"That's not exactly regular," Mark objected.

"I know, but it's a worthy cause, and it comes under the banner of community benefit. It would make a big difference to the town." He had to talk persuasively, and overcome objections from Mark and Roscoe, but in the end, Ralph agreed with him and that swung the other two around.

"Why don't you attend the dinner and do the honours, Ralph? I won't be there, but I've donated a painting to their silent auction. I could get you an introduction to Christos Antoniou, if that helps."

Ralph snorted. "I'm not a fan-struck groupie, but will I get a photo handing over a cheque? That would be something for the PR files."

"I'm sure that can be arranged."

"No promises, but I'll think about. I'll have to consult my calendar."

"Do that. Otherwise, I'll send you bank details for a transfer. I'm sure the donation would be tax deductible, if that sways your thinking. If we're finished here, I might grab a flight back to Adelaide."

"Stay for lunch at least," Ralph said as Harley rose from the table. "That will make up for no pastries."

The two men wandered down the road to a local Indian restaurant, one which had been a favourite in the past.

"You seem to have developed an affinity for that town," Ralph remarked. "I'm surprised you're not going back there."

Harley didn't reply immediately. "The journey I'm on fulfills a goal that I've had for a while. I'm not inclined to throw it away on a whim. I have thought about it once or twice,

258

but maybe the time isn't right. Maybe… maybe I'm not convinced that it would be the right thing to do."

Ralph looked confused, but didn't pursue the conversation, moving onto other topics instead. Later, as Harley sat in the airport lounge awaiting the departure of his flight. His phone rang.

"Harley? This is Adam. I've a proposition to put to you."

Lily ticked off her checklist. Her tasks for the dinner were under control. She was waiting to hear that Christos had arrived in town, and then she could relax. Eleni and Dion were driving down from Adelaide, and they promised to pick Christos up from the airport and bring him with them. Anh was alternately dancing with delight at the number of tickets sold and going into panic mode at the things that could go wrong.

As promised, Bryan and Meredith had bought tickets. They were already booked into the Regal Hotel, and Lily had seen them strolling through the main street of town. Meredith had also bid on the opportunity to sit at Christos' table, and currently, hers was the highest bid. The bidding closed in fifteen minutes, and then the winner could be notified. She glanced at her watch. As soon as that auction was completed, she could head back home. The room at the venue was set up for that evening, and she had distributed place names on each table, pinned up the table lists by the entrance door, and helped with the décor. The various auction items were displayed on tables to one side of the room. Guests would place their bid on the record sheet during the dinner.

She looked around with satisfaction. Event management wasn't her forte, but in this instance, she thought she and the others had done well. The room had a good vibe. It should be a fabulous night. As she adjusted the placement of Harley's painting, her mobile rang.

"Hi, Adam. Have you taken your dinner suit out of mothballs?"

"Sure have. I'll be there with bells on. Um… have you seen your emails?"

"No, why?"

"That second broker has responded. Because I was copied in on your application email, he also copied me in on his response. I just read it."

"And?"

"He's turned you down. He considers the risk to be too high, and that you don't have a high enough credit rating."

"Bastard! So now I lose my option fee?"

"You haven't run out of options yet. You've got all the paperwork prepared, so it will be easy to submit it elsewhere. You could always ask your father to go guarantor. That might sway the decision."

"I'm not asking my father to do that! I haven't depended financially on my father for years, and I'm not about to do so now. I'll stand on my own two feet."

"I thought you'd say that. It was only a suggestion. We can talk about it tomorrow. I knew you'd be disappointed about the finance, so I wanted to tell you now, rather than let you find out just as you were all dolled up and rushing out the door. Forget about this for now and focus on the dinner. You women have done a great job with organising this event."

"I'm not sure I can forget it so easily, but you're right. Tonight is not the time to fret about it. I'll save my fretting for tomorrow."

That was easier said than done. Lily fumed as she stood under a steaming hot shower, trying to ease the tension that tightened her shoulders. Would the response have been different if she had been a man? Was she silly for not approaching her father? Perhaps she would have to do that if she didn't find the money elsewhere. If he turned her down, she would be totally stuffed.

She didn't have time to wallow in her private pity party. She had promised Anh she would arrive early to help with greeting the attendees and ensuring everyone found the right table and seat. Simultaneously, she could direct their attention towards the tables with the auction items. Anh was in charge of the music and liaising with the catering team. Together, they should have the evening under control.

Lily slipped on an off-the-shoulder dress in midnight-blue jersey that finished mid-calf. The bateau neckline gave it some gravitas. Her mother had given her a string of her grandmother's pearls. Normally, she would have felt the necklace was too old-fashioned, but the pearls looked good with the outfit. She swept her hair up into a sleek chignon, and secured it in place with a comb. She had to repeat the process twice before she was satisfied with the result. That left her ears exposed, and she remembered a pair of sapphire stud earrings she had been given for a birthday and never worn. When she attached them to her lobes, she was impressed at the difference each component of her outfit made. Perhaps she should dress up like this when she had interviews with brokers. Maybe they would take her more seriously.

She suddenly remembered that with the internal drama caused by Adam's phone call, she hadn't checked who had won Christos' auction. She checked the app controlling the bids. Meredith had, as she had expected. The final amount she had bid left the competition way behind. The hospital would benefit, but Christos might be in for an interesting evening. This was a phone call she couldn't put off.

"Hi Meredith, just letting you know that you and Bryan will sit with Christos tonight. Thank you so much for your bid. It was very generous of you." She heard the muffled squeal of delight.

"I just wanted to do my bit for the babies. Will there be photographers present?"

"Yes, the press will be in attendance, and of course, the PR department from the hospital has organised a photographer to take photos at each table." Lily paused a beat. "I can also take a photo with your phone, if you like."

"Lily, that would be fantastic. Just for the family album, of course."

Lily knew it would be on social media before the night was out. The next call was to Eleni to confirm that she and Christos had arrived in Sandy Bay.

"Sure have. We're all here and the family is getting ready. See you soon."

That was her cue to return to the venue. Anh was already in the dining room, compulsively checking everything and generally faffing around. The musicians arrived, and that gave Anh something else to do.

Lily moved Bryan and Meredith's place names to the head table. Those two seats had been left un-named in anticipation of the highest bid. People began arriving, and milled around in the foyer area with pre-dinner drinks. Ever one for punctuality, Adam arrived early with Maisie on his arm.

"You okay, kid? You look smashing, by the way."

"I'm fine. You look pretty good yourself. I'm disappointed, but I'll cope. I haven't had time to explore Plan B, mostly because I don't know what that is."

"Plan B? What's that about?"

Lily pivoted to find Eleni and Dion standing beside her. The two women embraced. Dion satisfied himself with a nod. "Long story. Are you here tomorrow? We can catch up then." Dion swiped two champagne flutes off a tray, and handed one to his wife. Lily didn't dare drink this early. "I'm on duty now, but I'll chat when the pressure's off." Their attention was taken by other guests, and with a half wave in Lily's direction, they were absorbed into another conversation.

"Lily!" Meredith called out a greeting as she approached, ensuring that people in the vicinity turned to look at her. "Darling, you look divine." Before Lily could react, Meredith air-kissed her on either cheek. "Mwah!"

She backed off slightly. Bryan hovered behind, and now he leaned forward and give her a light kiss on one cheek. "Good to see you, Lily. I take it you've got a place for us at the main table?"

"Sure have. Christos isn't here yet, but should be at any moment. I'll show you to your table if you like. It's the head table, so it's number one. The CEO from the hospital and her partner will also be at the table, and Adam and Maisie Grant. You should have a lovely evening."

He smiled at her, though she wasn't sure that he looked forward to the table seating as much as Meredith. Someone seized her from behind, and as she twisted in the grip, Christos planted a smacking kiss on her mouth.

"Christos… look this way please. Stand closer."

The roving photographer snapped their photo, while his assistant moved forward to ask for and record her name. Meredith looked daggers at the missed opportunity, as the photographer moved onto the next group. Lily was glad she was facing Meredith front-on. If not, she might have been removing a dagger from her back.

"Christos, I'd like you to meet Meredith and Bryan Wilson. They'll be joining you at your table this evening. Bryan is the art dealer who is representing your brother in the art world. You might have met him at Dimitri's exhibition in Pt Reilly."

"Of course, I remember. Good to see you again."

Christos pumped Bryan's hand enthusiastically while Meredith hovered to one side. Christos's manners were impeccable. He turned to her and offered his hand also, with a more sedate shake. "Can I fetch you both a drink?" he asked as a waiter glided past. Meredith looked delighted, and Lily slid away, being sure that her presence was no longer required.

At a signal from Anh, Lily shepherded the diners into the dining room, directing them towards their particular tables. She hung around in the foyer area, in case some latecomers showed up. The main door swung open, and a figure in a dinner suit burst through, hurrying towards her.

"I didn't book. Is there room for one more?"

"Harley! What are you doing here?"

"Hello to you too." Grasping her shoulders, he gave her a kiss. "You look absolutely stunning. Love the pearls. Sorry, everything happened in a rush. I had to come down to present

264

you with this." He handed her a bank cheque for ten thousand dollars. It's from Logistical Solutions. Ralph was going to come, but his timetable clashed. Hopefully, it goes some way towards compensating the town for the shut-down at the co-op."

"You could have posted it, or given it to Bryan and Meredith."

"I could have, but some things are better done in person, don't you think? Do we stand here all night, or do we have a seat at the table?"

"Now that Bryan and Meredith have moved to the head table, there is a spare seat at mine. Follow me, but you have some explaining to do later."

As they took their place at the table, joining the rest of the Antoniou family, Eleni looked up with a grin and gave her a wink. It's not what you think, she wanted to say. Harley reached for her hand under the table. Who was she fooling? She was no longer sure what to think.

22 – Fundraising Dinner

"… AND I ESPECIALLY want to thank Logistical Solutions for their generous donation. They supply the operating software on which the local fishing industry depends, and in recognition of the role of fishing in this town, wish to support this fundraising event."

The crowd whistled and applauded. Harley heard Mavis comment at the adjoining table. "And so they should after what they put me through." He half expected she would tell him that in person.

Christos listed the donations and funds received so far, and warned everyone that the silent auction was about to close. "You have five more minutes in which to secure yourself a fabulous painting by Harley Mendelson, who is present tonight; two night's accommodation at a waterfront B&B donated by Professional Coastal Rentals; a garden makeover by South Coast Native Plants; and many more offerings."

People leapt from their seats and clustered around the bidding sheets, either making a last-minute bid, or checking that nobody had outbid them. Harley sat back, watching in amazement as people lined up at the sheet in front of his painting. He wouldn't have said he suffered from imposter syndrome, but he was still surprised at the figures people would pay for one of his paintings. He noticed that Meredith was talking the ear off her dinner companion. He saw Lily use Meredith's phone to take some photos of those at Christos' table, and he was sure they had hit Instagram already. Bryan was lined up by the holiday rental. Presumably, he planned future visits to the town. Not surprising if he was representing Dimitri.

Bryan and Meredith had looked equally astonished when they looked over at his table and noticed him. He hadn't told them he hoped to attend the dinner, and until the last moment, hadn't even been sure he would. Bryan slipped over to him during a lull in proceedings.

"You're a sly dog. Why didn't you mention you were coming down? You could have come with us."

"You two are having a couple's weekend away. I didn't want to rain on your parade. Make the most of it. I hired a car, so I've got wheels."

"Sounds to me like you had your own plans." He winked. "I'll make sure we don't rain on *your* parade."

By that, Harley assumed Bryan would keep Meredith occupied elsewhere and not intrude on him and Lily.

After the silent auction results were announced, the dinner wound down. Some people left, and others clustered in groups, catching up on local gossip. A few die-hards clung to their drinks and looked as though they were settling in for the night.

Lily and the other organisers began packing up the auction tables, and attended to any last tasks for the evening. South Coast Native Plants had supplied the floral arrangements on the tables, and Harley observed some people removing them from the vases and taking them home. Better that they were still appreciated while they lasted.

Christos came over to Lily. "It's been a good evening. A few of us are dropping into the cocktail lounge at the Regal Hotel for a nightcap. Are you and Harley coming?"

She glanced in his direction. "I'm not sure… we may do, but don't rely on that."

She spoke to Harley in a low voice. "I'm not sure what your plans are now. I assume that Bryan and Meredith are both joining Christos at the Regal, and are also staying there. Do you want to join your friends?"

"I didn't come down here to see them. I've just spent the last week with them. Can we go somewhere and talk? Preferably not the Regal, though I had better check in there. I'll need a room for the night."

Her eyes widened as she absorbed what he'd just said. "Not much is open in town at this time of night. We can go back to my place. I'll just finish up here, and then we can go."

It took another thirty minutes for the band to pack up, the last of the revellers to leave, and for Lily to say it was okay to leave. She exchanged a hug with Anh, and then turned to Harley.

"Ready to go? You can either drive with me, or follow in your car."

"Best if I follow. I don't want to leave the car here."

By the time he climbed out of his car and locked it, Lily had the front door open and the hall light on. She stood silhouetted against the glow beyond, one arm folded against her chest and the other hand supporting her cheek in a pensive gesture. As he approached, she turned and led the way inside.

Lily kicked off her shoes and promptly lost a few centimetres in height. "What would you like to drink? I can offer you wine, a whiskey, beer? Coffee or hot chocolate if you'd like."

"What I would like is this." Seizing her by the shoulders, he pushed her against the wall of the passage and kissed her, soundly and passionately. She looked dazed when he finally released her, but she had responded, hesitantly at first and then with more obvious fervour. Harley pulled back so that he could see her face. "I've wanted to do that all night."

The way her breasts heaved in that dress with the expanse of neckline made him think of other things he would like to do, but he was there to talk. "In answer to your question, whiskey would be good."

Lily pushed herself away from the wall. She looked slightly dazed as she headed towards the drinks' cabinet in the kitchen. She glanced over her shoulder a couple of times as though half expecting him to seize her again. He might, but not yet. Now that they were alone, and the time had come to explain why he was in Sandy Bay, his stomach churned slightly. He hoped the whiskey didn't make it worse.

She poured two glasses, added a single ice cube to each, then directed him to the lounge room. While he sat on the three-seater sofa, she sat at the other end of, swivelled slightly to face him with one foot curled beneath her. It was a defensive pose. She sipped her drink and waited.

Harley relished the smoky peat taste of the fiery liquid as it slid down his throat. He looked up from studying the amber liquid as he swirled it around in his glass until his eyes met hers. "I thought I would be in Port Lincoln by now, but had to go back to Sydney during the week. There was some residual business to address following the hacking incident. That's when I picked up the donation for the fundraiser."

Lily nodded and blinked. "Thank you for that. It was very much appreciated."

"While I was there, I received a phone call. I was updated on the progress of your plans... getting finance, buying Serendipity, launching the business... Rather, I was updated on the stalled progress."

"Adam? Adam rang you? He didn't have any right to do that."

"He probably didn't, but he did. He told me the first finance broker had turned you down, and based on the feedback, he expected that the second broker probably would as well. He rang me earlier today and confirmed that was the case."

Lily uncurled her leg and leaned forward. "I know you're aware of my plans, but he should have told me what he was doing." She sounded miffed.

"Adam said you were going to need another option, and knowing of our earlier discussions, thought I could help."

"What can you do that I can't?"

"I can back you... financially. There are options. I can offer you a loan or I can come in as a silent partner. I know this is your dream, and I don't want to muscle in on that. If you want a deckhand, I can do that too. I want to stress that there are no strings attached to this offer."

He waited for her to scream at him to get out. As he ran through the various scenarios in the car on his way to the dinner, this was one he considered the most likely. Lily was an independent woman and liked to be in control. Taking a loan from him might make her feel that control was being taken away from her. She stared at him, and still hadn't said a word.

Harley took another sip of his whiskey. Liquid courage. "It would be under contract, of course, and I would expect you to engage a solicitor to look over it on your behalf. It would be your business; nothing would change about that."

"But why?" She finally found her voice. "Why would you lend me anything? You're sailing around the country following your own dream. I don't understand."

"If the question of me investing like this had arisen some weeks ago, before I ended up in Sandy Bay, I would have laughed at you. I'd never even heard of Sandy Bay for a start. It wasn't until spending time here that I understood the underlying stress in my life. I wasn't just following my dream; I was running away. Running from corporate life, from the nine-to-five grind that was more like seven-to-seven."

He monitored her expression, trying to judge her reaction to what he was saying. Guarded was probably the best way to describe it. She swirled the ice block around in her glass, making a clinking noise, but didn't speak. He pushed on.

"I began to appreciate that there is another way to live. In Sydney, I hardly know my neighbours, and rarely see them anyway. Everyone's too busy. Here, after only a short time, so many people knew my name and stopped to ask about my day. It was refreshing."

"You still haven't explained your offer."

"Leaving Sandy Bay helped me to gain some clarity. I don't want to go back to my old way of life, and if I return to

Sydney, which was my ultimate intention, then I would. And then there is you."

Spots of colour appeared high on her cheeks. This was coming to the challenging bit.

"I wasn't looking for a relationship; it was an unnecessary complication. That was before I met you. You're unlike any woman I have ever met, and I found myself falling for you. I didn't want to act on that or say anything, because I was reluctant to intrude on your life. You have your plans, and I respect those. I believe in you, and I'm sure you will be a success in your business, provided you get the start-up funding. That's where I can help. After Adam rang me in Sydney, I checked my investments. I can make that money available to you, under terms we agree."

"I'm confused. You can bankroll me, either as a loan or as a silent partner; you say you're falling for me, but I don't understand what you want from me?"

Now it was his turn to gather his thoughts. "I didn't come here to pressure you, but I want to know what your feelings might be for me. That night we shared was not something I expected, but blew me away with what I experienced. Before I left, I had the impression that the attraction was mutual. Was I wrong?"

"No." It was said in a whisper. Lily cleared her throat. "No," she said more strongly. "You weren't wrong, but you were on a mission of your own, and only here briefly. I didn't have the right to hold you back from a trip I understood you needed to make."

"Lily, I've learned that I don't need to live in the bright lights to be happy or fulfilled. I can do that just as happily in a small town like Sandy Bay, particularly if it's with a woman who feels for me as much as I feel for her." If she also shares my love of the sea, even better."

He took a larger gulp of his whiskey than he meant to. "Lily, would you object if I hung around in Sandy Bay for a while?"

∾

Hung around in Sandy Bay? Did he mean hung around with her? "You would live here?"

"I would. Sometimes I might fly back to Sydney for business reasons—I still have the apartment there—and sometimes I might need to travel somewhere if my artwork is being exhibited in another city, but my base would be here."

Whatever thoughts had run through her mind when he said he wanted to talk to her it hadn't been what she had just heard. He had a questioning look in his eyes. He might have a different definition of *hanging around* in the morning, but tonight, she had her own. She sucked on the remains of the ice cube, resulting in swollen and chilled lips. Sliding across the sofa towards him, she slid an arm around his neck and drew him towards her. Kissing him with chilled lips sent a hot wave coursing over her body as her tongue sought his.

"Do we have to talk about this tonight?"

"I thought we did, but now I'm not so sure." He leaned back against the end of the sofa, pulling her with him until her body lay with his. "Some communication is non-verbal. I think we're doing just fine."

She relished the sensation of his hard body beneath hers, providing a pulsing base over which she strained to reach his lips. His fingers danced a path down her back to the base of her spine, tapping a pattern that made her quiver. Who knew that was erotic?"

"Are you comfortable?" she asked, drawing back slightly so that she could look into his eyes.

"Yes… I mean no, but…"

"I didn't think so. Come with me." Wriggling off his supine body, she adjusted her dress where it had slithered up, and held out her hand. "Some conversations are better held elsewhere."

His eyes asked the question, but she let her actions provide the answer. If she stopped to think about what she was doing, she would probably freeze with embarrassment, but this was her night. Harley was here; he said this was where he wanted to be, and he wanted her. She had not admitted it before, not even to herself, but she wanted him. She led him to her bedroom and shut the door.

Lily lay quietly, watching the sleeping figure beside her. Waking to a man in her bed was a novel experience, and she revelled in it. His chest rose and fell in time with the soft snuffling noises he made, and she had an urge to run her fingers through the light forest of hair. She examined the eyelashes fanning his cheeks, indecently long for a man. He had a bad case of bed hair, but she adored the curls with sun-bleached tips which crept around the base of his head.

She wanted to feel his skin against hers. Easing herself closer, so as not to wake him, Lily carefully slid her body closer, feeling the heat that radiated from him. Suddenly, he rolled over and grabbed her in a bear hug, stifling her squeal with his mouth.

"You were awake," she protested when able to speak again. "You must have been watching me."

"It was only fair. You were lying there watching me."

Lily snuggled more firmly against him, slinging one leg over his to extend the connection as she felt a heat of her own.

"Good Lord, woman… what are you doing to me?"

Lily opened her eyes wide in mock innocence. "Why don't you find out?"

Later, as they sat in the dining room sipping coffee, him wrapped in her bathrobe and she in a baggy t-shirt, they resumed their conversation from the previous evening.

"As I tried to explain in my tongue-twisting way, I think your business idea has merit, and I'm offering you the outstanding finance you require. It would still be your boat, your business. As a loan, it would be interest free for a set period, six or twelve months. That would ease the initial financial pressure on you and would give us the opportunity to see if working together is feasible." He reached for her hand. "If it does work out, that can be my investment in your charter business. I can either be a silent partner or can work with you as deckhand."

"You, a deckhand?"

"I don't see why not? I can say 'Aye, aye Cap'n' with the best of them."

"If it doesn't work out between us?"

"Then, I'll be on my way, but the finance stays. The terms would be covered in the agreement."

Lily's head spun with ideas and possibilities. She couldn't sit still any longer. She rose, and clutching her mug between both hands, stood in front of the window, looking out over the garden. She'd known that if her scheme came to fruition, she would need to employ a crew, but had never imagined it would be Harley. He would be a fantastic partner. He had a combination of charm and business smarts. He was an experienced sailor and gave confidence he would remain calm in a crisis. Best of all, he would be living in Sandy Bay as her man.

She turned back to him. "You're serious about this? You've thought it through? What about your trip, the one you planned with your grandfather?"

"That doesn't have to be now. I can do it anytime. There will be quiet periods in the charter business, and we can always do some legs then. You can also come to Sydney with me during the off-season. Have you ever explored that city, or the east coast? My apartment is overlooking the Harbour, so you'd still be near the water. What say you?"

He voiced the question lightly, as though it was of little consequence. Looking at the hope in his eyes, Lily knew the significance of her response was every bit as great for him as it was for her. "I say yes. Yes, to my new deckhand; yes, to the finance; and yes, to us."

He leapt from his seat and grabbed her in a tight bear hug. One hand slid down her back to clasp a firm bun, holding her tight against him. "While we're still in control, I think we should have breakfast at Maisie's to celebrate."

23- The Launch

THE WEATHER HAD been variable throughout the day. Lily scanned the sky, watching for telltale signs that might spell doom. Uncharacteristic nerves grabbed her in a steely vice. Forcing everyone inside would destroy the vibe she sought. A twilight cruise was supposed to be a pleasant experience, with calm seas and no more than a gentle breeze. She crossed her fingers and sent a silent prayer to the gods who controlled these things.

So much planning had gone into this day, but there was still an hour to go. She watched as Jordan wheeled a trolley towards them, carrying the finger food Adam had organised for the occasion. The man in question moved forward to meet his son and supervised loading the food and storing it in the galley. That was another tick off her list. She checked the remaining items. One un-marked line stood out. Adam passed her, and she caught hold of his sleeve.

"Adam… the drinks. They haven't arrived."

"Settle, petal. We've got the non-alcoholic under control. Jordan's gone back to the car to load up the soft drink. The hotel is delivering the alcohol. It's been stored in their cool room. I'll call them and check it's on its way."

Lily took a deep breath and slowly let it out. Her father was on board already. She couldn't keep him away.

"I thought you'd had enough of boats, Dad."

"I wanted to be here early in case you needed help."

Her mother, sitting under shade on the deck with a cool drink that Adam had already provided her, rolled her eyes and patted the seat alongside her. "Stan, get out of your daughter's way and come and sit down. You're retired, remember?" He grunted, but Lily noted he did as he was told. Her mother was setting the ground rules in this next phase of their lives.

A pair of arms slid around her from behind. "Relax, Lilipie, it will all go like clockwork."

She grabbed the hands that circled her, desperately wanting the reassurance they gave, but needing, on this day of all days, to look professional and under control. She leaned back for a moment, relishing the warmth and strength in his embrace. Reluctantly, she untangled his arms. "How is anyone going to respect me if you call me that? Captain, if you please, and perhaps you could salute while you're at it."

Harley laughed as he let go of her, but gave her a salute anyway.

"Giving her grand ideas, aren't you? You'll be downtrodden forever if you behave like that." Davey stood beside the boat, with hands on his hips. He gave a cheeky grin. "Permission to board, Cap'n?"

278

As if she could keep him away. "Of course, Davey. Have a look around. Not a smell of fish anywhere."

He grunted, but took her up on the offer, inspecting every part of the boat and the controls before coming back to join her. "Bit flash, but should give a comfortable ride. Best of luck for the new venture. I brought you a present." He thrust a box wrapped in brown paper at her.

"Davey, you didn't need to do that."

"I know, but I wanted to anyway. We've known each other for a long time. You worked hard for your dad, and now you deserve this opportunity for yourself. Open it."

She tore off the paper wrapping to find a box containing a pair of marine binoculars.

"I thought you might need these for bird spotting on your cruises, or something like that."

"That's so thoughtful." On impulse, she leaned forward and kissed him on his cheek, grateful that for once, he had shaved. He ambled off to sit with Stan.

Dennis directed passengers through the marina gate and along the pontoon towards Serendipity. He both looked and behaved like an admiral of the fleet. He wore a new navy jacket and Lily was sure that he had polished the brass buttons. He'd even grown a moustache in recent weeks. Despite his usual dress, including the captain's hat, he rarely left shore. Perhaps he never had. This time, he was definitely on the passenger list.

Lily shielded her eyes as she watched people coming down the pontoon towards her. These were the people who had supported her and had to be invited today. There was one man she didn't recognise. He looked uncertain, as though not sure he was in the right place. Even at a distance, she could see that his clothing was a cut above what most of her guests were wearing, and his sunglasses looked as though they cost a week's salary for some. He scanned the people already onboard, and spotting Harley, called out, "Hello, sailor!"

"Ralph! You made it! Come and meet Lily."

Ralph slid his sunglasses to the top of his head, and she was engaged by the deepest brown eyes she had seen in a while. When he extended his hand and smiled, Ralph flashed a row of perfect pearly whites. "Lily, I've heard so much about you. My respects to any woman who can spark this man up as you've done. You've given him a new lease of life."

"Ralph, Welcome aboard. I've heard about you as well. I believe I need to thank you for your part in donating to the local hospital. I'm pleased you came today. Where are you staying?"

"At the Regal Hotel. Harley offered me accommodation on Ocean Dream, but I leave the boat thing to him… except for today, of course."

Lily saw Bryan and Meredith hovering behind Ralph. Presumably, they all knew each other already. She nudged Harley. "Probably Bryan and Meredith have checked in there as well. That's where they usually stay."

Ralph spun around and there were more greetings all round. Meredith even gave her a warm hug, before exclaiming on the monogrammed polo shirts that she, Harley, and Adam all wore. "Love the colour. If you need more uniforms designed, I'm sure I could help you out." She glanced around at those who were filling the deck. "Is Christos coming?"

"No, he couldn't make it. The rest of his family is here, including Dimitri. They're chatting to Mum and Dad." Lily assumed that from her comments, that Meredith didn't think their shirts were upmarket enough. She may be right, but for now, they would do. "Harley, why don't you show these three around? I'm sure they want to see the galley and the cabins."

He gave her backside a reassuring pat before leading them into the galley. Her smile was still plastered in place when she turned around to greet Mavis. The woman gave her a bear hug. "Hey girl, you've got yourself a flash-looking boat here. Better than gutting fish for a living, hey?"

Lily agreed, although she had never gutted fish for a living. "I'll get you a drink as soon as the hotel delivers it. Any minute now. What would you like? After we cast off, Adam will be around with the food. It came from Maisie's Café."

"This is living the high life. I'd love a champers, thanks. Wait 'til I tell everyone back at work about this. They'll all be wanting to book a cruise."

"I hope so. I'll have to give you a commission on sales." Mavis beamed and took herself off to chat to Stan and Davey.

Lily checked her watch. Most of the invited guests were on board, but there were still ten minutes to go before cast-off. Alyssa Finchley and Max Saunders headed in her direction, and were followed by Delia Kennet and Ben Benedict. The only person who was still missing was Maddie Masters. She couldn't leave until Maddie arrived. Her friend had been a support in recent weeks and had promised to promote the cruises to her holiday tenants.

She checked her phone in case Maddie had left a message. Nothing. Dennis was now walking in their direction, presumably with the assumption that all guests were on board. Surely Maddie hadn't forgotten?

"Ready to launch?" Adam stood at her shoulder. "It's time for your father's star turn."

"We can't go yet. The hotel hasn't delivered the wine."

"I did ring them. Give them another five minutes."

She nodded, but pulled him aside for a quiet word first. "I'm sorry if I sounded tense before. None of this would have happened if it weren't for you."

"Don't underestimate yourself. Your idea and your energy, plus you've given me a job. Retirement was driving me—and Maisie—crazy."

"It's a big change from teaching."

"And that's what I love about it." He nodded towards the gate. "I think that's our alcohol arriving now."

She saw the van from the hotel pull up beside the gate. The driver jumped out and began loading his trolley with cartons. That was one more thing ticked off the list. "At last! I'll wait until everyone has a drink, and then we can get going."

He nodded and went to meet the driver. The cartons were quickly loaded and Adam broke them open and began distributing drinks of choice.

She had wanted to ask Adam to say a few words and cut the ribbon, in recognition of the help he had given her with the business plan, not to mention contacting Harley behind her back. He insisted it would be more appropriate if her father did, a symbolic handing on of the baton, so to speak. Stan had been astonished when he learned she had purchased the catamaran, but after initial misgivings about whether she had lost her mind, was now supportive. He had even offered to act as crew for her, if the need arose. When she asked him if he would do the launch, he was delighted. She now waved him over.

"You ready, Dad? It's time." She placed the scissors within reach.

Stan moved to the bow and tapped the side of his glass with a spoon he had retrieved from Adam. "Family and friends," he bellowed, "if you step this way, I'd like to say a few words."

"Don't go! Wait for me!" Heads swivelled in response to the cry. Maddie broke into a trot as she hurried down the pontoon. "Sorry… last minute phone calls. I'm here now."

She was panting by the time she reached the gangplank. Stan waited until she was on board before he began again. "My daughter, Lily, has grown up on the sea and knows these waters as well as I do. When I sold Sea Witch, I thought I was doing her a favour, telling her there were other things in life for a young woman rather than early starts and hauling in fishing nets. I thought she would find herself a nice occupation or business on dry land. She has proven me wrong in the past, and she has proven me wrong again."

He paused, looking over at Lily. "I guess she's a chip off the old block, because she doesn't take no for an answer. Unbeknown to me, she researched a charter business, put together a plan, organised finance and bought a boat… the one you're standing on. Not only that, she's found herself a crew for her new venture, with Harley as her new deckhand, and Adam looking after passenger catering and services.

"I wanted to smash a bottle of champagne on the hull, but decided against wasting good champagne. Dennis has a thing about broken glass in the marina as well, so on that basis, I now cut the ribbon and officially launch *Serendipity* and Sandy Bay Coastal Charters."

He took up the scissors and cut the ribbon with a flourish. "I now ask you all to raise your glasses in a toast. To my clever daughter, Lily, her business partners, and their new venture. Cheers!"

Davey leaped up and, crossing to the control panel, sounded the horn. Everyone raised their glasses in salute, and Adam moved to slide the gangplank onboard and shut the gate. Lily started the motor. Vibrations rumbled through the decking, and the gap between the boat and the edge of the pontoon widened. Her first cruise had begun.

&

"That went well," Harley remarked as they secured the last of the rubbish bags. "The reporter from the South Coast Chronical seemed to enjoy himself. I noticed him chatting up that young receptionist from Alyssa Finchley's office."

"I guess that's what sea air and a glass of champagne will do for you. He'd better give us a good write up in the next edition."

"I'm sure he will. It was a better junket than he usually gets."

"My cruise could hardly be called a junket."

"If you're a small-town reporter, I bet it is. If we're going to join our out-of-town guests, we'd better hurry." They turned off all the lights and locked the cabin door. "Before we join the others, there's something I want to show you over on Ocean Dream."

"Now?"

"It won't take a minute. The others can wait." He led the way to the mooring and jumped aboard, turning and offering

284

his hand to Lily as she did the same. She stumbled slightly, colliding against him on the deck. It gave him an excuse to wrap his arms tightly around her and claim her lips with his. She tasted of champagne, salty air, and promise. He wavered about joining the others for a moment.

Lily slid her arms around his waist, lifting the shirt at the back so she could feel his skin. "Is this what you brought me over here for? There's no time for that. We're expected for supper."

"Wishful thinking, but no, it's not that. Wait while I unlock the door." He turned on the lights inside and beckoned her in. "I started this weeks ago, and wasn't sure when to show it to you, if at all. Bryan saw it on our trip to Kangaroo Island and said I had to. I got it back from the framer today."

Harley propped the painting against the wall, so they could stand back and absorb the detail. "This is my gift to celebrate your new business."

For once, Lily was speechless. A few moments passed before she spoke. "It really looks like me."

"It's supposed to. It's up to you what you do with it, but it would be better kept at the cottage."

"This is an amazing surprise. You're so talented. You should do more portraits."

"That's what Bryan tried to tell me. This one is special. I'm not sure I need to do any more. I haven't forgotten that your father wanted a painting of Sea Witch, by the way. I'll do that one next as his retirement present."

"You started this weeks ago?"

"I did. When I left, I wanted to take something of you with me."

"But you came back."

"The lure of Sandy Bay was strong, but not as strong as the wonderful, passionate woman I found here. Was I wrong to respond to your siren charms?"

"Not at all. I'll remind you of that often."

"This town provided me with a safe harbour when I needed it, but best of all, it introduced me to you."

Harley locked the cabin again, and they wandered slowly back along the pontoon, this time, arm-in-arm. They paused once more before the gate, when Harley grasped her should and spun her around to face him. He kissed her once more, and then they turned and walked through the gate and out into the night.

Don't miss out on your free download!

If you enjoyed this story, you might like to read a collection

of short stories in

Romance in the Stone

To receive your *free* copy, and keep up-to-date with news

about future releases,

copy and paste https://bit.ly/3qQdbqR into your browser.

Sandy Bay Series

THE AUSTRALIAN COASTAL town of Sandy Bay is close enough to the Adelaide that its residents can access the city if they need to, but far enough away that they can ignore the city too. The town swells with visitors on weekends or during the holiday season, but at other times it's quiet and the locals like it like that.

In a small-town environment, everyone knows everyone else, and secrets can be difficult to keep. It's astonishing what things some people manage to hide for so long. Either in Sandy Bay, or the adjoining hub of Port Reilly, the unexpected may still surprise the most cynical resident.

No matter what the current crisis, the lure of the Bay and the pristine Australian beaches will continue to delight, not just the characters but the readers as well.

Secrets in Sandy Bay – an introductory novella

IT WAS LATE on a Friday afternoon, but was that any excuse?

Property Manager Maddie's heart sinks when she realises that she has given Alex Isherwood the wrong keys to his rental cottage. It's already dark and the weather is foul and promising to get worse. There's no other option – she has to drive out to Seaspray Cottage and sort out this mess.

Give him the keys – that was all she had to do. So how was it that an hour later, she was sitting in front of an open fire, minus her own clothes, and sharing a meal with a man who didn't take 'No' for an answer? The tempest outside was nothing to the storm that was stirred up inside the cottage.

With a shared history in the town, they had a few things in common, but didn't know how much. It's amazing how tightly held some secrets can be, even in a small town where everyone knows everything.

Maddie's world disintegrates as the secrets of her past are revealed.

Escape to Sandy Bay

ALYSSA NEEDS TO escape… from her job, her dreams, and her man. She flees to coastal Sandy Bay to lick her wounds. The town of her childhood holidays provides a job and a place to stay.

Her new-found sanctuary is shattered when she learns of a controversial proposal that will change the face of the sea front forever. When she sees a man undertaking preliminary site investigations, Alyssa springs into action, determined to thwart the development.

Max is focused on caring for his young son and building the reputation of his business. He's not looking for trouble, but in the guise of a lawyer who is quick to react, trouble comes looking for him. She stirs the emotions in ways he didn't expect, but when she neglects his son, he is quick to lash out.

Leaving the past behind is not so easy, especially with unfinished business back in the city. Should she forgive and forget, or forge a new life so different to the one she'd always imagined? The responses of the men in her life influence the decision she needs to make, but which choice is the right one?

Return to Sandy Bay

DELIA FLED SANDY BAY with a secret she couldn't share. She left behind the carefree life that young people enjoyed in the coastal town. She also left behind the man she loved, resolutely forging a future and career in the city.

Work draws her back to the town in which she grew up, forcing her to confront her past and the people who shaped it. Some facts are easily manipulated, and not all actions are honourable. She can't hide the truth from Ben any longer, but there are surprises in store for both of them.

As one door in her life closes, another opens in the form of a new business opportunity, potentially bringing them closer together. She hadn't counted on the changing family dynamics when she made this move.

Will she give Ben a second chance, or will the fallout tear them apart?

Safe Harbour in Sandy Bay

WHEN A YACHT'S ELECTRONICS fail, corporate escapee Harley Mendelson is forced to dock in the close-knit fishing town of Sandy Bay. His gleaming vessel, Ocean Dream, carries not just his lifelong sailing ambitions, but the weight of a past he's desperate to outrun.

Local fisherman's daughter Lily Jardine has salt water in her veins and cynicism in her heart. To her, Harley is just another city slicker playing sailor—more suited to a kiddie pool than the open seas. But as engine repairs stretch from days into weeks, she discovers depths in the quiet stranger that make her question her hasty judgment.

As Sandy Bay's rustic charm begins to crack Harley's carefully constructed walls, an unexpected connection sparks between two souls from different shores. Yet Harley knows his demons make him unworthy of the fiery, free-spirited Lily. And she knows that dreamers who chase the horizon eventually sail away.

But sometimes, the heart drops anchor when you least expect it—and the biggest adventures begin when you stop running from your past and finally find your way home.

Emily Hussey

EMILY HUSSEY HAS lived in several Australian states, and that experience has provided useful backdrop for some of her novels. She spent her twenties in Alice Springs, which became the setting for the Red Centre Series. She now resides on the coast in the city of Adelaide, and is exploring the writing options in every café in walking distance.

Emily was a marriage celebrant for 24 years, and has married couples in many different locations, ranging from private gardens, to beaches, to caves, or rural locations. Many of her clients remain friends to this day. She usually writes with Iris, a black and white cat at her elbow, demanding her share of attention. Writing tends to be fuelled with regular coffee boosts, and occasional squares of very dark chocolate.